Runaway

KATIE CROSS

KCW

Contents

To Ryker.
For all your love, safety, and loyalty.

Chapter One

Drizzling rain pattered my windshield as I stared at a two-story cabin built of wooden logs stacked on top of each other. Faded white lines lay between each log, making it look ancient. Rain stained the wood a darker shade of brown, and a little wisp of smoke rose above the chimney despite the moisture.

Charming, if I wasn't so terrified the owner would kick me out as soon as he saw me.

The longer I sat out here in my beater car that didn't even have a real license plate yet, the weirder this whole situation became.

And it was already *pretty* weird.

Still, there was one man that could help me, and that man both resented my existence and desperately needed it. He also proudly lived the life of a hermit in the mountains—I mean, who bragged about that?—and hated all details.

Mark Bailey.

That alone seemed pretty ridiculous, but so was this entire situation.

A few more moments passed while I rallied my courage. In

fact, I prepared myself like this every time I had to talk to Mark. I'd clutch the phone for a few minutes, think through every sentence that I *had* to say, and then hope that he didn't wander off on a list of ideas. Eventually, he would wander. That much was inevitable. He'd talk things out, and I'd have to pull him back to reality with the main points he'd called for anyway.

Lately, he'd called a lot more often than usual.

Today would be very different, however, because we'd be face-to-face for the first time. I stalled this inevitable confrontation while trying to picture what he looked like. Mark and I had always spoken on the phone. He called me out of the blue one day, declared his need for an accountant, and proceeded to tell me about every business venture he'd ever started. For a man that hated details, he had a mind like a steel trap.

Plus, I'd seen his tax returns too many times. He was overly generous on charitable contributions to the point he sabotaged profit from his company. A bit of a bleeding heart, really.

Blonde, I'd guess. He sounded nice enough on the phone, so probably straight-laced, with short hair like a businessman and crisp clothes. He was single, at least his tax returns weren't filed jointly, and had no other income besides his own. Slight of frame, maybe. Like Ryan Gosling?

With a jolt, I shook my head. No, I had to stop assigning actors to everyone I met. It just . . . made people easier to approach.

With a shove, I forced myself out of my little car and into the pounding rain. It slammed into my shoulders while I shut the car door, then skirted the edges of a dirt path filled with water. Mud squished under my shoes as I scuttled under an eave and forced myself to knock. The only thing that kept me moving was momentum. If I thought too hard about this, I'd just leave.

Ten seconds after I knocked, the door flew open. Out of sheer nerves, my heart fell all the way to the pit of my stomach.

Then I burst out laughing.

A tall, broad-shouldered, bear of a man glowered at me. He had brown hair, almost black, that stuck up in odd angles from the back of his head. It was at odds with his hazel eyes in a lovely way. His beard hadn't been trimmed in days. He wore no shirt and gray sweatpants with a pair of flip-flops on his feet. My glance was quick, but he certainly wasn't *slight* or *business-like* in any sense of the word.

A hibernating bear came to mind first. Hardly Ryan Gosling. Hardly what I always pictured on the other end of the phone. Somehow, though, this was better. First, who would mess with me if *that* scowl came to the door? Not Joshua. At least, I'd hoped not. For years I thought I knew Joshua, but the last few weeks had been revealing.

Second, I could fit Mark's voice with this guy.

This was a wild Mark Bailey.

Quickly, I drown my amusement in the face of his dark annoyance. Now that I thought about it, this may not even be Mark. He spoke about a twin brother, JJ, often enough. Behind him was a warm-appearing cabin, with a snapping fire that let out heat. A trickle of rain ran down my back, and I shivered.

"Are you lost?" he asked.

"No, I . . . I'm looking for Mark Bailey."

His eyebrows lifted. When he said nothing more, I realized that was the only response I could expect.

"Are you Mark?"

He nodded. I rolled my lips to school my laugh. No, I couldn't laugh at him again. He'd hear the wild hysteria. The tinge of desperation and fear and uncertainty that belied everything in my life now. Then he'd turn me away.

"I . . . I'm . . ."

My name hovered on the end of my tongue. *Stella Marie.* Did I dare say Marie? I'd always run my accounting business through my middle name because I didn't want the world to know my first name. It felt too much like an invasion. The two names together may not clue him into my identity.

But maybe the sound of my voice *and* the name Marie would get him thinking.

In a perfect world, I'd get through this confrontation without him knowing me. Mark tried to hide it, but he ended every call frustrated. Didn't like when I curbed his wild ideas with sound financial sense. If there was one thing Mark felt like he didn't have, it was time. He was in a hurry for everything even though he was what, thirty-one? Two years older than me.

Money didn't always run at the same speed as Mark, and that galled him to no end.

"My name is Stella Marie," I finally said.

You are Stella Marie, grandma Marie always insisted. *Not just Stella. Be proud of your heritage.*

His gaze tapered further.

I swallowed a squeak of fear and the desire to ask if I could come inside. No, of course I shouldn't ask that. I wouldn't let me inside if I were him. He hadn't let go of the door, giving me unparalleled access to his abs. By sheer willpower, I kept my gaze on his face.

"What are you doing here, Stella Marie?"

"I need some help. I heard you might have a cabin to rent."

Confusion clouded his annoyance. "Who told you that?"

No one, I thought. *Just the hope deep in my heart and what I know of your world.*

"Oh, just driving through town." I waved an airy hand in the vague direction that I thought Pineville would be. "I need a place to stay and I'm willing to pay cash. Maybe just for a month or so?"

His brow furrowed.

Please, I thought. *Please don't care about these details. You never have before . . .*

"Who in town told you to come here?"

Dagnabbit. Of course he had to ask questions now of all times. The conversation we'd had a few days ago when he said he wanted to start a ride-a-horse operation ran through my mind. He hadn't asked how much it cost to keep a horse alive or pay vet bills or bring hay into his canyon or any of that.

No, he just found a horse he thought was handsome and wanted to try it out.

Thankfully, I'd backed him out of the idea. He hadn't been happy at the time. *Now* he had to know who sent money his way? Mark needed money as desperately as I needed to disappear. Why didn't he take the offer?

Perhaps he'd be deterred away from how I came to know him and focus on the dollars.

"$500 a month for a small cabin? I can pay in advance if you want the cash now."

The money burned a hole in the back pocket of my jeans, but I didn't reach for it yet. He leaned against the doorframe instead, unbothered by the misty fall air that flowed past him into the cabin. No one else had stirred inside, and I caught a vague peek of furniture and a can of something pried open with a spoon sticking out of it.

Bachelor, for sure.

"Why do you need a place to stay?" he asked.

"Does that matter?"

His brow lifted. "It does now."

My nostrils flared. I wasn't good at this. Lying, deceptions, sneakiness. I just wanted to find a place where I could hole up and not see anyone for a while. Maybe I'd been naive to think this would be easy. To show up on his doorstep and ask if I could live with him? The man lived in the middle of a mountain canyon. No one drove out here unless they had to, which was why I wanted to stay. Why I'd driven all the way across the country on a desperate prayer and a crappy car not yet registered to my name.

My breath was shaky when I let it out. "I just . . . I need someplace to disappear for a while, and I've heard that you have cabins to rent and no one comes out here."

He snorted. "You're hiding."

Yes, I thought.

I didn't answer him, just studied his face. Beneath all that beard and wild hair, I sensed a general kindness about his eyes. The same kindness that I heard in his voice on the phone when he wasn't rattling off plans. His gaze had an edge to it, however.

He straightened up. "Look, I'd love to help. I really would. Being the nice guy used to be my favorite thing, but I'm kind of over it now. My brother just got married and moved out and I initiated this plan to go full mountain man this winter. The last thing I need here is a renter."

I blinked. *Full mountain man?* What did that mean? The words rushed out of me before I could stop them.

"But why?"

He shrugged. "I don't know! Seems like a good idea. We'll see how it pans out. I'm full of ideas, and sometimes the ones that seem the most stupid are actually the greatest in the end. Regardless, I'm not harboring a sketchy fugitive from the law that's lying about someone in town telling her I'd rent a cabin for $500 a month on my property. Sorry. No one in town would have sent you here to rent."

My heart raced as he reached for his door and began to close it.

"I go by Marie sometimes!"

Two inches before it shut, the door stopped. His fingers tightened around the edges, but I couldn't see his face now. A lump filled my throat and I swallowed it. My voice rang out clear despite my worry. I shivered but wasn't entirely sure it was from the cold.

"If you listen hard, you might recognize my voice. My full name is Stella Marie Lee, but I do business under Marie Lee. Mark, I know you're always annoyed with me because I stifle your ideas and I honestly have no idea why you still pay me to do your books, but I . . . I need some help."

Slowly, the door opened back up.

Chapter Two

MARK

A shiver passed through me before I pulled the door open again.

Marie Lee, the most frustrating, safest-playing accountant on this planet. The woman who probably rolled her eyes every time she saw me call, but spoke such calm sense I couldn't help but listen. Even if she never said what I wanted to hear.

Now she stood on my doorstep.

She clutched her arms under a wet, red parka. Hints of light blonde hair peeked out from behind her ears. Her eyes were wide, uncertain, and a gentle brown. She was younger than I expected. I'd always pictured her in her late fifties. No, if I had been given a lineup, the last person I would have chosen as Marie was this girl.

Plus, it changed everything about her sketchy request. I mentally berated myself for letting her stand on the rainy porch. JJ may have left me, but I didn't have to be a jerk.

"Come inside." I opened the door wider. "It's freezing out there."

With a grateful half-smile, she stepped onto a towel I'd thrown on the floor as a rug. Lizbeth and JJ married six weeks ago in an outdoor wedding near his favorite local climbing rock.

It had taken all of seven days for this place to devolve back to the chaos it had been before her arrival.

I missed it.

Marie—no, Stella—skirted out of my way as I closed the door behind her. She didn't bring anything inside with her. Then again, she probably didn't know what to expect from me, so why bring her bags? I gestured toward the fire with a tilt of my head.

"Have a seat. I'll warm up some crappy hot chocolate, unless you want coffee this late?"

"Hot chocolate sounds great."

While her parka rustled as she peeled it off, I grabbed a half-gallon of milk from a tiny refrigerator and reached for the crappy hot chocolate packets that were, frankly, insulting to my taste buds after JJ's real-deal homemade stuff.

I shoved that cranky thought away. Lizbeth and JJ were perfect together. I was happy for them. Jealous, but happy.

The cabin remained quiet while Stella peeled out of a pair of fuzzy white boots and padded over to the fire, shivering. Without her parka, she looked as normal as anyone. Blonde hair with darker streaks in a bob around her jawline. Soft eyes. Wiry body. A runner, maybe. It occurred to me that, as my accountant, she knew almost everything about my business. Enough to find it on a cold fall night. But I knew nothing about her.

Talk about unfair advantages.

The microwave dinged, so I pulled the mug out, grimaced when I realized I'd forgotten to wash the old coffee stains out of it, and grabbed a clean one. I'd take the dirty one.

"So." I leaned back against the sink while the microwave hummed away, then realized I still didn't have a shirt on. No wonder she wouldn't look away from the fire. As casually as possible, I grabbed a shirt from the back of a chair and pulled it on. "You must be in pretty bad shape if you're coming here."

Did I imagine that grimace? Her throat bobbed as she swallowed, her profile silhouetted against the bright flames. Outside, the rain began to ease.

"Yeah."

I waited for more, but she didn't elaborate. Once the milk finished warming, I dumped the chocolate powder inside, grabbed two spoons, and headed her way. She turned, giving me another tentative smile that didn't quite reach her eyes.

A veritable damsel-in-distress?

Well, maybe I didn't mind being the good guy so much.

"Thanks." She accepted the mug from me. I sat on the couch a few feet away to give her some space. She sat on a recliner across from me, glanced at me over the top of her cup, then looked away. The spoon clinked against the side of the mug as she stirred.

Oh, she seemed docile, but I'd been on the phone enough with her to know that something else lived under all that uncertainty.

Wildcat.

"Of course I'll give you a place to stay," I said, just to dissipate the tension in the air. No bruises colored her skin, and she didn't jump at unexpected sounds so far. Didn't seem like she'd been in an abusive situation. No, why would she run to a single male in the middle of nowhere?

But something was surely up.

"Really?" she asked.

"Of course." I ran a hand over my beard and held back my own grimace. At least I'd showered, but not much else had happened for grooming the last two weeks. No wonder she burst out laughing.

"Thank you."

There it was. A hint of that confidence again.

I shrugged.

"What would you like me to pay you?" She reached for her back pocket. "Like I said, I have—"

I waved that off. "We'll figure it out later.

She stifled a smile. "I insist."

"You will. We just don't need to deal with details tonight."

My phone buzzed against my thigh and I ignored it. An incoming text message from the *Hearts on Fire* dating app, no doubt. Stupid thing wouldn't stop buzzing, feeding an endless stream of girls that, once I started messaging, lost interest too quickly. Easier to message them back from the computer, anyway.

"So." I leaned forward, scrubbing hot chocolate off my mustache, which *definitely* needed a trim. "There's a small cabin behind this one that you can take. Lizbeth lived there until she married my brother and moved out. I haven't stocked it with firewood yet, but I can do that pretty quick." I lifted an eyebrow. "I assume you have clothes?"

"Yes," she said quickly. "I have a few bags in my car."

"Good. Anything I can help with?"

She hesitated, then said, "I just . . . I came here because I wanted to be left alone for a while. I don't want anyone to know I'm here."

"Sure."

She blinked. "You're really okay with this?"

"Of course. Is someone after you?"

"Not yet."

"But will be?"

"I'd rather not go into more details."

"Are you in danger? I won't ask any more than that."

"You wouldn't be."

She didn't answer my question, but I could tell she wouldn't elaborate, so I let that one go. I did love a challenge.

"It's no secret you avoid my calls and get frustrated with me on the phone," she said as she set down her hot chocolate. "I wasn't sure what kind of reception to expect, to be honest. But you need cash, you live in the mountains, and that's a good fit for both of us right now. I figured it was worth a shot, at any rate."

I grinned, and it seemed to surprise her. There wasn't a single person on this planet as stubborn as Marie Lee—Stella Marie Lee, I meant—or as fit to do my accounting. She told it like it was, and most of the time, I didn't like reality.

But I still went with it.

"That's true." I toasted her with my mug. "Our conversations are frustrating. But I haven't gotten rid of you yet, have I?"

She blinked. "No. Why is that?"

"I need people that challenge me." I stood up and set the hot chocolate near the sink. Then I pulled a coat on and stepped into a pair of muck boots by the door. "Help yourself to whatever you want. There's some food in the fridge. I need to get the fire going in your cabin so you don't freeze tonight. It's still warm during the day, but the nights get cold."

"Oh." She nodded. "Thanks, I appreciate it."

Without another word, I walked outside. What else was I supposed to say? She was far more charming in person than I'd expected. Although she was clearly in an uncertain situation now, it didn't seem to change the inner core of strength I'd always sensed on our calls. Though I couldn't reconcile the frustrating woman on the phone that rarely backed my investment ideas with the confident woman before me now.

And, for some reason, I didn't want to.

Chapter Three

STELLA

The twitter and call of a bird outside woke me the next morning.

I stirred, wrapped in the warmth of a sleeping bag that Mark had dug out of . . . somewhere . . . after starting a fire in a small fireplace. The cabin he'd given me wasn't large. Barely had room for a small bed, a square desk, a chair, a pole to hang clothes across the far wall, and a tiny bathroom with a standup shower. It had just been built a few months ago when a woman named Lizbeth had moved in here. But it was oddly perfect.

Small. Isolated. Quiet.

Heaven.

My new phone chimed. I grabbed it off the ground where it charged near a plug in the wall and yawned to find a text message.

Grandma: You've arrived safely at your mountain retreat?

Stella Marie: Yes! My friend is here and all is well. Love you.

My finger hesitated over the *send* button. Was Mark a friend? That would be a generous interpretation of the word. But *client* sounded weird, and he was more than just an acquaintance. He had, without pressing much, taken me in when I needed it the most. If that wasn't a friend, then what was? I sent it.

Her response came moments later.

Grandma: Love you.

With a little yawn, I stretched my arms over my head. The dying fire kept the room warm. Outside, fresh sunlight streamed through the naked tree branches and onto the ground. A little wind drifted by, and the soft scent of fall lingered in the air. Beyond my cabin lay a summer camp—Adventura—but I didn't know much else about it beyond annual income, operating expenses, and a few other ratios that had nothing to do with reality. I knew Mark and investors had sunk money into this, that he'd had a bad second summer, and those investors had left at the end of the summer. A guy named Maverick took over those investors in a last-minute save that prevented Mark from losing everything.

Several big churches had pulled their reservations at the last possible minute in July, and now Mark still scrambled to come up with cash. With a shake of my head, I pushed those thoughts away.

Work would come later. It never had before. Work had always been first. But now it couldn't be.

Because I had no job anymore.

Right now, it was time for a run. Running here would be far different than a city park or long blocks, but there had been a road that brought me here.

Last night, Mark had wordlessly helped me lug my two suitcases and rolling laptop case inside. I riffled through them now, yanking out a pair of black pants and my favorite socks. Even so little luggage cluttered the available area. I'd have to buy hangers at some point, but living out of bags was acceptable for now. My gaze drifted outside. I'd also have to confront Mark again at some point.

Perhaps it wouldn't feel so daunting now that I knew he wouldn't kick me out. At least, not yet.

Once ready for my run, I rooted through my laptop bag, grabbed a stack of sticky notes, and scrawled my goals for the day on top. Then I slapped them on the wall on my way out.

1. ~~Notify grandma~~
2. Buy food, hangers, and chai mix.
3. Check on my clients.
4. Go for a run.

Maybe hiding in the mountains wouldn't be so bad after all.

Chapter Four

MARK

If Stella had made anything clear last night, it was that she wanted to be left alone.

So did I.

A craving for isolation, or maybe something else entirely, drove me to declare my official mountain man status after JJ's wedding. The summer camp season had ended at Adventura, which made the timing perfect. Justin winterized the most remote cabins and ran off somewhere with my little sister, leaving me alone with a lot of ideas and thoughts and . . . other things.

What *mountain man status* actually meant, I had no idea, but the vague idea in my mind involved isolation, snowy nights, and a really big beard.

So far, the experience had mostly been itchy and silent. Being alone at Adventura wasn't too bad. This wasn't my first time. It involved pacing the cabin, prowling the trails to find a cougar that kept wandering too close, and trying not to explode from the sheer quiet. Ideas stacked up in my brain like dust without JJ here to talk me through them. Which had, for a time, driven me to call Marie more. By some miracle, she actually answered each time.

Now that she was here, I couldn't help but wonder if I'd given time to some of those random ideas just so I could talk to her.

On one hand, the fact that she seemed close to my age, was definitely confident, and absolutely single, was great. On the other hand, it was also massively embarrassing. My financials had taken a swing in the wrong direction this summer. Not only had the spa idea fizzled out, thanks to an overzealous city council after I'd sunk money into the build-out, but Adventura lost two big clients and took devastating hits as well. Only Maverick's curiosity and deep vision kept me from being homeless, but my problems were far from over.

Embarrassing.

Now, I had to figure out a way to save Adventura and survive the winter alone. Or maybe not so alone.

With a sigh, I cleaned up the bathroom, swept up the remains of my ghastly beard—which now was trimmed and wouldn't try to grab all my food—and ran a comb through my hair. Even that improvement might drastically change her response to me.

I mean . . . she *laughed*.

My pride still stung, even though I didn't really blame her. When I stepped back into the cabin, my phone chimed. I grabbed it, then grunted at the *Hearts on Fire* notification. Two new messages.

StephLuvsDogs: Hey Mark! Saw your profile and just wanted you to know I love hiking. I think we'd have a lot in common.

A snort bubbled out of me. Six months on and off this

stupid app had quickly taught me that most women thought that *hiking* and *living in the mountains* equated to about the same thing. But once they saw Adventura, they skittered off.

Too isolated, one girl said. *Are you like a hermit or something?*

Nope. If I can't hear sirens, it's not for me, said another. Which still didn't make sense to me. Did they not read my profile where I was very clear about where I lived? What did sirens have to do with anything?

Or maybe it was me they avoided.

Another message waited below that one.

AbbyKessler65: Sorry for the late response, Mark. I got caught up with some work stuff. Hope you're doing great!

My fingers tightened around the phone. Clever girl. Yes, she hadn't responded to my follow-up message after our first date ten days ago, and now she expertly ghosted me here. Apology. Explanation. Well wishing. Now I had nothing to really say back, and if I did, which I wouldn't, she'd ignore it.

Classic move.

For the thousandth time, I considered ending my time with *Hearts on Fire,* but I'd already done that three times. Eventually, I wandered back. Because what else was there? Sitting alone in the mountains while I stewed over my money loss and desperate need to gain it back?

Besides, I was my mother's son, and couldn't dissuade my natural optimism about people in general.

There was always a bud of hope that the next woman would be someone I could talk to. Someone that didn't mind my crazy ideas. Wasn't intimidated by my energy. *Dynamo,* someone had once called me, and it hadn't been kind.

Someone to just *be* with.

A memory of JJ and Lizbeth snuggling on the couch, reading their separate books, rose in my mind. I sent it away. JJ deserved her. They were perfect for each other. And now I was insanely jealous that he was the first Bailey brother to cave. JJ, the one that didn't care about love and never talked about having a family. Of course he'd be the one to break because he was the one that didn't want it so bad.

With a shake of my head, I pitched my phone to the couch. I'd talk to Stephanie about her alleged love of hiking later. For now, I needed to lift. Heavy squats. Maybe some presses. Something to push against.

Stella Marie filtered through my mind, but I forced her back out. She wanted to be left alone, so I'd honor that.

Even if I was intrigued.

A quick tap came on my front door and I pulled it open. Stella stood there. Sweat rolled down her face and she breathed heavily.

"You good?" I asked.

She grinned. "Fine. Just went for a run. You look . . . less like a bear."

My fingers raked my beard. "Thanks."

"I need to go to the store. Is there somewhere I could store food? Like a . . . kitchen or something?"

My head tilted toward the combined kitchen and dining hall through the trees. "Big building down that trail. I don't winterize the kitchen, so the power should be on. There's a massive fridge, so help yourself."

"Thanks." She turned to go but stopped. "Need anything at the store?"

"I'm good, thanks."

Stella hesitated, nodded, and disappeared around the side of the cabin. My mouth opened to call her back, but not knowing what to say, I shut the door. No, I had to leave Stella Marie alone. She was my accountant. Saw my tax returns. And she'd come here needing help. She'd asked for space, I'd honor that and act as if she wasn't here.

Meanwhile, I had someone else to swoon in town.

* * *

"Adventura is going great."

My lack of enthusiasm sparked a hint of amusement in Maverick's eyes. He sat across from me at the Diner, where a plate of rubbery eggs, butter-soaked toast, and watered-down ketchup awaited him. I used my fork to cut into a pile of pancakes as he grabbed a knife.

A waitress named Dagny set a cup of orange juice in front of me and I thanked her. Dagny had tucked us into the back of the diner against the wall. Fading yellow flowers drooped in the middle of a cheap vase that I pushed out of the way to make room for maple syrup.

Our fourth-quarter meeting had just begun, and what a bangarang report.

"I figured as much," Maverick said, "but I also think you're holding back. What's going on? How did Q3 play out?"

Maverick, a previous corporate powerhouse turned small-town-business-guru loved a puzzle. When my brother married his adopted daughter, we'd become good friends. No one gave me the truth as hard as Mari—Stella, but Mav came a close second.

The words stuck in my throat like needles, but I forced them out. "I had to put the staff payroll on my credit card to get them paid after the loss. It closed out payroll, at least, but I got nailed on the payroll taxes."

He grimaced.

Mav had started talking to me about his interest in Adventura last April. When things started to tank in July, and my other investors decided they didn't like the risk after the second year of sketchy returns, Mav swooped in, bought their shares, and now had a controlling interest in the company.

Also my life.

"I worried about that," he said.

"There is still the mortgage to pay and the minimum balance on the credit card. The camp can't sit all winter, and JJ isn't renting anymore to do his catering, so Adventura effectively has no cash flow until spring."

Doubts assailed me. Maybe Adventura had been a mistake. Summer camps made no money. This wasn't feasible. I let them roll through, then back out. Too late to have doubts. Time for action.

Maverick lifted one eyebrow and silently indicated for me to continue. He held a controlling interest but acted more like a mentor. So far, he hadn't solved any of my problems except taking the shares. Thankfully, he didn't want to control Adventura—just advise and then make money. After two years of summer camp management, it was clear that Adventura wouldn't survive on that alone. Which meant it was time for me to generate some new ideas. Sometimes, I thought Maverick invested out of sheer curiosity about me.

Now I had to prove him out because who knew where a partnership with a guy like Maverick could lead? Anywhere.

While I laid out the numbers with clinical sterility, I could feel his thoughts churning behind his eyes. I paused only to take a few bites of bacon and pancake every now and then. By the time I finished, he gave a low whistle.

"Tough situation, Mr. Bailey."

"Tell me about it," I mumbled.

He shrugged. "I've seen worse."

"I have a couple of apartments and townhomes I rent out to tourists in Jackson City and some other places. I could sell one and use it to pay the mortgage through the winter, but that drops the money that feeds me. Plus, I don't want to give up long-term assets."

He punted a few more questions back and forth. I rolled with them, even as I hated the punch to my pride. Business was like that. High and low. The highs felt amazing. The lows were a deep crash. I'd always pulled through somehow, but this time I wasn't so sure I'd pull through the *way* I wanted to. It wasn't a matter of surviving.

It was what *surviving* looked like at the end.

"So what's your plan?" he asked.

Something sparked back to life inside me. Yes. Ideas. I had no lack of ideas. "My gut tells me I need to focus inward. Make use of what I have." My brow furrowed. "But how do I repurpose Adventura?"

He reached for a glass of ice water with a sudden, mischievous gleam in his eye. "If anyone can figure that out," he drawled. "It's Mark Bailey. I have faith in you, brother. How is the mountain man life?"

I snorted. "Quiet."

He laughed after taking a drink. "Want my six-month-old? He doesn't stop babbling."

Yes, I thought. *I'd take your family life in a heartbeat.* Instead, I grinned. "Fatherhood too much?"

"Nah. It's everything I wanted. Just need to update my tattoos now."

"Everything else okay?"

A cloudy expression followed the question. "Ellie is struggling lately, which affects Bethany, but things will eventually even out."

"Yeah?"

"Devin Blaine left." He set the water aside. "Joined the Marines unexpectedly and is gone." He snapped two fingers together. "No real explanation. They had plans to attend state university together, but he joined without telling anyone, then left two weeks later."

I leaned back, stunned. "Devin did? I had no idea. They're close."

"Were."

I winced. Ellie, Lizbeth's sister, and her best friend, Devin, were loose figures in my life. They came to Adventura every week to see Lizbeth when she lived there. I liked them both. Devin would make a solid soldier. Ellie was a veritable mountain goat, and I'd been embarrassed when she almost out hiked me.

There was definitely something electric between them. They claimed to be best friends, but it didn't take an idiot to see there was more. An unexpected departure would be ugly, particularly to a girl like Ellie. She trusted at glacial speed and had a sharp wit for survival.

"Sorry about that," I said.

Mav smiled. "I think it's a good thing for both of them, to be honest, but Ellie can't see it yet. With time, she will."

The conversation devolved into his latest business project, revamping The Boulangerie bakery in Jackson City that JJ had worked for in late winter and spring. Didn't seem like they'd pull through with their current strategy, and brought Maverick in to save their cash flow.

While he told me about the details, a movement behind him caught my eye. A familiar woman with a bright smile, slightly crooked front teeth, and trailing brown hair sat in a booth across from us. A thin, clean-shaven man with glasses sat across from her. They smiled in that warm, lovey-dovey way that made my stomach queasy.

Abby Kessler.

The latest girl to ghost me on my messages this morning.

Half my attention kept the conversation going with Maver-ick, the other half tracked her. Abby and I had messaged for two months on the app before we finally found a time that worked to meet up ten days ago. I'd liked her more than I thought I should for never having met her and she seemed to feel the same way. Our date had been easy. A fun hike, some easy rock climbing, and lunch on top of a massive boulder.

Then she'd ghosted.

And now, if her entwined fingers and googly eyes with that guy meant anything, she'd found someone else.

A sardonic mixture of amusement and annoyance filled me. If she found someone else, good for her. But the timelines were pretty squished. She would likely have known about that guy while messaging me—unless, of course, they moved at light speed. Our date was only a week and a half ago, it's not like it had been an eternity. She'd been very careful with me, too, and seemed that way in general. Was she hesitant because she had this other guy on the line at the same time?

Had it been a pity date with me?

She had no obligation to me, of course. Let her date five guys at the same time if she wanted to. But the same frustration arose again regardless. Why was I always the loser in this equation? The one that *didn't* get the girl?

I must be missing something.

When Maverick slipped to the bathroom, his prosthetic legs drawing a few surprised stares, Abby looked up. Her eyes tangled with mine for half a moment. Shock came to her face first, then uncertainty, and finally a forced, tight smile. She turned back to her date, but her eyes flickered to mine a few times. She shifted in her chair, although she tried to hide her discomfort.

Oh, yeah.

That was definitely guilt.

You led me on, I thought, *and then you ghosted me. Hope that feels good.*

"R-ready to give me money?" Dagny asked, hand held out. I gave her my credit card between two fingers.

"I'll get both of ours here." Even though I didn't have the

money for it, I gestured toward Abby and her date with a tip of my head. "And put those two on my card too, but don't tell them until they leave. Just tell the woman it's a parting gift from a friend."

Dagny snatched the card and swiped it. "Got it, boss."

Maverick returned, we parted with a handshake, and I left the diner without another backward glance. Closure felt good, but an unforgettable exit from a woman's life felt even better.

Chapter Five

STELLA MARIE

"Stella Marie?"

A smile broke my lips, the first true one in weeks. "Hey, grandma."

"How are you?"

Her warm voice, smooth as honey, made my stomach catch. I settled on the edge of my bed with a sigh. Just hearing her eased my prickling stomach, which felt constantly on edge these days.

"I'm good. How are you?"

"My stock has dropped," she muttered. "I'm not happy about it."

With a laugh, I sprawled back on the bed. My cabin door was propped open, and one window cracked, admitting a warm autumn breeze that shuffled through the little cabin. It smelled roughly sweet, like decaying leaves and incoming rain. The sun settled lower on the horizon, hidden from the high mountain walls that were a backdrop behind me. I shivered and shut the door gently.

"I wouldn't be happy either."

"What happened to your old phone number? I'm having a

devil of a time getting you programmed into my phone under the new one, even after you texted me."

"My phone broke. Had to get a new one." My throat thickened with the lie, but she didn't need to know the truth yet. Grandma had created a lovely, safe life within her retirement community. No need to pop that yet.

"Oh. I'll ask the nurse to reprogram this number in."

"Good idea." I balanced the phone on my shoulder and reached for a log on top of the pile Mark had put in my room. Sparks flew up the chimney when I jabbed the wood inside. "How's the Bunco group?"

Our conversation spiraled into her most recent exploits. Ranger, the retired military man that lived next door, followed her to their weekly crafts meeting again. His attempts to flirt weren't very subtle, but grandma had never been one to turn a man away. She lived a far more extroverted life than I did.

"Don't worry about me," she said. "I'll keep Ranger on his toes."

I laughed. "I never do worry about you, Grandma."

"Any husband prospects yet?"

"Not yet."

Mark riffled through my mind, but I shoved that back out. Nope. Noooope. He was my client and not at all my type. Although, granted, I didn't exactly know my type. Dating hadn't been high on my priority list the last few years, and Joshua certainly hadn't made it easy.

That whole married-but-possessive-of-other-women thing got in the way.

"Well, what are you going to do about it?" Grandma asked. "How can I be a great-grandma if you don't have babies?"

I laughed again. "You can adopt some from one of your friends there. You basically run that retirement home."

"It's not the same, Stella Marie, and you know it." The

chiding in her voice softened. "He'll come. He'll probably surprise you, but he'll come."

"Love you. Thank you for answering. It's always good to hear your voice."

"You too, honey. Love you. Be safe!"

With a click, she was gone. I set my phone aside as a blast of wind slammed into the cabin wall from the west. Disturbed coals glowed a bright red in the fireplace but didn't seem to catch onto the log I'd shoved inside. This whole Laura Ingalls Wilder setup was new to me. Charming, but I needed a guidebook.

In a crouch, I blew on the coals. They flared to burnt orange, and a small flame licked up the side of the wood.

But would it stay?

For several minutes, I stared at the coals to will them to life, lost in thought. Was Grandma safe? Yes. There was no paper trail to her through financial or public records. Joshua hadn't heard much about her except that she existed, and Grandma could pay for herself for now. Phone records existed, but would he dive into those? I snorted. Okay, that was a step too far. I kept blowing this whole situation up in my head.

Well . . . maybe not.

With a sigh, I glanced up and realized darkness had settled outside. Several store bags littered the room, still unpacked. I flicked on the lamp that I'd bought, filling the cabin with a warm glow. A new winter coat hung across the back of the desk chair, and packaged clothes hangers waited for me to unpack my two suitcases. Maybe Mark would let me stow my empty suit-cases somewhere else.

At some point, I needed to eat dinner.

Just after I started a movie on NetShows to run in the back-ground while I worked, a gentle tap came on the door. By the time I pulled a jacket on and got the door open, no one stood outside.

A single mug of hot chocolate sat on the ground just outside my door, steaming in the cooling night air.

* * *

Five days of blissful quiet passed.

Mark and I blithely avoided each other, like we'd created a game to see as little of each other as possible.

A mug of hot chocolate appeared at my doorstep every night. Instead of catching him on delivery, I paused to give him time to escape. I left an envelope filled with five 100 dollar bills and marked *rent* on his table after his ancient truck roared away. Because who would lock their door out here?

Sometimes after I grabbed some coffee in his house and slipped out the back door again, the cabin smelled like a faint hint of pine, as if he'd just slipped upstairs when he heard my knock and didn't want to be seen. When I returned from making lunch in the kitchen, fresh firewood was stacked in my room.

Strange, like a dance.

But nice all the same.

By the sixth day, however, I was silenced out. The utter stillness of the mountains, while soothing, became grating. Although I'd caught up on a lot of the movies that I'd missed while throwing my world into the accounting firm I suddenly left without explanation, I didn't feel accomplished.

Or relaxed.

The absence of bustle, activity, and people had been rejuvenating. Now, it was too quiet. Suffocating. What was I doing with my life? The four remaining clients I had—Mark included —wouldn't need much until the end of the month. No unusual local or national headlines caught my attention. The quiet should have been a relief.

Now, I just felt restless.

And how much longer would this last? Weeks? Months? I really should have bought that RV. At least there was adventure and movement in driving around.

That evening, I dressed in my warmest running gear. Wild, gray clouds piled on the horizon, whipping in on a cold wind. If I didn't get this excess energy out, I'd never sleep. My cabin wasn't big enough to pace, and I didn't want to intrude on Mark and his mountain man world.

Whatever that meant.

No, there was a strange skein of ice between us, and I didn't want to be the first one to break it.

A chill raced through me when I stepped outside. Gravel ground underneath my shoes as I headed for the road, doubting the intelligence of this decision. It was a few miles to the bridge and back, which would be just right in terms of length. Dark would just be falling in earnest by the time I returned if I hustled.

As I headed around Mark's cabin, buttery light in the windows, a voice startled me.

"It's a bit late for a run."

Mark stood on his porch, one leg tucked behind him in a stretch. He straightened the bent leg, shaking it out. Like me, he wore long pants, sleeves, and ear coverings. Only his face was flushed red, as if he'd just gotten back from a run.

"Hi." I stopped. "Yeah, I just . . . need to get out. I won't be gone long."

He frowned. "Where are you running?"

"To the bridge and back."

A beat followed, then he started toward me. "Mind if I come?"

"Um . . . why?"

"Because there's a mountain lion that's prowling around here at night. It's not safe for you to run by yourself when it's dark here. It'll be dark before you get back and rain is supposed to be blowing in, anyway."

Several responses flooded me, but none of them made it to my lips. Dadgummit, but I definitely hadn't considered the furry type of predator. At least, not near the camp and a road. But then, why wouldn't they be here?

"Oh." I swallowed, realizing how ridiculous that sounded. "But it looks like you just came back."

He shrugged. "I did."

"You want to go again?"

"It's only five miles round trip."

Only. Spoken with the casual arrogance of someone that ran often. How far had he just run? Did he race or something? At first, I was tempted to reschedule the run for later, but the idea of returning to that tiny cabin made my stomach churn. No, I needed to tire myself out first.

"Sure." I managed a smile. "Thanks."

"You set the pace. I'll follow."

Running with another person felt oddly intimate. I forced myself to focus on my body and my pace, the way I always did, instead of whether he thought I was fast or slow. Even with darkness creeping in every minute, and the bare tree branches rattling in the wind that brought it, there was a stark beauty to an autumn forest. Even if it was ready to kill me at any moment.

Suddenly, mountain lion eyes seemed to be everywhere.

We didn't speak at first. Mark followed at my side, but slightly behind. Eventually, my body warmed into the movement. The cool air ached when it spread through my lungs as I breathed faster. Foggy breath trailed behind me as we moved. By the time we arrived at the bridge, the storm covered the sky with slate. Somewhere behind the mat of impending moisture, the sun set. The mountains had already fallen into darkness.

"Thank you," I said. My breath puffed in front of me as I stopped at the bridge. Headlights from the highway on the other side slid by, round, yellow orbs glowing. For some reason, knowing that civilization was close enough to touch made me feel better. I wasn't *so* gone, so lost in the folds of the mountains, that I couldn't find my way back out.

"Thank me for?" he asked, hands set on his hips. He breathed heavily, but not hard.

"Coming."

I turned around and picked my pace back up. Standing around would only chill me, making it harder to start again. Besides, I was sort of terrified to plunge back through the dark tunnel of trees that now faced us and really *did* feel grateful to not be alone. "I wouldn't have been comfortable out here by myself. I didn't realize it would get so dark."

"No problem."

He said it casually, so easily that it broke some of the reservations I felt over even talking to him. Would it change our silent dance if we spoke to each other?

Actually, why didn't we talk more?

"You were gone for a long time today," I said, grabbing the easiest conversation string I could think of. To my surprise, when I tugged it, he didn't unravel.

"Yeah." He matched my stride now. We were perfectly even, our legs thudding the ground in simple synchronization that I enjoyed. "A date."

My brow lifted when I turned to him. "Oh?"

He shrugged again. "Didn't go well."

"No?"

"Her name was Stephanie. She wanted to go on a hike together, so we did."

"Sounds like a great date."

"I thought so too."

Silence fell while I waited for him to elaborate. The dark trees seemed to reach for us, the world obscured in the shadows.

My pace increased ever-so-slightly. Even with Mark at my side, maybe that tiny cabin was a better place to be right now.

"What is it with women saying one thing and meaning another?" The words burst out of him all at once. If we hadn't been running, I would have been shocked. The movement kept me from reacting strongly, however. I took it in stride, like I usually did with Mark.

"What do you mean?"

"Stephanie said she loved to hike. We messaged for a few days, she picked the place, and we met there. Then we started hiking and she complained the whole time. Her shoes hurt. She got bored on the trail. She was tired by the end. The leaves smelled funny."

"How far did you go?"

"Less than two miles."

"Oh."

He shook his head, clearly agitated now. But he seemed to warm up to his words and they flowed as if they'd been pent up for too long.

"She messaged me about her love of hiking. In fact, it was the first thing she said, but she clearly hated it when we started. By the time we finished, and I even cut it short by a mile, she was miserable. Apparently, she doesn't like being sweaty."

"So when she said she loved to hike, she really meant she loved the idea of hiking?"

"Exactly!"

A little chuckle peeped out of me. What a hilarious side of him that I'd never imagined before. This frustrated, trying-to-date-but-hates-it side. He'd inadvertently started to run faster as he told his story, so I pushed my pace to keep up with him. The burn in my chest felt oddly good, even if I wanted to collapse. Pride kept me going.

"Why couldn't she just be honest?" Agitated breath puffed in front of him. "If she doesn't like to hike, that's fine. I don't need her to like everything that I do. But can't she just be honest about that?"

"How long have you been talking to her?"

"A few days. Since you arrived."

"Maybe she's insecure."

"About what?"

I shrugged this time. "I don't know. Lots of people are afraid of not being liked, so they mimic the other person." My breath was more strained, but he didn't seem to notice. "Eventually, it falls apart. She did you a favor. Now you know it's not a good fit because she doesn't even know herself."

His shoulders settled a little bit then, even though his brow had wrinkled. He seemed to think that over for a few minutes before he mumbled, "Probably."

"Not probably. Definitely. What if she had pretended to love hiking and you thought it was real?" My breath huffed in earnest now. He dialed back his pace a little and I went with it in silent exultation. "You'd keep dating her, thinking it was a good fit, and then it would crumble beneath you later. Now it can crumble before it began. Reality sucks, Mark. But sometimes you have to be grateful for it."

Advice I should take myself.

This time as he considered my words, his annoyance calmed. We'd inadvertently fallen into the same back-and-forth we often had as client and accountant. It seemed so easy. In person, his long silences weren't so weird. I left him to think about it as we rounded a bend. Wind blew gentle rain in our direction and sprinkled my hair with a chilly staccato.

"You're right," he finally said. "We weren't a good fit, but I wouldn't have seen that right away."

"It sucks."

"It's frustrating."

"Very."

That seemed to calm him further and we settled back into

the run. When the lights of Adventura were visible through the dark underbrush, I glanced at my watch, startled to see minutes shaved off my time. Maybe I should run with him more. He certainly pushed me.

We slowed at the parking lot entrance, not far from where both our cars were parked and walked in silence to cool down. Before I could veer to my path with a vague *thanks, have a good night,* he nudged me toward his cabin with an elbow.

"Come inside," he said. "There's more room to stretch at my place."

Chapter Six

MARK

A low bank of coals greeted us when we returned to my place.

While Stella stood on my towel-rug and rubbed raindrops out of her hair, I brushed water off my shoulders and headed for the pile of firewood near the fire. Cold had already started to seep in between the chinks in the wooden log walls and through the windowpanes. Keeping this place warm was a part-time job.

"Have you eaten yet?" I asked over my shoulder.

"No."

"Great. I'll make grilled cheese."

She didn't protest, which I took as a good sign. Instead, when I turned around, she'd become engrossed in a picture of me, JJ, and Lizbeth on the wall. JJ had his arm around both of us. While he and I laughed, Lizbeth stared up at him with utter adoration, red hair glimmering in the summer sunshine. Lizbeth had tacked it onto the wall as soon as she'd printed it, and it had been there since the spring. With them gone, I couldn't bring myself to take it down.

"JJ?" she asked, still studying the photo as she gripped one foot behind her in a stretch.

"Yep."

"You're not identical, then?"

"Not even a little."

With a little tender care, the fire flared back up around the small kindling and my driest logs. I abandoned it to grow slowly and grab a drink of water, then tossed her a cup to help herself. She did, and I was relieved. I wanted a friend, not someone to take care of. She seemed perfectly happy to do it herself.

"You plan to shower?" I asked, leaning on the back of a chair.

She nodded.

"Great. We'll both shower, then I'll fix dinner. Once I'm done, we're watching a movie."

An eyebrow arched. "Are we?"

Taking command was natural in some aspects of my life. Work. Travel. Lifting. Mom had always said I was born a natural leader, while JJ assumed I just couldn't help myself. But dating was my fuzzy realm. The place of uncertainty. The place where my dreams went to die because some women didn't like male leadership. Or maybe I came on too strong. Maybe *that* was why everything failed me.

"You don't have to," I countered. "But you'll regret it if you don't. I'm just about to start a James Bond marathon and that's one stud muffin you don't want to miss."

I held out my hands as if to say *just saying*.

Her gaze tapered. "Which Bond?"

I scoffed. "Don't insult me. We start at the beginning and we watch from Sean Connery to Niven to Lazenby to Dalton to—"

"You forgot Moore."

A hint of color brightened her cheeks when I grinned, a hand pressed to my chest. "You know your James Bond actors?"

She scoffed. "Don't insult me."

"Ah, a woman after my own heart. You passed test number one. Get that stinky smell off you, my friend. We have grilled cheese sandwiches, potato chips, and Twinkies to destroy while we watch the world's greatest superhero in action."

* * *

To my relief, Stella Marie gave no peep of annoyance at the old video or my junk food. We sat on opposite sides of the couch, gazes fixated on the TV mounted on the wall while the studly Mr. Connery flashed onto the screen.

"He's my favorite one," she whispered.

My curiosity was piqued. First of all, she might be the *only* woman I'd ever known to be able to name all the 007 actors. The ones that knew anything about James Bond almost exclusively knew Craig—sometimes Brosnan.

"Not Daniel Craig?" I asked, scandalized.

She shrugged. "Meh."

"Why?"

"It's the drawl." She dropped her voice in a poor imitation of the famous *Bond . . . James Bond* line, and ended up laughing at herself.

"You must live like ten secret lives," I said in shock. "Where has all of this truth been hiding all these years? You're a closet Bondie. We should have been best friends years ago."

She smirked and had another bite of greasy—but delicious—grilled cheese. I'd already wolfed down my third. "Somewhere beneath reconciliation charts and spreadsheets?" And I thought I heard her mumble, "with the rest of my life."

"Fair."

We fell into a relaxed back-and-forth, with the movie absorbing most of our attention. Or, at least, appearing too. I had a hell of a time keeping my gaze forward, and she remained mostly quiet. Every now and then a tidbit would arise. A question. A snarky comment about a love of bouffants. But unlike the pressured dates I was used to, this almost felt like a movie with JJ or Megan. Maybe I was too tense and ready to impress on dates. Maybe I should run ten miles before *every* date, just like this one.

A voice in my head couldn't help but wonder if I was too wound up. People said it too much all the time. *Be patient.* Or *wait it out a bit.* Or *calm down, Mark.* Maybe I should have had more dates out in the middle of the wilderness.

Now *there* was an idea.

My thoughts narrowed in the familiar churn that meant I was onto something. Dating in the wilderness? No. Too unsafe for women. But there was a sense of escapism in the mountains. Some people might want to escape out here. Some people— the *right* people, like Stella—might pay to . . .

With a shake of my head, I flicked those thoughts away to focus on the movie. Tonight, I could just enjoy the fact that I didn't watch this movie alone.

Halfway through, Stella grabbed her twinkie, broke it in half, and sucked the cream out of the middle. It must have gone straight to her windpipe because she started to hack. I reached for her water and handed it over. Flushed, she accepted, and the coughing spasm quieted.

Trying to hide my laugh, but failing miserably, I said, "Twinkies fight back, Stell."

Lips pressed, she nodded. The high color in her cheeks had nothing to do with the blazing fire on the other side of the room. Wet strands of hair rested around her ears, still drying after her shower, and the light scent of something floral wafted by every now and then. Under the easy ambiance, I relaxed.

Eventually, she did too.

And the flickering lights pushed the dark, cold night into the back of my mind. I didn't think of Adventura slipping away from me. From my supposed failures. From anything like that.

At least for one night, I wasn't all by myself.

* * *

For the next four days, we acted like movie night hadn't happened.

I delivered her nightly hot chocolate. She answered the door after I'd already left. One day, I returned from stalking the stupid mountain lion to find lunch—tomato soup and a delicious turkey breast with swiss cheese sandwich—left in tinfoil on my table. When she disappeared in her car for a few hours, I restocked her firewood and de-iced her path.

Like we wanted to live around each other for a while but not be *with* each other.

On a random Thursday that shivered with sleet, I shoved a hand through my hair and groaned into my phone. "Justin, just bring your dog back. I don't care if you move in with Megan, I just want Atticus."

His rolling voice laughed. "I'm glad to know where we stand."

"Don't act like you thought you ranked above your dog."

"Never."

"The stupid mountain lion is back and growing bolder. I need another animal around. I wouldn't care as much if it were just me, but I have a . . . friend staying here now."

Interest piqued his voice. "Oh?"

"Yeah, I have friends outside of you ugly buggers."

He laughed again. "Good to know. With such a rosy personality, I'm not surprised. How close has the big kitty gotten?"

I frowned and glanced out the window. Leaves scuttled by on the dry ground, stirred up by a brief vortex of wind.

"Prowled outside the kitchen for a while, but no claw marks on the door. The tracks are pretty clear until they disappear back toward the lake. It seems curious, not hungry, but I don't want it to get used to this place. I can't bring campers here when there's a giant cat prowling around."

With a shudder, I recalled last summer, Adventura's first year open, when Atticus had gone missing. My little sister, Megan, found him up the canyon with slash marks on his ribs. She carried him back on her shoulders and saved his life. Justin always joked that that's when he'd fallen in love with her. I'd always assumed Atticus had chased off a black bear and gotten in a fight, but now I wasn't so certain.

"Silly kitten," Justin murmured. "We're coming back soon, I promise. Watch close at dusk, keep the garbage tight."

"Yes, Mom." I rolled my eyes. "Of course I'm doing all that. The garbage is all inside. I need slashing, angry dog teeth."

"Good. We'll be back soon."

A knock sounded on the door when I ended the call a few minutes after getting updates on my sister—who never called now that she had Justin but thought it was acceptable to update me on her life through him. That would never be acceptable and Megan and I would have words over it.

Stella pushed the door open a few inches and peered inside. "Mark?"

"Come in."

Her hair was pulled away from her face. She wore a pair of jeans and a black pullover that brightened the light streaks of blond behind her ears.

"I need to run to the store." She jerked a thumb outside. "Need anything?"

I held up my hand where my keys dangled from my finger. "Just leaving myself. Ride with me? We can go in together. There's a winter storm warning for tomorrow night. A little snow, but mostly ice in the canyon. I need to stock up on a few things in case we lose power."

She blinked. "Is losing power here a thing?"

I nodded. "Oh yeah."

She hesitated for a moment, eyed her car, then mine, and finally nodded with a shrug that suggested she thought she went to her death. I'd be offended if I didn't get it. My truck would give a person tetanus if they just looked at it.

Still, it was a dependable old tanker.

"Sure," she said. "Thanks."

* * *

The Zombie Mobile rumbled as I steered it down the dirt road toward the highway. It wasn't quite 11:00, which gave us time to get supplies before the rush of Pineville citizens got off work. We'd grab something for lunch on the way home.

With nothing to talk about, we said little. While I might miss having people around—mostly JJ and Lizbeth, 'cause they were special—that didn't mean I wanted small talk. Stella didn't seem inclined either, and the companionable silence took us all the way into Pineville.

Once we rumbled down Main Street, which was the largest of three roads in Pineville, I pointed out the very few landmarks. "Grocery store on the left," I said. "The Frolicking Moose on the right. Great coffee. But they're finalizing renovations after a fire last winter and will hopefully open soon. The Diner is our main restaurant and the bar is just down the road. The pizza place is total crap."

A sign that said *Under Construction* hung across the porch of the Frolicking Moose as we passed. Inside, a few bodies bustled around.

While we walked through the grocery store parking lot, Stella spun around, looking all around her. The reservoir that drew people into Pineville in the summer, and ice fishermen in the winter, hadn't iced over yet. Dark waters and mountains decorated the background behind us. Seemingly satisfied, she faced forward again with a sheepish little smile.

"Bank?" she asked.

I tilted my head across the road as we stepped inside the grocery store. "Just over there. Want to share a cart?"

"Sure."

The wheels on the cart issued high-pitched squeals as I pushed it around the produce, tossing bananas, apples, and salad into bags and slinging them into the cart. She followed behind, carefully inspected each piece of fruit—grapes, avocado, and organic blueberries—before setting them inside.

When I reached for the instant hot chocolate box down another aisle, she put out a hand to stop me. "That is utter trash," she said. "It's not that hard to make. I'll get the ingredients."

"You'll own my heart."

She snorted.

While she gathered powdered milk, cocoa powder, creamer, and sugar, I tossed some protein bars and BBQ potato chips inside.

"See?" She gestured to the ingredients as if I was born in a barn. "It's not that hard. But those chips will probably give you a heart attack."

Before I could quip something snarky, her phone buzzed. I steered us toward the toilet paper—that was one disaster I'd never let happen again—while she poked at her phone. When she didn't catch up with me, I glanced back to find her standing in the middle of the aisle, frowning.

"Stella?" I sang.

She startled, looked up, and her face cleared. She started to walk again as she tucked her phone into her back pocket with a confused expression.

"Everything all right?" I asked.

"Fine."

But the lines remained in her forehead as I grabbed eggs and milk and too much bacon. Her phone must have buzzed again, because she pulled it back out of her pocket, frowned, and pushed her lips to one side as if putting together a mental puzzle.

"Do you need to make a call? You might have to go outside. The reception in here kind of sucks."

As if in a daze, she looked at the cart. "No," she said slowly. "I just have two more things to get. I—"

Her phone vibrated in her hand. The dark expression on her face deepened. For some reason, it reminded me of *Hearts on Fire* and how I hadn't logged in today.

"Stell?"

"Tampons," she murmured as she tapped away on her screen. "I just need tampons and girly pain relievers. Then I'm done."

"Regular or super?"

That totally should have been a weird question, but wasn't. Either her distraction was too great to be embarrassed, or Megan had trained me way too well.

"Regular."

"Long-lasting girly pain relievers or regular?"

"Long-lasting."

She bit her bottom lip as the phone buzzed *again*. Something definitely was up. "Go make your call," I said. "I'll grab your lady things and meet you outside."

She spun and headed down the aisle without taking her gaze off her phone. She must have been distracted or else I had a feeling she would have protested me paying for her organic blueberries.

Not to mention her tampons.

Chapter Seven

STELLA MARIE

My heart pounded as I sped walked to the front of the store, vaguely aware of mumbling something to Mark before disappearing. The incoming text message occupied most of my brainpower.

Unknown Number: How long is your retreat? I just heard from HR that you submitted resignation papers. That's not a retreat, my love.

My heart sped up. No, this couldn't be Joshua. How would he have found my number? I'd only been gone twelve days. At first, I'd lied to him, said I went to Canada on a big retreat with a friend. A few days after I'd gotten the apartment off my hands and left, I'd submitted my official resignation.

My stomach felt cold as I stopped near a cracker display and typed out a response.

Stella Marie: Sorry, you have the wrong number.

His response came seconds later.

Unknown Number: We both know that I don't.
What's going on, Stella love?

My stomach twisted as if a knife had entered it.

I tried to remember Joshua. To picture him outside the small world I knew. To me, Joshua had been a supervisor. Surrounded by cubicles, people, and stress. Maybe not entirely trusted by most of us, but extremely good at what he did. Tall, charismatic, and perfectly aware of the power of his smile. He'd inspired more uncertainty than awe in me from the beginning, unlike other accountants in the firm who adored him, but even that hadn't been enough to keep me safe from his natural lure.

There was something drawing about him.

Until there wasn't.

It didn't seem entirely unreasonable that he'd be upset with me once I left and he realized I wasn't coming back. Didn't seem unreasonable that he'd be furious and try to reach out. To my old number, maybe.

But how did he get my new number?

For a moment, the world seemed to swirl around me as all the implications settled down. Did he know where I was? Was I safe? Was *Mark* safe?

Just in case, I turned my phone on silent and closed my eyes. Now, the store felt too warm, smelled too much like slush and dirt and metallic carts. By the time I hurried outside, I was afraid I'd crash. But I didn't. I stepped into the cool air and drew in a deep lungful. It centered me. Calmed my racing heart. My vision cleared.

This is part of the plan, and that's good, I thought. If grandma taught me anything, it was that belief was power. Whatever I told myself would probably come true. *So always tell yourself good things, Stella Marie,* came her chiding, loving tone.

My breath puffed out in front of me while I headed back to the Zombie Mobile to get my bearings. While my mind raced, my body had calmed. Several things worked to my advantage here. Anonymity, for one. I was Stella here. No, Mark had been calling me Stella Marie. I'd go to just Stella. Sacrilege in Grandma's eyes, but this situation called for what she'd jokingly call *extreme measures*.

Second, Joshua had friends in high places. He may have pulled some strings at a phone company or something. I wouldn't put it beyond him. But that didn't mean he knew I was here, in the middle of the mountains.

Just when I'd gotten ahold of my thoughts and realized I'd actually asked Mark to grab tampons, my phone buzzed again. Frustrated, I glanced back down to see a different name this time.

Tatum: Some guy named Joshua called me this morning —didn't know it was your birthday! Happy birthday!

I had to read the message four times before my brain comprehended it. Tatum was my oldest client. He ran a used bookstore on the other side of the country and always struggled with moving inventory. My birthday? Just as I moved to reply, a second message came from a different number.

Antoine: Is everything okay? Just got a message from a guy named Joshua. He claimed to be your assistant. Had some weird questions for me, so I wanted to check in before I answered any of them.

My hands shook now, and not from the cool autumn air. Somewhere in the distance, a truck roared by, splashing slush onto the sidewalk in front of the store. Two teenagers emerged from the grocery store, laughing. Their hilarity sounded oddly hollow in my ears.

Joshua wasn't my assistant.

It wasn't my birthday.

Which meant something very ugly was just about to happen.

The feeling of a stone crushed my heart as I dashed off a quick text telling Antoine to say nothing, then shoved my phone in my pocket. Before I could hurry back into the store, a hand touched my arm. I whipped around with a muffled cry in my throat to find Mark standing there. Concern darkened his features.

"Stell?"

"The bank," I croaked. "I need to get to the bank right now."

* * *

My hands trembled long after we left the bank. Long after I shoved the $20,456 dollars that constituted everything in my old business and my life into the inside pocket of my jacket. Long after we turned out of the parking lot and I sank lower in my seat to plead quietly, "Please take me back to Adventura."

Then I rolled down the window when we crossed a bridge and I chucked my phone into it.

Mark asked no questions while we rushed down the winding canyon highway. The farther civilization fell away behind us, the better. My mind moved too fast to be productive. Unable to do anything, I let the thoughts run amok for a while.

Paper trail, I thought. No more phones. Nothing but email now. Could I call the feds back, tell them what happened? No. What would they do?

Besides, I didn't have a phone now. Maybe that had been a bit too rash. What about Grandma?

By the time we made it back to Adventura, the mess that had become my brain had already populated a to-do list. I lacked only post-it notes to make it all very clear. Without a single word of explanation, I jumped out of the Zombie Mobile. Before I sped-walked to the cabin, I skidded to a stop and whirled around.

"Call me Stella now, not Stella Marie? Never Marie."

Mark blinked, halfway out of the truck. He shrugged.

"Sure."

"Have you received any phone calls, text messages, or emails from someone unknown? A Joshua?"

He glanced at his phone. "No."

Relief made me momentarily weak. "Good. If an unknown number calls, don't answer. Don't answer any text messages or emails. Okay?"

He nodded.

I spun around and jogged back to my cabin with the silent promise that I'd explain everything . . . eventually. Once there, I shut myself inside, grabbed my computer, and flung it open.

While it booted up, I let out a long breath and forced myself out of panic. Out of fear. Before anything else could be done, I had to write these emails. They would dictate what I needed to do next. I pulled up Tatum's email, clicked on the new message icon, and started to write.

* * *

Two hours later, my brain felt fried.

Forcing a positive, normal tone while writing to my clients, except for Mark, whom I hadn't seen any sign of since the store, had been harder than I expected. Some of them emailed right back and proved my hunch right. Joshua had been innocuous, maybe strange when he spoke with them. Enough for them to want to call me to ask me about him but without saying anything identifiably wrong.

He'd been fishing for information on me, clearly. Perhaps he had gotten my number from one of them. But how had he gotten *their* information?

He was playing a game. Always a game.

He *wanted* me to know something was wrong. He might even know already that I'd seen something I shouldn't. Did he realize I'd turned him in? He had to be suspicious that I was hiding from him, at least. I wasn't on a retreat, and now I'd never return. By now, he probably even knew I'd sold my lease to someone else and moved out. Of course, he could think I was tired of his constant chase and I wanted away from him.

Which would only make him chase harder.

So I shut down everything else.

My old accounting company I'd started after college then stopped growing to work at corporate. The bank accounts. The social media accounts. I wiped out every trace to my company, changed every password I'd ever known. Registered a random PO Box in Texas and routed all my mail there. With tears in my throat, I emailed my clients that I had to take care of a family emergency that would be a while. I referred them to a trusted friend and said goodbye.

These were my first accounting clients from six years ago. Before I'd been lured into a big firm with exciting opportunities and bigger pay. These were the salt-of-the-earth people that I held onto because they were good.

That lump sat in my throat all day.

The hours raced by while I typed away on my computer, peeling sticky notes off the wall as I accomplished each task. 2:00. 3:00. 5:00. When darkness fell and a whistling wind began to pick up, the lump in my throat grew. I shut my laptop on an email that confirmed the bank accounts would close in 72 hours. Heat prickled at the back of my eyes as I stood, unable to dismiss the ugly truth.

My old life was gone.

I had no job, no clients, and no hope of getting one in the future.

What few friends—more like acquaintances—that I'd held

onto over the years might not even notice that I'd gone off the radar. Not for a while, or until something big happened. Then they'd remember that they'd forgotten me, which was fine.

Frustrated, I let the tears finally fall. I'd held onto them long enough—for at least three weeks, since the day I first figured out that the companies Joshua had me applying for a government program for weren't real.

Sniffling, I grabbed a sweater and yanked it on.

Stupid Joshua.

Stupid men.

Stupid corporate greed.

Dadgummit, but I needed those pain relievers and those tampons.

A knock came at my door. It was so tentative at first, I almost didn't hear it. But the door groaned open slightly, and that's when I realized it hadn't totally shut, which explained the whistling wind. That my room felt icy cold because I'd forgotten to attend to the fire.

Mark stood outside, a mug in his hand. He'd frozen as if about to take a step back when our eyes met through the thin crack.

"Stella?" he asked. "Sorry, I didn't mean to interrupt. I'm a little early, but I was worried. Are you—"

I reached out and pulled the door open further. Cold wind raced past him, shocking me. He straightened, hot chocolate in hand. His gaze hadn't left my tear-stained cheeks. The fact that I looked like a mess didn't even matter.

"Stella?"

With a wave, I beckoned him inside.

"C'mon." I folded a jacket more tightly against me. "I have some explaining to do."

Chapter Eight

MARK

We sat on the floor, our backs braced against the twin bed that Lizbeth had replaced the old metal cot with a few months ago.

The wooden floor was creaky and cold, but the fire I'd prodded back to life was crackling fast now. The heat came with it, filling the small space almost instantly. Stella stared at the flames with the dazed, exhausted expression of someone that had just been through hell. Night had fallen, and with it came a massive drop in temperature. The wind brushed by outside, heralded by rain on her windows. She'd drawn the blinds, but the *plunk plunk* left no doubt.

"Three weeks ago," she said suddenly, breaking apart the quiet, "I went to work just like any other day. Sat at my desk and answered some emails. Joshua, one of my supervisors, brought some paperwork by and said some of our smaller companies needed to file for government assistance." She waved an airy hand. "Nothing massive, but it seemed odd that there were so many to fill out."

A dark feeling started in my chest then, and I could already see where this went. I stayed silent, however, and listened while we both stared at the fire. Several inches remained between our shoulders, but the cozy cabin felt intimate all the same.

"Anyway, I decided to look into the companies because some of the paperwork didn't quite line up. Eventually, I discovered that the companies weren't real. They were fake. Joshua wanted me to obtain government assistance for businesses that didn't exist."

"Money laundering," I murmured.

Dejected, she nodded. When she took a sip of the hot chocolate, her eyes closed briefly while she savored it. I fought back an exultant shout. It had taken me five tries to make a single mug of "real" hot chocolate off a googled recipe. The previous four had been disgusting. She had another sip before she continued.

"Once I realized that it wasn't some fluke, of course, it wasn't, but I kind of wanted it to be, I wasn't sure what to do. For a few days, I just kept going to work and pretending everything was fine. Joshua checked on me daily but he had always done that. Always been . . . *too* attentive."

My body immediately tensed, but she didn't notice. Just kept speaking, every now and then tucking a piece of hair behind her ear in a nervous gesture.

"Joshua didn't seem overly suspicious of my behavior and didn't ask about the applications much. But there was . . . something there. So I just tried to figure out what to do and how to gain the evidence.

"By the end of the week, I felt like I had all the proof I needed. So I stayed late, cleaned out the important things at my desk, erased everything that could show my deep research off my computer, and met with a woman named Anya. A federal investigator. I gave her everything."

I whistled low. She snorted.

"Yeah," she muttered. "Real brave, wasn't it? I ditched all the evidence, called in sick the next morning, and requested a three-week sabbatical to go on a retreat to Canada with a friend. Since I'd left a few things there, no one thought anything of it, I would imagine. I didn't have friends at work to notice, anyway. Joshua's attention was an effective isolator. That night, I packed up all the important things at my apartment. An old college friend of mine had been crashing at my place for a few days and wanted the lease. I signed it over and left."

My eyebrows rose. "Left left?"

"Left left," she repeated with a little twitch of her lip. Like she wanted to be amused, but the reality was just too ugly. "My furniture was minimal anyway. I didn't really . . . I didn't really *live* in my place." She frowned, running the tip of her finger along the top of her mug. "I worked a lot. Shayna bought all my furniture and plates and that stuff for $2,000. I packed up my car and drove away."

"To here?"

She hesitated, chewing her bottom lip. "To here," she said without looking at me. "I needed someplace to hide. Eventually, Joshua would figure out I wasn't coming back and maybe even realize I was the whistleblower. I thought about buying an RV and just driving around the country, but . . ."

She trailed off.

I leaned my head back against her mattress as I tried to comprehend all she'd revealed. Of course, she'd been running from *something*. That much had been obvious from the moment that she showed up. But this wasn't what I had expected.

She sighed heavily.

"Then," she muttered, "today happened."

While she explained the text messages she'd received and the calls that dipwad Joshua made to her clients—which call I never got, but calls rarely come through here—my mind raced.

She was good and stuck.

"Joshua is in love with you?" I ventured carefully.

She sighed. "I guess? If that's called love. He's married. But ever since I started the job, he's made it very clear that he's interested in me. At first, it was subtle and not a big deal, but it's grown in the last year. If I hadn't found the fraud, I probably wouldn't have quit. But his attention . . . it's been so slow. So steady. He's . . . possessive of me, in a way."

My fists clenched. "He's an asshole."

She laughed mirthlessly. "That too."

The situation was bleak and infuriating. No job. Just closed her business. No way to venture into the outside world until all of this was set aside. No wonder she came to Adventura. It was out of the way and she had some sort of trust in me. Even if I was likely her most frustrating client, at least she knew me enough to be fairly certain I wasn't a creep. The thought of her on her own, in an RV, sent a shudder through me.

Bad idea.

The silence rode for several minutes once she finished. She sipped the rest of the hot chocolate and didn't seem so bleary afterward. I lifted the fire poker and shoved a teetering log back. As always, I had ideas.

Lots of ideas.

But of all the ideas whirling in my head, filling me with that heady exhilaration that I hadn't felt in a while, was one that really made the most sense—even though it made absolutely no sense at all.

"Well," I said with a steady breath out. "Sounds like you're here to stay."

She recoiled. "Mark, did you just hear all that? What if Joshua comes after me? You could be in danger."

"And since you're here to stay," I continued as if she hadn't spoken, "I think it's also time that you realize something."

Wary brown eyes studied me as she drawled, "Yes?"

No doubt she heard my tone. The cheshire cat tone. The tone that said *oh yeah, I have ideas and you're about to get all of them.* When I smiled, she grew more serious, which is just where I wanted her.

A little shock-and-awe never hurt anybody.

"I think you've got a bunch of time on your hands with nothing to do and the need for free rent. Not to mention someone that can kick Joshua's ass if he comes by. For the record, that's definitely my job."

My grin grew even as I felt a shot of trepidation. What was I thinking? I couldn't pitch this. She'd never go for it. I reached into my back pocket anyway and handed over the folded envelope I'd been carrying around for days, waiting for the right moment to give her the $500 rent back without seeming like a weirdo. There had always been a clear line between us. Client. Accountant.

This broke that in a big way.

And, frankly, I couldn't wait for that weirdness to dissolve. So I handed it over to her. The words barreled out of my mouth like they had their own power.

"We're both in a jam right now, and I may have already thought of my way out. Except I'm going to need some help. Lots of help. So you can stay here free, Stella. I'll keep you safe with a roof over your head, and you help me save Adventura."

Her face dropped into shock when I gave the big finale.

"You save me, I save you?"

Chapter Nine

STELLA

For a full fifteen seconds, I tried to comprehend such an offer.

You save me, I save you.

Well, there was a line I hadn't heard before. Did I need saving? My first response was *no, I got this*. But that wasn't true either. The $20,000 in cash hidden in a small, plastic box I'd dug out of his kitchen and shoved underneath a loose floorboard seemed like a large amount of money, but that kind of cash disappeared quickly on the run. If I tried to buy anything with it —like a crappy RV—I would use a good chunk of it, and the problem of food and gas still existed.

Even that $500 he was trying to give back was precious.

So, yes. I needed help and free rent and big muscles. Desperately.

Did he need saving?

Yes. Desperately.

I licked my lips, locking him in an uneasy stare. "What does that mean, exactly?"

Amusement flickered through his bright eyes, like this sort of trespass into uncertain territory gave him great delight. Knowing Mark, it *did* delight him.

"I'm not propositioning you, geez. Don't look so scared. Stell, I'm about to lose Adventura. You know that as well as I do. But I may have thought of a way out. I'll just . . . need help getting there." His gaze darted around. "Turns out I suck at housekeeping and details and we'll need all that and more."

His casually spoken sentence nearly made me choke as I laughed, half in disbelief, half in confusion. But then I realized he was serious and I sobered quickly.

"What is your idea?"

Fire leaped into his eyes, mimicking a sudden smile. He jumped to his feet and started to pace as if his legs were somehow attached to his vocal cords.

"In order to save Adventura, I have to do more things with the real estate that I already have. Obviously, I have no money to invest in something else. Which means I need to do something to make money with Adventura through the winter. My Home-BnB's rent is pretty steady, as you know. It will pay for both our food and electricity. But to pay off the monthly mortgage, we need more money."

"I know all this already."

He flapped an impatient hand. "I know, but I have a process. Go with it."

I pulled my legs out of a very cramped place where we'd been together and straightened them out. He didn't seem bothered by being able to pace only two steps at a time. He continued, his face a mask of concentration.

"Not many people would want to come to Adventura in the winter. Unless, like you, they had a reason. Someone . . ."

"Desperate?"

He stopped, thought it over, then shrugged. "Maybe?"

"You're going to put out an ad that says, *running from a psycho boss? Stay with us!*"

The daft man actually looked like he was considering it.

"Mark . . ." I drawled.

He shook his head, snapping out of it. "No, of course not that. But . . . maybe. I hate throwing away ideas. Anyway, what if we rented out this cabin to people that needed to escape their everyday life."

"Parents?"

"I was thinking artist, but I can go with that!"

I blinked. Now that had taken me by surprise. Artists? How oddly . . . specific.

"Artists?"

"Yeah. We rent out a cabin or two and prep it for artists." He gestured around us. "Take this homey little number. We make it cozier if possible, you and Lizbeth have done a great job, and prep it for art. Get a big drafting table—"

"A drafting table?" I cried. "That would take up the whole space here."

"Okay, so we do that in a different one. Whatever, those are details we'll figure out later. We advertise it as an artist's retreat. Maybe we have the wifi turned off for them during the day, or . . . food!" he exclaimed all of a sudden. "We provide all meals and delicious food. JJ could cater!" His face scrunched. "Those details can come later, too. But we have a winter retreat for the crazy creatives that feel like they can't create in their usual spaces."

This conversation had instantly pushed us back into the Mark-and-Marie that I knew so well, and that calmed me. For a moment, it felt like we were on the phone, worlds apart. Now, however, immersed in his life, his vision seemed so much brighter. The idea ran through my head a few times, accruing statistics and numbers as fast as I could form a thought.

"Do you have supplies to 'cozy this place up'?" I asked.

"Maybe. I also have a Justin."

"What's a Justin?"

"Justin. The camp ranger."

"Oh!" The name finally surfaced in my mind from his

payroll paperwork. It struck me—not for the first time—how oddly intimate a relationship between accountant and client could become. We saw most people in a light they didn't even comprehend themselves. Behaviors, statistics, impulses, challenges, all laid out in numbers.

To see it in real-life was disorienting, at best.

"Justin." I nodded. "Right."

"We'll need to do most of the work." He ran a hand through his hair. "Lizbeth nearly perfected this little cabin, not to mention the addition of the bathroom, so we could spruce it up a little more with an artist in mind and try here first."

His ideas flowed so easily now I almost missed the *we* in there. When had *we* become an official thing? Drywall? No thanks. Then again, this cabin wasn't too bad. Maybe people would pay to live here.

Hadn't I?

I cleared my throat.

"If we rent this place, then what about me?"

"The attic," he said immediately. His brain really did move fast. He waved his hand in that direction again. "I'll crash on the couch or something. I've done winter camping before. It sucks, but with the right gear, it's livable."

My mouth opened to protest, but I stopped. Winter camping? Okay, this was going sideways somehow. His phone was buzzing incessantly in his back pocket, so I pointed to it with the hope of a mental break. He was hard to keep up with.

"Do you need to get that?" I asked.

He shook his head. "Just the app."

What app? I wanted to ask but figured it must be his online dating one. He'd mentioned it vaguely one day when leaving for a date or something. Because we were client and accountant, I hadn't asked. Stupidly, I had to shake off a flare of annoyance that came with the thought of him on a dating app. I forced myself back into his idea.

"Give me a sec," I murmured. "I need to think."

He said nothing but kept pacing. Because he moved, I closed my eyes and tilted my head back on the mattress. With the chance to stop talking came more thoughts, and with them, more clarity. Finally, I pegged what had me most stymied here.

What Mark was really asking—though I couldn't be sure he realized it himself—was a dissolution of the client-accountant boundary. Mark wanted to approach our mutually-messed up situations as . . . *friends*.

Why did that make my throat tighten and feel like a bad idea?

I had no idea. Friends were in short supply these days, and I needed more of them. Or just one really good one. Fortunately, Mark had all the underpinnings for that. His offer was mostly innocuous but hid so much more. Was I willing to live *and* work with Mark? To be his . . . buddy? We were water and fire when it came to details. The details he brushed off so easily were the ones I hyperfocused on because you *had* to. Those were the parts of a project that could make or break the entire thing.

But he'd also offered me a safe spot. Himself, on some level, as protection. And I couldn't deny that it gave me an unexpected level of comfort to know I'd be near him. He was a gentleman, indeed, and had no absence of strength or ability. At the very least, he could keep me physically safe, which felt like too much of a selfish ask. But one I would gladly take.

In fact, Mark was far lonelier than I would have ever imagined. Like a puppy stuck in the store, staring out the window and wishing someone would just take him home already.

Once again, I had to force myself back to his business idea when my mind wandered into deeper territories. Thankfully, he left me in blessed silence for almost ten minutes. I kept my eyes closed, but quietly cataloged all my thoughts around it until I had no more.

Then I opened my eyes. He sat on my desk chair and stared at the ground. When I shuffled, his gaze locked on mine.

"You know, Mark . . ."

He stopped, eyes wide. "Don't tell me! You love it."

"I don't *hate* it."

He let out a whoop. "That is definitely a first." He bounced back to his feet and rubbed his hands together. "We're going places. So what do you say? You hang out here and help me get organized and prep these cabins? I'll run the errands in town so no one can see you, Justin will help with the big stuff, Lizbeth will do the website and social media management. My mom probably knows crazy people that want to escape. Dad definitely knows crazy people."

"Mark. Stop."

I stood next to him and he stuttered to a standstill. For two seconds a strange expression crossed his face as if he braced himself, but it faded soon into a silent question.

With firmness, I said, "It's a good idea."

His shoulders dropped. Until that moment, I hadn't noticed how tense he was underneath all his energy. But the absence of it left him glaringly obvious. He really *did* have a hard time finding people that would listen to his ideas. Which was understandable on some level. The man was like a fountain that didn't shut off. On the other hand, I could see a lonely little space of him existed in the vacuum of people that could twist his gear and slow it down.

Something like hope showed on his face. I tucked a strand of hair behind my ear.

"I'll . . . help you however I can. As a friend."

The word didn't strangle me. In fact, it slipped out easily.

His brow dropped, and the softening in his gaze made him look so much like a happy little boy I almost lost my composure. Dagnabbit, but why did he have to be so *rugged* underneath all those layers of entrepreneur?

This was a bad idea. I didn't know why and I'd have to figure it out later, but this was a *bad* idea.

Now that I'd started, however, I couldn't stop it.

"But I won't put my accountant support behind it until we prove it out in the numbers and . . . we find someone to rent this cabin."

He nodded, hands held in front of him as a concession. "Fair. I'll take that offer. Shall we 007 tonight after we crunch the numbers?"

His eyebrows waggled. My lips twitched.

"What's your draw to this place?" I finally asked, just to seal the final uncertainty. Would we work hard together just for him to decide to sell it on a whim? He'd certainly done that in the past.

Mark blinked. "Adventura is home. Forever. I'll never sell my home. I'm going to live on this piece of land and be that smelly old guy the summer camp kids always laugh at because he farts so loud and doesn't realize it."

Unbidden, I giggled.

He grinned.

And then the decision was made: Mark and I were going to save each other.

Like *friends*.

MARK

Stella let out a heavy sigh behind me the next morning as we strode toward the commissary, which happened to double as a garage in the winter. We kept most of Justin's supplies in a back room that he'd roped off.

After our second 007 movie night and her relentless grilling of details, Stella had curled up on the couch, absorbed in her tablet, and mostly fallen quiet. I didn't mind. The silence wasn't so deafening when someone shared it. So I'd scribbled more ideas onto paper, mulled over our options, and, in general, had the best night in a while.

Pale morning light tinted the horizon as we quietly walked through Adventura. Both of us had been up early. We normally didn't even attempt to interact before noon, as if both of us couldn't sleep. Most of the time, it was easy for me to put off the enormity of tasks that I took on, but this was different. Never in my adult life had I formed any attachment to a place. JJ and I had literally lived in an old bus for a while. For nearly all of our twenties, we bounced around the globe, living on JJ's climbing sponsorships and whatever money I could scrub up on my early, failed business attempts. When my parents divorced, the house I grew up in was the first thing to go.

Adventura was *my* first home.

And now I could lose it.

Which is why I finished my workout by 7:00, showered, had breakfast, and responded to two new *Hearts on Fire* messages. One from a girl named Shanti that was driving through tomorrow, and another from Sunni, who needed some money but really hated to ask. Shanti—that one had hope.

At 7:30 on the dot, I paced the floor to work out the broad logistics of this plan. By the time Stella snuck in through the back door at 8:00 and peered around the corner, as if afraid she'd disturb me, I'd already moved past basic cabin redesign and onto website construction. My sloppy notes covered four sheets of paper. Even I couldn't read two of the sentences.

But this morning seemed to have brought a change in her. Deep lines lived in her brow, and a growly expression covered her face. Was she the kind of girl that got hangry? Because she hadn't eaten yet.

"Regretting it already?" I quipped as I nudged her to the left, toward the commissary. She grumbled something as we approached the door.

"What are we doing here again?" she asked as I pushed open the door and motioned her inside. She tilted her head back to look at the two-story rafters overhead. On the far right were warehouse-sized shelves that stored and separated meals for campers in the summer. Workers organized and stored the food with weekly deliveries. Now, they lay empty, like a skeletal structure forgotten in the zombie apocalypse.

I yanked open a side door off to the left. Steel scratched across the cement floor as it swung toward us.

"Just checking what Justin's kept here so we know how much we'll have to pay for, as you put it, *dolling it up.*"

She made another sound, her focus back on her tablet,

which she clutched like I'd take it from her. As if electronics and I had ever been friends.

A dusty lightbulb did a poor job of illuminating the closet, which was as perfectly organized as I expected. Nothing out of place except dust. A quick scan confirmed all the tools we would need. Basics like hammer, nails, spackle, every imaginable size of screwdriver, and more. Paint cans. Brushes. Rollers. Tarps.

Man land.

I freaking love this closet.

"Listen, Mark, I've put together a rudimentary cost analysis based on your current profit and loss—"

"English," I muttered.

She sighed. "Me know your numbers."

My back was to her as I attempted to wrench an old cardboard box off the shelf, which made it safe to grin.

"Tell me more, cavewoman Stell."

"Okay," she drawled, "to summarize in Mark terms, you need about $4,000 a month to pay off credit card debt and the mortgage. Right now, you have $1,000 in savings and $15,000 in credit card debt. You have three weeks until both the mortgage and the credit card are due again. You pay $2,000 for the mortgage and a minimum of $1,200 for the credit card."

Those numbers normally wouldn't bother me. Money was fluid and came and went, but a long, lonely winter awaited me with little to do. There had been years in my life when I grabbed any job I could just to eat, but that kind of work wasn't available in Pineville. Now, I had nowhere else to go.

"Not bad," I muttered as my finger caught the edge of the box. Dust trickled on my nose and made me sneeze when I finally yanked the box off the shelf. The lid tipped to the floor, scattering dead moths. She eyed them and stepped back to the doorway, which she leaned against.

"Setting aside income from your HomeBnB's to pay electric and food, if you plan to open one cabin—mine," she added with an edge of tightness that made me grin further, "—you would need to earn $3,000 from renting that cabin in the next 21 days. That requires you to book out the next three weeks for $152 a day." She hugged the tablet to her chest. "Starting within the hour."

Marie—Stella—had always had a slice of self-righteousness to her tone just when we were about to start arguing. Her depth of belief in numbers was a sure foundation. *They don't lie,* she always said to me around gritted teeth.

But outside forces could skew numbers within seconds of discovery. A winning lottery ticket. A new investor. An idea that built with sheer work instead of monetary investment.

That same tone built within her now and gave me a little thrill. It's why I secretly loved to talk to Stella: we always did this back-and-forth. While I dreaded it because I never won, I adored the path to my demise.

"You assumed we need to make $3,000 this month," I said. "Drop that to $2,000."

Her frown could be felt through my back. "The only way to do that is to use your savings?"

"Yep."

"But then you have no savings."

"Yep."

She paused. The silence stretched so long I thought she'd left. When I looked back, she still stood there, eyebrow quirked.

"But..."

"Savings are meant to be used in the worst of times, right? I'm in the worst of times, Stella. Calculate please?" I asked.

With another grumble of assent, her tablet pen poked away. I turned half my attention to the box I'd just pulled down. Though dusty, a few tidbits still lived in there, half-eaten by mice. Nothing usable. With a grunt, I tossed it into the commissary to throw away with the next trash run, and moved onto the next one.

"$95 if you book out every day," she said.

"Try for 14 days."

Another dramatic sigh. "$143 per day."

"Perfect!" I wiped my dusty hands on my jeans. "That gives us one week to find enough people to pay $143 per night to stay in that tiny cabin for two weeks."

"You make it sound so easy," she muttered.

I glanced back at her. Her lashes were low as she stared at the tablet, lips quirked to one side of her face as the tablet pen tapped against the side. When her gaze lifted to mine, I gave her a lopsided smile.

"It doesn't have to be that hard."

"I think you're underestimating how much marketing you need to do to *find* someone," she said. "Do you have a social media presence?"

"We don't have to market."

She glared at me. "You're going to conjure them out of thin air?"

"Yes."

At my simple response, her mouth shut.

"You're going to cut and dye your hair so you blend in better?" I asked, to cover the fact that I'd been staring at her a little too long.

She snorted. "My life is not a *Loveline Channel* movie. So no."

Her attempt to keep it lighthearted wasn't a failure, but I saw some tension in her response. Maybe she wasn't full-on witness protection program yet, but what if it turned to that? I couldn't discount that it was possible.

Honestly, the cougar scared me more.

"Can we return to the numbers?" she asked. "And the details? I need to know *how* you conjure clients out of thin air. Most companies require money in marketing to generate leads."

"I'm not most companies."

She snorted. "Whatever. I'd like to pad these a bit. I don't want to use up all your savings. Let's assume we can charge $160 a night. It buys us a little leeway."

"I'm going into town tomorrow." Another rain of dust showered on me as I gripped the third box to pull it down. "I'll start talking to people. I texted Lizbeth this morning and she's already starting on a website and social media page."

"Just like that? You don't have the money to pay her."

"I'm not." I shrugged. "They love me. It's what family does. We're going to try listing the cabin as a HomeBnB first, see if we can get traction there since I already have a profile she manages for me for now."

Stella quirked an eyebrow. "Lizbeth sounds pretty amazing."

"She is."

"How long have you known her?"

"Less than a year."

"So fast?"

I shrugged. JJ and Lizbeth moved faster than even that. I didn't mention the fact that they spent only two months dating before they were engaged. For them, it fit. Plus, Lizbeth had loved JJ forever. Stella didn't seem like the uber-trusting type. She made a sound low in her throat, but kept her eyes on her tablet.

When the third box joined the other one to be thrown away, I clapped the dust off my hands in resignation.

"There's nothing here. I thought we had some odds and ends we could use to clean up one of the other cabins—lamps, light fixtures, that kind of thing—but nothing is here so far. I'll have to buy some things in town."

"With the savings you plan to spend for a minimum credit card payment?" she asked sharply, throat bobbing. Stella stared outside, though there was nothing there, and I recognized the tight, pinched part of her voice.

Did risk scare her?

Maybe it should scare me more, but this wasn't the tensest situation I'd ever been in. Things always had a way of working out.

"Something will pop up," I said easily. "Now that it's warming up outside, let's hop on the four-wheeler. I'll tour you around the camp. Let's see if it triggers any ideas for either of us."

Chapter Eleven

STELLA

Twenty minutes later, we bounced down the road on a tired four-wheeler that gasped every time Mark pushed the accelerator too fast. I sat behind him, the autumn sun warm on my face. His back felt firm against my chest even though I tried hard to keep space between us. The bounce of the ride made it almost impossible. Eventually, I gave it up and enjoyed the feeling of him close to me.

How long had it been since I'd had physical touch with someone?

Too long.

My mind shifted away from that and tried to quell the rising panic.

This is Mark's responsibility, not mine.

This is Mark's responsibility, not mine.

Even though Adventura wasn't actually mine to save, a rising sense of responsibility had grown within me overnight. The feeling of being in this together ever since he gave the $500 back. Besides, if something happened to Adventura, I wouldn't have a hiding place *or* anyone in the world I could safely rely on.

More than that, however, was I wanted this for Mark. He

was a good guy. Misunderstood. Energetic to a fault. But a good guy.

And his laissez-faire attitude was going to kill me.

Touring Adventura didn't help my anxiety, either. The land, tucked into the folds of the mountains and still thick with blooming green and gold, took my breath away. Fresh air brushed past my cheeks and removed some of my desperate fright. But under it all lay a sense of vast emptiness.

There wasn't much here to fix.

The kitchen was the largest building, with an attached dining room and open seating space to feed the campers and staff, but the shingles on the roof were in need of repair and a good slapping of stain on the dry wood. The cost of the stain alone would be hundreds of dollars.

A few outbuildings and smaller sheds dotted certain areas. No pavement appeared anywhere outside of the highway miles away—even the parking lot was dirt. Outside of the cabin where I slept, a few others I hadn't gotten a good glimpse of were tucked out of sight. Were those the ones he also wanted to rent? They seemed sort of close together. The commissary was the only other building. He had other perks, like the lake and the river and hiking in the canyon, but there wasn't much *at* Adventura.

My stomach sank with every mile Mark put on the engine. He'd point at something, slow down, and explain it. Campsites. Stream access. A place where a black bear had been spotted. Twice we crossed a burbling stream, shady parts edged with crackling ice. The entire place truly was lovely. A definite home.

But could he *sell* it as a retreat that people would pay for?

Finally, Mark took me up a trail that was clearly created by the four-wheeler. Eventually, he stopped it and killed the engine, then swung off. He extended a hand to me with an eager, bright smile.

"C'mere. There's a view of the whole camp."

I slipped my hand in his and he tugged me off the four-wheeler. My skin thrilled to the contact of another human, even if wholly without romantic affection. Only a few paces away was the edge of a rock face that looked down. The tops of the cabins were visible from here, dark slopes against the green and spiny-branched backdrop. I'd seen the lake from the ground, but not so high. Rolling green spread out the other side of it, disappearing into more ridges and trees. The canyon walls were closer than I'd thought, leading back until the mountains disappeared in themselves.

The wild beauty took my breath away.

Mark sat down, a broad grin on his face. How was he this calm? How could he stand to look at all of this when he could be a few bad payments away from losing it? And why was he so unconcerned about the blatant problems in his plan? Mark usually came to me with his broad strokes ideas. Rarely did I get into the nitty-gritty with him, like now. Instead, I oversaw, advised, and he left to do whatever he thought best.

He drew me back to the present with a loud breath.

"Amazing." He lifted both hands. "Isn't it absolutely amazing?"

We stared at the mountains, and they stared back. Somewhere around the rills of the peaks across from us would be the highway, hidden by twists and turns. I had absolutely no sense of direction, grateful that only one road led in and out, or else I would have gotten lost long ago.

"Very," I murmured.

Mark leaned back on his palms, the backs of his shoes thudding against the rock his legs dangled off of like a little kid. I chose to sit back a little farther, legs crossed. The sheer drop below sent my stomach into a tumble at the mere thought.

After several moments, the quiet worked its magic. I lost the trail of anxiety that I'd been walking and let myself get lost in the quiet whisper of wind. My thoughts skittered like the leaves behind us. I closed my eyes, letting the sun warm my face again. When had I last sat outside to feel the sun?

Too long.

Grandma would never approve.

Mark kicked his heels in an alternating rhythm now, but it had a sort of cadence that seemed accidental. Even though he didn't speak, I could hear his thoughts moving. Likely, they never stopped. I could tell that some sort of calculation moved behind his eyes. Although overcome with doubts that he'd be able to save this place, I appreciated his moxie at trying.

Adventura was lovely, but its prospect was bleak. If he really wanted to make stable money off of it, it would need far more upgrading. My lips twitched as I thought of his idea a few months ago.

"Horses, Marie," he'd said. "I think I need to invest in horses. There's a lot of grazing land out here, and we could use them for the summer camp. What do you think? Horses may draw in more people. My investors are thinking it over."

While he rattled about horse therapy and autistic kids, my mind had gone down the trail of insurance needs, care, grooming, and basic maintenance. We'd spoken for over an hour about it, and he'd happily paid my consulting fee. Until now, I hadn't realized that Mark did nothing with the horse idea. Maybe it wasn't the worst concept, but the practicality behind it would be more detailed than he'd like.

No, that was a dead end.

My mind spun through other possibilities. How else could the land be used but still maintained for the money-making summer? My thoughts must have spiraled deep—or perhaps my face just betrayed me—because his voice broke into them. My thoughts scattered like grains of sand.

"It's going to be okay, Stella."

When I looked at him, he peered at me with a curious, but steady, gaze. For a second, I was tempted to smile and lead him down a different track. Tell him that fear and concern weren't even on my mind. But that would be a lie, and I never lied.

"I hope so."

"I always figure it out."

That much *was* true. He figured something out usually, even if it was patchwork and eventually abandoned. His life was littered with bandaids, but even those had slowly side-stepped him places.

Where did the steady trust in himself come from? How could he so easily spin ideas and just *hope* to find the money? There needed to be a firm plan. A path to find the people that would do the rentals. A known, trusted source for each step that we could logically move into next.

"It's pretty simple, really," he said as if he were talking to himself now. "We already have the space to rent since you are kind enough to move to the attic. There are no upgrades that need to happen aside from basic cozying up, which is easy. So we have one week to find someone—or several someones—to rent it. The path is clear."

"Right," I said, my tone deadpan. "As if that were so simple. As if companies don't spend thousands of dollars every day in lead acquisition."

He laughed. "We don't need thousands of dollars."

My frustration was palpable. "How are you going to *find* those people? Leads? Paid traffic? Do you have some sort of . . . connection in Jackson City or . . ."

He grinned, which stopped me short. There was a little too much rugged attractiveness about his beard, his quirky hair, and the bright set of teeth behind his lips. Lips that, I admitted to myself, I looked at a few too many times today.

"With the steadiest, most reliable asset I have," he said.

"What's that?"

"My unflappable charm, of course."

* * *

Turned out, he wasn't kidding.

Two hours later, we drove back down the highway toward Pineville but pulled off before we arrived in town. Mark didn't say where we were going as we bounced down a paved road that turned into dirt and eventually a worn two-track with dead weeds in the middle. Instead, his forehead remained slightly puckered with thought. I held onto the seat and tried not to panic.

When Mark had ideas, sometimes they got *weird*.

Fifteen minutes later, he stopped at a small, gray house with two windows framed by dull red shutters, a porch with a swing, and a giant gray truck. The charming little place was tucked up against a hill at the foot of a sprawling mountain, like everything here. When I stepped outside, I could hear the tinkle of a creek nearby.

"Where are we?" I asked as I stepped out.

A man with salt and pepper hair and a lined face stepped onto the porch in a pair of cowboy boots and a long flannel shirt. The screen door slammed shut behind him with a *crack*. The knees of his jeans were worn to soft white patches. He half grinned, and it looked so much like Mark that I knew immediately who he was.

His father.

"Hey, Dad." Mark started around the front of the truck and toward his father, who stepped down a few stairs, gaze on me.

"Hi."

Mark motioned to me. "This is my friend, Stella. She's staying with me for a while. Stella, this is my father, Jim."

I nodded. He returned it. A fishing pole leaned against the front of the house near the screen door. Mark stopped a few feet away from the porch and half-tucked his hands into his pockets. He seemed at ease. Jim, at first sight, didn't strike me as a talker.

Mark dove right in.

"Is your Cuban friend, Camilo, still painting these days?"

If Jim noticed my sudden surprise at the question, he gave no indication. Instead, he frowned at the dirt. "Not sure," he finally drawled. "Why?"

"Trying something new."

Jim snorted, but his lips twitched with a smile. "I can ask him."

"Do you have his number? I'll call. No need for you to break your quota and talk to more people than me for the next week."

Jim snorted with warm amusement, then pulled a phone out of his pocket and tossed it to Mark. Mark scrolled through and seemed to text something to himself because I heard the buzz of his phone a second later. Meanwhile, Jim glanced at me again. A silent question lived there. One I didn't want to acknowledge or have to answer, so I pretended to study the creek.

Why are you living with my son? he seemed to want to say.

"You like to fish?" I asked him.

Jim nodded. I couldn't help but wonder if Mark had so much to say because he felt that he had to fill the silences his dad may leave behind.

Mark tossed the phone back to his dad. "Thanks, Dad. Good to see you. Need anything?"

"Nope."

And just like that, we were back in the truck, rumbling back toward the highway. Jim disappeared inside with a brief wave, and I blinked.

Wow. That was . . .

"What?"

Mark asking the question made me realize I'd spoken out loud. "Oh." I shook my head. "Sorry, I . . . I'm just . . . that was so quick."

He shrugged as he flipped on the blinker and turned toward the highway. Cars whizzed past. The Zombie Mobile needed a lot of land to get its slow engine up to speed, so he had to wait for several minutes. On our way here, he'd driven on the side of the road to get going fast enough.

"I see him pretty often," Mark said as we chugged along in a break of traffic. "He actually wanted to live at Adventura because of the river running through the canyon, but the fish aren't great there."

"Really?"

He laughed. "Really. Fishing is his life right now."

"You could have just called him."

"Yeah, but I like to see him. He doesn't get a lot of human interaction since the divorce. Doesn't really want it, to be honest, but he loves to see us."

Divorce. I filed that away in my head for later. Something I hadn't known.

He glanced back at me. "You don't visit your parents for short periods of time through the week?"

"No. They're dead."

"What?"

His shocked cry gave me a sense of relief. Most people were awkward at moments like that, and I always ended up attempting to soothe them for what happened in my life. At least Mark owned his surprise.

"When I was five." My breath whooshed out of me. "They were in a car accident. I don't remember much. Grandma raised me. We had already been living with her for a while, which made it a lot easier at first."

"Bet she's amazing to turn out someone like you."

I grinned with my whole face. "Yeah. She totally is."

Mark's gaze darted to mine and back to the road several times before finally focusing again. I cleared my throat to soften a sudden tension in the air.

"So, Camilo?" I asked and turned slightly to face him.

Mark laughed. "Yeah, probably a dead end, but I'll pursue it out. There are a few other options that we're going to chase in town, but they're in neighborhoods. You'll be out of the way of town so no one has to see you."

"It's not that extreme, Mark."

"Not yet," he said easily as if running from your boss and his twisted attraction was so normal. Still, I appreciated his attention to these sordid details of my life. It made it seem more real because some days I still couldn't wrap my head around this being a thing.

I couldn't help but feel a bit intrigued with what I had already seen of his plan. I'd always seen the results of Mark's attempt to salvage his life back together, never the actual grasping for straws. Seeing him in his element—which appeared to be uncertainty—was a whole new game. Although I still felt uncomfortable with all the murky details, I couldn't help but wonder if maybe he knew *exactly* what he was doing.

In the end, I didn't ask, because I wasn't sure I wanted to know.

Chapter Twelve

MARK

The next morning, I stood just outside my cabin home and frowned. Nestled amongst broken pine cones, pebbles, and a few slivers of pine needles lay a subtle set of tracks. They marched past the cabin, about three feet away from the door.

"Kitty cat," I murmured. "What are you doing here?"

At one point, the cougar seemed to have stopped, started toward the porch, then decided against it and veered away. A bit too bold for my liking. I grabbed my phone, thinking of Stella. I'd have to remind her not to leave her little closet alone at dusk or in the early morning.

Maybe we should schedule runs together. The thought of her in the mountains alone didn't sit well with me.

Mark: Seriously, Justin. Where are you? This cat is now at my place and I need your dog.

The message to Justin was sent but didn't deliver right away. My gaze narrowed. Where was he anyway? Justin spent way too much time with my sister as it was. They'd been "officially" dating for almost a year now. Plus, he rarely took Atticus with him. The dog belonged in the mountains.

Before I could text him again, a new *Hearts of Fire* notification popped onto the screen. Shanti. She wanted to meet up for dinner. I hesitated, thoughts settling on Stella.

Did I want to go with Shanti?

Yes. But . . . I'd rather watch another 007 movie with Stell.

As a rule, I rarely turned a woman down that seemed non-crazy and who also put effort into meeting. The women that expected me to do all the work had never been good news. Shanti was going two hours out of her way to meet me for dinner in Jackson City on her way across the country to see a friend in Seattle. We'd been writing back and forth for a few weeks now, and she always made me laugh.

Shanti: I'm still up for Mexican if you are. I'll be at the junction that takes me your way and need to know if you're still willing.

Mark: You bet. I'll send you a pin on where to meet on Maps.

Shanti: Yes! I'm excited to officially meet you tonight, Mark Bailey!

Her text was accompanied by practically 5,000 heart emojis, then the Mexican flag and what appeared to be a burrito. I sent back a thumbs-up as the front door opened and Stella peeked out. She wore her running gear and a questioning half-smile.

"Hey." I shoved the phone back in my pocket. "Listen, the cat is back."

Her eyebrows rose.

"You have a cat?"

"Not one I'd recommend you petting, and if you can hear it purr, you're probably already dead meat. Literally."

I gestured to the prints with a toe, careful not to disturb

them. Her eyes widened as she appeared to comprehend what it meant. Then I snapped a picture and sent it to Justin with a thumbs-down emoji.

Mark: Get back here before I have to buy myself a dog.
Or at least send Atticus.

Stella grimaced, then shivered as she stared into the trees across the parking lot. "So that means a run by myself is not an option."

"I just wouldn't recommend going alone while it's wandering so close. Once Atticus is back, you can run with him. He'll keep you safe."

She shifted, warily eyeing the prints. I motioned inside.

"Let me change and we can go together."

* * *

Stella was quiet for most of the run until we slowed to a walk not far from the parking lot on our way back. My concern over the cougar washed away with the exertion. If I didn't hear back from JJ, I might borrow Thor, a Rhodesian Ridgeback, from Ellie, Maverick's other daughter. That dog would scare off an African lion.

"Who is that?" Stella asked.

She froze. Her panting slowed to hard breaths. She had her hands on her hips as she inclined her head toward Adventura, where two people climbed out of a small, eco-friendly car. A cluster of trees mostly obscured the view of us from where we stood on the road. Such a hippie car meant only one person.

I forced a smile, but couldn't help a sudden tension all the same.

"My brother."

Stella started to walk again but eyed me as if I had a weird look on my face. I tried to act like nothing unusual had happened. JJ and Lizbeth hadn't come around much since their wedding, which was probably for the best. I loved them both for different reasons.

And that was a bad thing because some love was strictly forbidden: like my twin brother's wife.

"Oh," Stella said.

Lizbeth and her bright red hair appeared out of the passenger seat. JJ glanced over his shoulder as we turned into the parking lot, then waved. A bright smile from Lizbeth and a little squeak of surprise followed. She jumped a little, waving.

"Mark!"

I pasted a smile on my face and hoped they wouldn't be able to tell it was a tiny bit unpleasant. Seconds later, Lizbeth had run up to my side and wrapped her arms around me, sweaty clothes notwithstanding. My heart beat a little too hard, and I prayed she wouldn't notice. Instead, she stepped back, a woman full of sunshine, sparkles, and moonbeams. She turned to Stella with a bright smile, her hand stuck out.

"Hi! I'm Lizbeth."

"Stella."

"Good to meet you. Jim said he liked you, which is high praise."

Stella blinked as if she couldn't comprehend Lizbeth's words. I didn't blame her. Dad didn't say much, but after working as the county sheriff for decades, he read people unusually well. It was the real reason I'd taken Stella by. I'd wanted him to meet her, even briefly, just to get his thoughts. He'd texted me later and said, *She seemed nice.*

Which really *was* high praise from Dad.

"Oh." Stella managed a similar smile. "Thanks . . . I think."

Lizbeth beamed further. She loved making friends. JJ jogged over. If the smile plastered across his face meant anything, married life had been good to him so far. We collided in a hard man-hug, and it felt really good to see him again.

"Mark," he drawled as he stepped back.

"My favorite hippie JJ."

He socked me in the arm and I instantly felt better. I put a hand on Stella's shoulder to introduce her, then almost regretted it. We'd had a strict, silent, no-touch policy since she'd arrived. Aside from me grabbing her hand yesterday to help her off the four-wheeler, we hadn't touched skin again, and that had felt like an afterthought. This was on purpose. And she didn't flinch away, which felt like progress, so I left it there.

"JJ, this is my friend, Stella. Stell, this is my hooligan brother that I've probably talked too much about."

JJ smiled warmly, extending a hand. I expected a little bit of a glazed-eyed stare from her. Quick, startled blinks. Something. Girls always had reactions like that to JJ, with his high cheek-bones and long hair pulled away from his face. He was a hand-some god amongst men, particularly on the rocks.

Stella just smiled with the same casual warmth and took his hand.

An unexpected sense of relief followed. With Stella here, everything would be different. For maybe the first time since Lizbeth wandered—or, more aptly, crashed—into JJ's life, I wouldn't be the third wheel. The one that ignored their making out or giggles or snuggle sessions while I desperately tried to bury myself in the business.

The one that also hid how he really felt because reality was disastrous.

Even if Stella was only a friend, that went a long way. Separating from JJ had been harder than I'd expected. Like peeling apart the sticky parts of two pieces of smashed duct tape. Something was going to get shredded. With over thirty years of our life side-by-side, there was a chasm without him. One that no amount of mountain man life could ever fill.

And maybe there'd even been an empty spot *with* him around.

Lizbeth hooked a loyal arm around JJ's waist and leaned into him. He took her weight and rested an arm across her shoulders with a smile. His fingers toyed with her hair that fell like glimmering strands of fire.

Lizbeth's gaze focused on me, then her jaw dropped.

"Mark," she cried, "did you trim your beard?"

I tugged at it a little. "Yeah. Needed it."

Her eyebrows rose. "Looks nice. And a haircut?"

"I'm not a caveman."

"I thought you were going full mountain man," she said.

"I ran out of flannel."

She snorted. I motioned to their car, then started to walk toward Adventura again. "So, to what do we owe the pleasure?" I asked. Stella followed to my right, a step behind, while JJ and Lizbeth fanned out on the other side.

"I have updates on your website and HomeBnB listing," Lizbeth said as she twined her fingers with JJ. I kept my gaze ahead and wondered about the mountain lion.

"Brought you some lunch, too," JJ said. He cast a quick glance toward Stella, but she was looking up in the trees. Wondering about the cougar as well, perhaps? "Thought you might like some company. But if we're—"

"You're not," I said brightly. "You know I love it when you come."

His shoulders dropped a little bit. Was it relief? Was he struggling with the change too, or was he too happily distracted? Even Lizbeth kept glancing at Stella, then me, as if trying to sense whether there was some sort of undercurrent there. Well, she wasn't wrong to wonder.

Sometimes I did too.

I clapped a hand on JJ's shoulder, able to push those

thoughts away because it's what I did so well. "Thanks, brother. I have a date tonight, so lunch is perfect."

Stella stiffened next to me as we came to the split in the path, but when I looked up, she had her usual smile on.

"Thanks for the run, Mark." Her gaze moved beyond me. "It was good to meet the two of you finally. Mark talks about you all the time."

Lizbeth opened her mouth to stop her, but Stella had already disappeared around the corner by then. I blinked, startled by the sudden escape. A tiny corner of my mind yelled at her. What was with the quick departure? But I shoved that away. No, Stella and I weren't like that. We were friends, but that didn't mean she had to hang around when my family came here.

Even if I wanted her to.

The elation I'd felt at not being a third wheel slowly died. I steeled myself for putting on a happy-go-lucky lunch with my usual suave charm. It would be harder this time. Way harder. Because I hadn't been around them in weeks and I forgot how nauseating it could be to see JJ holding her hand. Her bright smiles at him. The way they mutually adored and took care of each other.

Suffocating. Heart-wrenching. Soul-tearing.

Because dammit, I'd fallen hard for my brother's fiancee months ago and no amount of online dating, mountain climbing, or business-crashing had changed that.

And now she was his wife.

Chapter Thirteen

STELLA

Coward.

The word circled my mind over and over while I attempted, for a third time, to watch a new thriller movie that had come out ages ago. I'd put it on my mental list of *must-watch movies* as soon as I saw the trailer, but that list had come to be more of an *I must watch them within the decade* kind of list.

How had I gotten so behind? Movies were my happy place.

Oh, yeah.

I'd let life swallow me for a while.

That had never been more readily apparent than now when I had ample time to live life but no idea how to do it. Running only occupied so much space, and hiding only created *more* opportunity for time. My thoughts spun as I set my chin on my knees, a bit haunted by both these strange circumstances and meeting Mark's family.

Coward, came the voice again. *Coward, coward, coward.*

Leaving so quickly had been the cowardly thing to do. I could see the upcoming invitation from Lizbeth. The startled look in Mark's eyes as I quickly ducked away. In fact, I'd wanted to stay. Wanted to get to know Lizbeth and JJ, the infamous people in Mark's life. Wanted to just be around other humans again. Meeting them had been . . . interesting.

Or, should I say, *Mark* had been interesting.

He'd stiffened like a board as soon as he saw Lizbeth? Or was it JJ? I couldn't be sure. There seemed to be troubled water under that bridge. His smile had instantly changed, though I doubted I would have noticed if I hadn't been watching him so closely. And why had I been in such a deep perusal?

Nope.

Didn't want to go there.

My thumb hovered over my computer as I stared at the email I'd sent Grandma earlier today. She preferred texting but made email work. I'd told her my phone had been lost in a mountain stream and I needed to find another one.

Grandma: My stocks are up! And I miss you. How is my girl? When do I get another visit?

A warm smile found me.

Stella: Maybe in a month?

Grandma: It's never soon enough, Stella Marie. I miss you very much. Are you doing well? Are you happy?

My gaze lingered on the last three words. Grandma always asked those kinds of questions. The hard, heavy-hitting ones. The ones that made your insides curl and your stomach ache because she did it so casually, so openly, that you couldn't even fake-laugh it off. Trust grandma to hit at the festering core of what made my heart feel so heavy tonight.

Are you happy?

How could I tell anymore? Although stressful, the last few weeks with Mark had been unbound in ways I'd never experienced before. Back home in Cincinnati, I'd thought I'd been happy. Maybe I worked a bit too much. Most of my weekends were me crashing hard, running last-minute errands, and failing to have a true social life that felt fulfilling and rejuvenating. Every now and then there had been a date. Mostly it was cruising NetMovies and falling asleep on the couch.

But now?

Now I felt something stirring inside me. Something that said all of that had been fake. Like a waking dream. A slow movement of existing, but not life. Not what Mark had. Mark didn't play it safe. He was unbound and a little wild and lived on just this side of *is he crazy, or does he just not care?* Maybe I played it too safe.

Maybe I *wasn't* happy.

With another sip of chocolate milk—my recovery drink of choice after a run, even though it had been six hours ago—I emailed her back.

Stella: Happier now than I have been in a long time. I'll catch you up soon.

Grandma: Sounds like you found a man.

My heart did a double whomp.

Stella: Maybe just some clarity.

Grandma: And that's good too. Love you, my girl.

Mark came back to mind, but I dismissed the ensuing race of my heart as the result of a rustle from outside. Instantly, my mind went to the mountain lion. JJ and Lizbeth had left three hours after arriving. I'd heard Lizbeth laughing as they walked back to their car, then drove away. Not long after that, Mark left with the roar of the Zombie Mobile as well.

To his date.

With night rapidly falling, and no one else in the mountain with me, an extra-large twinge of discomfort filled me. I quadruple-checked my little cabin. Door locked. Windows firmly locked. Drapes drawn. Phone and computer charged. Internet working.

Safe.

Except . . . it didn't feel like it.

Being alone at Adventura in the daytime was one thing, but at night? That business was something else altogether. Dark mountains. Who knew how many kinds of animals—lots of them predators—foraging for winter. Were there grizzlies down here? I gulped and turned my attention back to the screen. Then I slammed it shut when I saw a montage of a girl running through a dark mountainside, pursued by someone with a flashing knife.

"Nope!" I cried.

The silence followed, and then I just felt silly. Mountain lions couldn't come through the walls, and the cabin was very sturdy. Still . . . I'd feel better in a bigger space where I couldn't hear every single sound. The rattle of a pinecone falling down the roof was loud enough to wake me up sometimes. Although I liked being set back in the trees, they sometimes rattled along the walls in the wind with a scratching sound.

Mark's house would feel safer, came the thought.

Although I vehemently shook my head to try to deny it, I couldn't deny that I wanted to be somewhere where I could smell him. For some reason, I knew it would comfort me. So would a much bigger space with a much louder TV and fewer branches scratching on the windows.

I eyed the doorway. To get to the main cabin, I'd have to cross the dark porch, skitter through the woods, and then let myself into someone else's house. So very Goldilocks of me.

Was I *sure* Mark was gone? Yes. There was no denying the crunch, pop, and snort of the Zombie Mobile. The path would be twenty steps at most. If I ran, it would be . . . maybe five seconds. A hint of daylight still lingered on the edge of the horizon, even though the rest of the mountains had settled into an inky band of black. The longer I waited, the scarier this night would get.

Coward, I told myself again.

Then I shoved my arms through my jacket, scooped my laptop against my chest, and darted into the night.

* * *

My heart pounded against my ribs when I slammed Mark's back door shut behind me, then locked it in relief.

Safe.

Mark had left a light on—no, he'd left *all* the lights on—which gave the place a warm, less-frightening look. As usual, stuff scattered in almost every available space. Living by myself meant an almost clinical feel to my world. The apartment I'd left behind rarely had a dish or spare piece of laundry. Grandma taught me to pick up after myself, which meant I washed the dishes as I cooked, rinsed as soon as I finished, and just reused the same one at each meal.

Mark's disorganization had a sense of . . . *home* . . . to it.

I checked the front door to make sure it was locked too—I'd open it again as soon as I heard the Zombie Mobile and slip out the back.

For now, relief filled me.

I set my computer on the couch, grabbed his remote, and turned the TV on. The noise filled the larger space, and when I wrapped a blanket around me, it felt like Mark sat nearby. One of his jackets hung over the back of the couch, so I grabbed it and took a deep breath in.

Pine. Outdoors. All the manly things.

All fear of the mountain lions disappeared, even when my computer chimed with a new email. When I clicked the icon, my stomach soured.

Stella Marie,

Had some news from work today, my love. Your normal love of detail has failed you. Each business application for government support has been rejected. Yet, when I look over the paperwork, I find no fault with your work.

I do wonder what may have caused that?

See you soon.

My eyes darted back to the door as I slammed the computer shut, breathing fast. The words *my love* ran through my mind like a ticker tape. The clearly sinister-sweet tone of his response. Of course, he had my old email—I should have anticipated that. Didn't think it was worth getting rid of that because too many important things came that way. Now I'd need to get rid of that, too.

The terror of the night pressed back around me, but when I caught a whiff of Mark on the air, I felt better. Joshua had received word of the rejections, which meant he was probably still in Cincinnati. He wasn't here.

Safe, I thought. *I'm safe.*

But it didn't feel like it, alone in the dark mountains. Banishing the fear of Joshua, I scrolled through Mark's list of stored movies, sighed in relief when I saw one of my favorite light-hearted romantic comedies, then started it. Then I pulled one of his jackets all the way around me and settled into the smell of Mark with a relieved sigh.

Chapter Fourteen

MARK

My thoughts were a jumble as I slipped out of the Zombie Mobile that night and headed for home. A breeze blew leaves around my feet as I crunched down the footpath, past trees, and toward my cabin. Shanti had been a refreshing change. Bright-eyed, filled with humor, and a sparkling wit I couldn't help but love, she was a date I'd been hoping to find a long time ago, but never could.

And now, as all good candidates went, she was out of my life. On her way to see a friend in Seattle, and staunchly non-committed.

Just like JJ and I had been once.

"I'm a mover," she'd explained with a wide, unapologetic grin that betrayed white teeth around her spiraling black hair. "I get itchy feet after just a few weeks, you know? But I figure I want to meet people as I head around. Want to see the world and all the people in it. A dating app is a great way to do it."

To my surprise, I wasn't as disappointed as I'd expected. Just as I wasn't as heartsick over seeing Lizbeth today as I thought I'd be. Tonight, I was more pained seeing their happiness together rather than her response to JJ instead of me.

It felt like . . . something.

The porch light was still on—I always forgot to turn it off—when I reached for the doorknob, then stopped. It wouldn't twist open.

Locked?

Blinking, I tried again.

Definitely locked.

Had I locked it on my way out? No. I didn't even lock it when I went out of town because who would come here? But it was definitely locked. Startled, I reached into my coat pocket to pull out my keys, letting out a breath of relief that I still had a house key on here.

When the door swung open, I stopped a second time.

A pile of short, golden hair spilled across the end of my couch. Stella. A blanket appeared to be snuggled up over her shoulder. Although a movie flickered across the TV, she was clearly missing all of it. My eyebrow lifted. Ah, one of Lizbeth's romances. She bought way too much of that garbage.

I quietly shut the door as I puzzled out what had happened, then felt a stab of concern. She'd locked herself in my house. Had she heard from Joshua? Had that jerk of a boss called again? No, she had no phone, which we also had to fix. We'd get her a line under my family's plan. He couldn't trace that. Before I charged in there to demand answers, I forced myself to cool down. Waking her up wouldn't change anything.

And I definitely didn't mind that she came here.

My keys were silent as I pushed them back in my coat to keep them from rattling, and peeled it off. Stella didn't even stir as I carefully built the fire back up to warm up the chill in the air. Wind huffed by outside, bringing in a pile of clouds that could spritz overnight.

Once the fire started rolling, I sat on the floor and leaned my back against the end of the couch while I logged back into the *Hearts on Fire* app to type Shanti a quick thank you. Two more potential dates—what a weird way to look at people in the world—had sent messages, but I ignored them for now.

After I sent it, I glanced back to Stella.

With her eyes closed, her face slack, she seemed younger, somehow. How old was she, anyway? I pegged her at 28. Her lips were slightly parted, her fingers curled beneath her left cheek, which she laid on. In the firelight, her highlights glimmered in different tones of blonde and brown. A lock of hair had fallen across her forehead and I had to stifle the urge to tuck it away.

My chest tightened.

The date with Shanti had been fun, but finding Stella asleep on my couch looking so peaceful was better. With a sigh, I answered some text messages from Mom, who had, of course, heard about Stella somehow—I blamed Lizbeth—and wanted all the details. Dad asked about a fishing trip. Camilo responded to my question about his painting career, which had crashed in a fiery plume of hatred when he *couldn't hack watercolor*. I crossed him off my mental list of potential candidates and sighed. For a while, I'd forgotten about our project to get the cabin rented.

While I skimmed through my messages, answering all of them, the room filled with warmth again. Eventually, after I sent off a few more messages to people that I knew needed a mountain escape (even if they didn't realize it themselves), Stella stirred.

I kept my gaze on my phone and waited for her to see me first. She'd wake up any second now and—

"Oh!"

Her gasp brought her almost off the couch. She bolted up, hazy with sleep, an adorable red mark on her left cheek from where she'd rested it on her knuckles. The blanket fell off her shoulders, and I realized it wasn't a blanket, but one of my zippered sweatshirts.

Stella blinked several times.

"Mark?"

"Hey."

"I'm . . ." She licked her lips as her eyes darted around, still a bit wild. They calmed as the pieces must have clicked back into place. "Oh, I'm so sorry. I didn't . . . I mean . . ."

"Is everything okay?"

She rubbed a hand over her eyes, then collapsed back against the couch with a groan. "Yes, it's fine. I just . . . I . . ."

She mumbled something I couldn't make out.

"You what?"

She sighed almost violently. "I got scared."

The back of my neck prickled. "Scared?" I asked quietly.

"Joshua emailed me." She covered her face with her hands. "But even before that, I was freaked out. It sounds so silly now but sitting out there alone in that cabin was . . . I don't know. Scary. I'm not used to the mountains and surely not by myself. It's such a small cabin that you can hear every single sound outside."

Understanding flooded me then.

"The mountain lion?"

She nodded, still hidden under her fingers.

"I don't blame you," I said. "That cat is a bit too bold. I'd be nervous too."

She peered at me from between split fingers. "You're just saying that."

I shook my head. "No. I'd be freaked out too if I didn't grow up here and live here full time. You get used to it after a while, but it's scary at first. A healthy respect isn't a bad thing."

Seeming relieved, she dropped her hands from her face. "I guess I felt safer in here. Sorry I sort of went all Goldilocks on you."

That drew a laugh out of me. How perfect—she was goldilocks. "Nah, not a big deal. I'm glad you came. You're definitely safe from the kitty in your cabin, but I can see how it wouldn't feel that way. There's a lot less noise in here."

She blinked away the last of sleep. Her eyes focused a bit more, but still drooped as she fought off a yawn.

"What did Joshua say?"

An instant scowl marred her face. "Just . . . a stupid email. The feds must be processing something because all the claims I put through were rejected. I think it's made him suspicious. I don't want to talk about him. How was your date?" she asked sleepily.

I shrugged. "Good. I mean . . . fun. I'll never see her again but it was worth the drive and the time."

"How do you know that?"

"Shanti just wanted someone to have dinner with on her way through here. Wasn't ever meant to be something."

"Oh."

She seemed to process that, but the last thing I wanted to talk to her about was my dating life.

"How long have you been home?" she asked with a light color on her cheeks.

"A few minutes. Wanted to get the fire warmed up so you didn't freeze, and before I went to bed." I paused. "Why don't you stay here tonight?"

She struggled against another yawn. "Really?"

"Of course. It's cold out there. You can take my bed or stay where you are."

"Here," she said quickly. "I'm not going to take your bed from you, but thank you for the offer."

I snorted. "Probably wise. Who knows what it smells like."

An amused smile threatened her lips. I stretched my arms over my head, my stomach still bursting with a delicious chorizo burrito and the memory of Spanish rice. A little color rose on her cheeks, but she yawned before I could make sense of it.

"This," she murmured as she snuggled in deeper, "is perfect. Thank you, Mark, for being . . . my friend."

I dashed up the stairs, grabbed my best pillow and favorite

blanket, and brought them back down. She snuggled into them with a grateful little sigh, another garbled thanks, and fell asleep seconds later.

With a warm chuckle, I checked the fire, loaded one last log inside to smolder, flicked the light off, and climbed the stairs.

But it wasn't where I wanted to be.

* * *

"ToasterTarts, SugarFlakes, and homemade french toast, but I only have one egg, so it'll be more like . . . toast. That's what I can offer you for breakfast here at Mark's HomeBnB. Can you see why Adventura might be lost?"

Stella's lips twitched.

We stood in front of my small fridge and stared at the less-than-desirable contents with mutual disappointment. She still had a blanket wrapped all the way around her, her hair adorably tousled and eyes still sleepy. Sunlight streamed in through the windows and warmed my bare feet. Outside a brisk wind blew, scuttling leaves across the dirt. In the distance, a deer and her yearling grazed by, oblivious to the nip in the breeze.

I tried not to think about how nice it was not to wake up alone in this cabin. To hear the shuffle of life moving around. The smell of coffee drifting up the ladder to wake me. There were a lot of reasons that I wanted to get that cabin rented, but the top of the list was closer proximity to Stella.

"Can we . . ."

She stopped herself. I lifted my eyebrows and scratched at an itch along my side.

"Can we?"

"Could we go into Jackson City? Isn't there a small diner somewhere or something? I'd like to try something different. We could talk about what Lizbeth said yesterday about her updates. We only have five days left of the seven days."

"Are you okay with that?"

She nodded firmly.

The idea of going anywhere with her sounded great to me, even with the pall of a five-day countdown hanging over us. Actually, civilization is what we needed. More networking was in order now that Camilo had backed out as a possibility. Overnight, a couple friends had responded to my text messages with interest, but nothing definite. I flicked the fridge door shut with my wrist, gratified that she hadn't scampered back to her place the moment sunshine hit the sky.

"Of course," I said. "Get some clothes on, girl. Let's get us some literally heart-stopping American diner breakfast."

Chapter Fifteen

STELLA

The decision to get out of Adventura had been, possibly, too impulsive on my part. My life *wasn't* a Loveline movie, and I did need to grab a few things, bars of dark chocolate to stash in my cabin included, but the thought of civilization wasn't as easy as it used to be. Even though I wasn't in apparent danger from Joshua, I didn't feel safe amongst unknown people in general.

With Mark though, it all felt so normal.

And right now, I desperately needed to feel normal.

My biggest fears used to be whether or not I'd get an account summarized in time, or whether Joshua would push me into a leadership position I didn't feel ready for, but always rose to the occasion to complete.

Now I feared mountain lions and boredom. My life had fallen apart, taking my personal company down in a blaze of sparks, and I had nowhere to turn except my only remaining client.

Who was *Mark Bailey?*

The guy that once thought a giant carousel in the middle of his small mountain town would be a massive success and bring in tourists. The world in which I found myself just felt too weird sometimes.

Besides, Mark had played my unexpected presence in his house off so easily last night. I wanted to take him to breakfast as a sort of thank you. And not at all because he'd had warmth in his voice when he spoke about Shanti. Or that he was on his phone all the time and I couldn't help but imagine all the girls he must be texting and maybe, just maybe, I wanted to be on *this* side of the situation for once.

Now, with the quiet muffle of people around us, I was glad we came. Mark, who of course knew the hostess, had given his charming smile and finagled us a spot in the back corner. Being able to see the traffic zipping by on the highway outside the diner gave me a reassuring feeling.

"Thanks." I peered at him over the top of my menu. "This is great."

His smile widened. He wore a pair of jeans and a long-sleeve black shirt that stretched taut across his shoulders. He'd trimmed the beard again. Instead of curls off his chin, it contoured his face now. Would he have the same facial structure as his brother? Because if he did, he'd be devastating. Which seemed almost impossible because I couldn't imagine him any more attractive than I found him right now.

The waitress came with an extra big smile for Mark, took our orders, and left us in the quiet booth with a little wink he didn't seem to notice.

"What did Lizbeth have to say?" I asked.

His expression momentarily darkened. "Just that there are a few more approval steps I'd forgotten about before we can list it on HomeBnB. We have to have some tax and licensure things to file for in the State. She's already getting them going."

"Wow. She's a dream."

A weird half-shrug/awkward grimace came next. "It's better

for everyone if I don't attend to those details. Lizbeth is happy to do it."

"Are you paying her? Because we'll need to—"

"Not yet. She was happy to help get it listed without pay. She's family."

As if that explained everything.

My immediate rebuttal surfaced: *that's not sustainable.* He couldn't just rely on family members to run his company without getting paid. They'd get frustrated and leave eventually, or not do great work. Although Lizbeth didn't strike me as the type, and this was a one-time deal.

So I stayed quiet.

Grandma had always been loving and supportive. For the burden she'd been left when my parents died, she rose to the challenge without fear. But age had taken most of her family away from her. Siblings. Friends. Her husband died a year before I was born. My father, her son, had been her only child. Now she was a spritely old woman living her best life in a retirement home and we supported each other.

But there had been no one else for us to fall back on.

No safety net like Mark's. No one outside of neighbors and friends that we could *truly* fall back on if we were in danger of losing our house, or something. The way Mark was letting me fall on him.

Did he know how lucky he was to have them?

"When is your next date?" I asked before the ensuing silence felt burdened. Then I grabbed my water, stirring the clinking ice cubes with my straw to have something to do with my hands. He laughed, then shook his head.

"Nothing lined up."

"Oh."

"Are you surprised?"

I shrugged. "You seemed to be pretty active in the dating world."

"Sometimes. It ebbs and flows."

"Does it ever stick?"

"Nah." He shook his head, but there was a flicker that accompanied it. "Not really. It's been years since I've had anything steady, and even that lasted maybe two months. I've only been really online dating for the last couple of months."

My head tilted to the side, unable to comprehend that a man like Mark didn't have girls lining up to date him. Sure, he wasn't perfect, and some of his quirks were absolutely maddening, but wasn't that everyone?

"You said your parents were divorced. What happened there?"

He leaned back against the booth and I wondered if I'd plunged too deep, too fast. The topic didn't trigger an immediate emotion on his face, and I wondered if that was a tell for him. If Mark was anything, he was expressive. So I let the question ride without pulling it back.

"Classic fall-in-love, fall-back-out kind of story." He spoke dispassionately enough that I wondered if repeating the story had become rote. Still, there was an undercurrent of something there. Shock, maybe. Lingering disbelief. I'd felt that way for years after my parents died. Shouldn't divorce be mourned as well?

"Mom and Dad grew apart and should have ended it sooner than they did. Finally, when Dad was preparing to retire, they realized they couldn't live together. So they split up."

"I'm sorry."

"Me too." He nodded. "It sucked. I'm the oldest and closest to my Mom. We're a lot alike in some ways, where JJ is more like my Dad. I spent a lot of time just supporting her through it. She's better now. Not quite so . . ."

"Needy?"

His lips twitched. "For lack of a better word, yes."

"And how long have you been in love with Lizbeth?"

He sucked in a sharp, sudden breath, his eyes a puzzle of shock. By sheer determination, I held his intensely questioning gaze. The question had been a calculated risk because I could be way off base and embarrass both of us. He may not be in love with her.

Except for the sudden paleness of his face gave him away.

"That obvious?" he croaked.

"Only to me, I think."

Mark studied me, jaw tense, for so long that I regretted asking. Did he hate me for noticing? Was he frustrated with me? So many emotions seemed to show on his face that I didn't even want to move.

"Months." His nostrils flared. He balled up the straw wrapper and rolled it between his thumb and index finger. He paused, as if thinking, then shook his head. "I don't . . . I know I fell for her. I can't say I'm *in love* with her because, to be honest, I'm not sure I know what it feels like."

"To be in love?"

"Yeah."

Our gazes met. For a tangled moment, my heart raced. There was heartbreak there. Sadness. The charming layers of Mark Bailey slid away for a moment before a half-smile shoved them back to where he must keep them hidden.

"Me either," I said.

His eyebrows rose halfway to his hairline. "What?"

I swallowed with a small chuckle that was more a nervous tick than amusement. "I think . . . I think I sort of lost myself after college. And in the losing, I forgot to live and date and . . . love. There have been plenty of boyfriends, but not real love. Crushes. Attraction. Flirtation. It all ended before it became too serious and happy. But I just . . . I guess I've put it off."

"What has been more important?"

Genuine curiosity filled his eyes now, and I felt something welling in my chest. Something hot and thick and oily and heavy.

It looked like my parents and grated, twisted metal and the quiet of Grandma's house. For a second, I felt sucked into a vortex where I couldn't breathe and I felt like a small five-year-old trying to make sense of the pieces of her life again.

The waitress reappeared with our plates, breaking the sudden sense of falling apart that had washed over me. One piece at a time, I pulled myself together. Syrupy huckleberry pancakes waited for me, a glob of butter melting over their golden tops. A massive omelet with four types of cheese sat in front of him. While he murmured *thank you,* I had a centering sip of cold water.

Before another word could be spoken, Mark's phone jangled on the table. The name *Lizbeth* flashed across the screen and he brightened, a finger held up. "This should be about the cabin."

With a nod, I gestured for him to take it, then shoved a bite of pancake in my mouth so I couldn't say a word. He stood and slipped out of our booth. The moment he was gone, I slumped down, closed my eyes, and shook off the weird moment. My thoughts were scattered and incomplete.

What had *that* been about?

Whatever it was, I had a tingly-not-so-good feeling that it was inextricably linked to the fact that my life wasn't as happy as I'd thought it had been. My life had been routine the past few years. Sheltered. Quiet. Lonely. While that seemed a small mimicry of the world Grandma had gifted me, the bright chaos of living with Mark made me realize that for me, down that unchanging path, there *wasn't* joy. Never had been.

Mark appeared again from outside as I poked and prodded at my pancake for several minutes, suddenly not that hungry. He stopped walking, then brightened as he cried out, "Hey! Seiko!"

The sound of laughing, a back slap or two, followed instead. I looked up to see him speaking with a woman not far away. The sounds of the diner made it hard to hear individual words, but I caught snippets of *music* and *practice* and *tour.* Five minutes later, the sudden appearance of Mark with his arm around the petite girl with jet black hair and thin eyes drew my gaze up. She had black leather pants and a bright pink top. The tips of her hair were an electric blue.

"Stella," Mark said. "This is my friend Seiko."

Seiko smiled and stuck out a hand with a skull and crossbones ring on the middle finger. "Nice to meet you," she said in a lyrical voice.

Mark didn't move his arm and I had to force myself not to look at it. He tipped his head toward her with a broad grin.

"Seiko is a literal rock star."

She grinned but didn't correct him.

"And," he continued easily, but his eyes had latched onto mine with an intent stare, "she's here to regroup before going on tour with the rest of her rock band. Needs some space to be alone."

Oohhh, I thought to myself.

The music scene wasn't one I dove into very often, particularly not any brand of rock. When I wasn't listening to nonfiction audiobooks, I'd throw on a movie to fill the noise, or maybe a soundtrack. I hadn't heard of or seen Seiko before, but had no trouble imagining her on a stage.

"Sounds amazing," I said.

Mark leaned forward. "She not only needs a place to stay but a place to *play*. An open floor where there aren't noise restrictions but space for them to lay out. I think we may or may not have an entire building that would serve that purpose."

The *we* in his statement gave me unusual comfort.

"Yes, the dining hall would be perfect."

While my head flooded with implications—noise ordinances in the mountains? Desired square footage?—Mark turned back to Seiko. They migrated to another table where two other people with equally bright hair sat nursing coffee cups. While Mark flexed his charm muscle, I tried to school a rush of hope. This wasn't a sure thing yet.

But it could be.

While waiting for him to work his magic, I kept an eye on the outside of the diner. The mountain peaks loomed to the south, giant, green sentinels still on fire with the fall leaves. Who would ever think I'd be here, running from a manager that ran a company I used to really admire?

No one.

A flash of orange caught my eye, and I glanced over to see a man standing outside a car in the parking lot. He wore a pair of sunglasses, his body canted away, but had an unmistakably familiar look about him.

My heart squeezed like a fist had grabbed it from behind.

Was that . . . Joshua?

My breath caught as I straightened. The man stood, a phone to his ear, as he sauntered farther away, just out of sight around a corner. Heart racing, I had to force myself to sit back down and not chase him.

The tousled golden hair, firm shoulders, and sharp way of holding his body had all spoken to Joshua.

But . . . maybe I imagined it.

For what felt like an eternity, I stared out the window in a half-stance, half-sit. Willed that person to show himself again. Five minutes later, and with the occasional blip of sound from Mark whenever he laughed, I still hadn't seen the man return.

The more time passed, the more I was convinced it had been a trick of my mind. Of fear. Eventually, my body unwound. Relaxed back.

Still, my insides felt cold at the thought of Joshua out there. His email surfaced back through my mind, unbidden. Emails from Joshua weren't unusual. There were twenty of them unread in my inbox. But that one had been oddly sinister. Combined with seeing him today?

No, I didn't *know* that was him. I couldn't play this game. Couldn't make up false realities that felt so real. But if it was real, the implications were terrifying.

Joshua had been more than just a manager. He'd shown interest in me to a level that, over time, equated with a stalker. Physical touches. Requests to have drinks. He'd happen to take his lunch break at the same time as me. I'd never gone with him on a date because I didn't date married men, and he wasn't my type anyway. Sometimes, I could sense his frustration, which only drove me farther away. Which seemed to make him chase harder.

Me, the forbidden fruit.

For a moment, I knew a shot of fear. What if Mark ended up being like Joshua? But I instantly dashed that. No, Mark was many things but he was *not* Joshua.

The man in question dropped back into the chair across from me with a wide smile that wrenched my heartstrings. I tried to conjure up one in return, but I couldn't. Something inside of me felt too cold.

MARK

Stella's face had gone white as paper.

"Stell?"

"I'm fine," she whispered. "I just . . ."

A jumbled explanation rolled out of her, but after a few quick questions, I was able to make sense of the conversation. Joshua at large, basically. Possibly here. I slid out of the booth.

"Be right back."

"Wait, no!"

Ignoring that, I stepped outside the restaurant, gazed around, and headed to the right, where she'd indicated she'd seen him. But nothing was there except the empty side of the building and the hill that dropped away from it, into a river ravine. I hung out there for a few minutes, watching for an orange parka. None appeared.

When I returned, she was an adorable mixture of furious and terrified. Her first question, however, was telling.

"Did you see anyone?"

"No one wearing orange or fitting that description."

She bit her bottom lip and frowned. She shook her head as she huffed a breath. "It's . . . it's kind of hard to believe, right? A little wild for him to be here of all places? I feel like I'm making a big deal out of something that isn't that big of a deal."

"Seems wild, yes. But has the potential to be a big freaking deal, Stell. You have to assume the worst in a situation like this. Joshua doesn't sound stable. He sounds like he seeks for power over women, and then exploits it."

She sighed. "I don't . . . I don't want this to come back on my grandma or on you." Her concerned expression lifted to mine. "I should probably go somewhere else, just in case. What if he is really here?"

Panic ripped through me at the thought, but I set that aside. "As the king of bad ideas," I said instead, "I think that one is the worst I've ever heard."

A twitch of a smile appeared before her hyper-focus on reality stepped in. "Mark, this could be an unsafe situation. Between the email last night and this today . . . but then . . . maybe it wasn't him? Maybe I'm paranoid. Or not."

She growled, more frustrated than ever.

"Which is why you shouldn't go anywhere. That would make it *more* unsafe for you. Who would ever look at Adventura, Stell?"

She shrugged. "I don't know? Who would ever do the things Joshua has done? He called my clients. Found my number. This isn't a game of logic and it never has been." She threw a hand in the air. "Joshua is possessive and brilliant and a little scary. I don't want that to have an impact on you."

"Could be positive," I reasoned. "Think of the free advertising we'd get from the news announcements if he came to Adventura."

She glared at me.

"Okay." I lifted a hand in surrender. She needed logic now. "Granted that's not a great spin either. Regardless, Stell, where else would you go and be safe?"

The image of her curled up on my couch filtered back

through my mind. My jacket covered part of her cheek as if she'd smelled it and then fell asleep. She hadn't even felt safe in her very-secure cabin. The thought of her in an RV in some forsaken park in the middle of nowhere was . . . not going to happen.

But Stella had to realize that herself.

"I don't know," she mumbled.

"Besides," I said, "you said you were my friend and friends don't just abandon each other when they most need saving. Adventura still definitely needs saving, so there's that. You're a cold-hearted woman if you leave me to handle this myself."

If possible, the smallest crack formed in her stubbornness. Maybe she felt awkward about being at Adventura or something. I'd always had family and friends to crash back on. I spent ten years of my life flopping around like a dying fish without any apology. To ask others for help bailing us out of a bad streak had sort of been . . . a Bailey-twins *thing*.

But not for her, obviously.

"Stell, I want you at Adventura. We have so many 007 movies to go through that I don't even want to number them. We haven't even gotten to Moore yet. I can't watch those alone now. Who's going to spit stupid movie-making accounting figures at me if you aren't there? They totally ruin the movie and it's way more fun that way. And who's going to stop me from renting land to horse owners? Because yes, that is *still* on my mind."

This time, she chuckled. She opened her mouth, then closed it again. Finally, her shoulders drooped.

"Plus," I added, just to frost the cake. "Justin just called me before I came back in and found Seiko."

"Does your phone *ever* stop ringing?"

"No."

She laughed again, but I had been totally serious.

"He's on his way back. Was helping Meg do some home improvement things and went to visit his Mom or something. I don't know. That means Atticus will be back too. Not only will Atticus be helpful for the little kitty we've adopted, but also for any strangers. Atticus is a tank. He'll keep you safe too. If anyone comes to Adventura, we'll know. Justin is the gladiator and a stud. Nothing could get through him. He can't out-lift me, but he tries," I tacked on, just to be gracious.

Not to my surprise, she did seem a little more relieved. More trusted eyes—and canine ears—were only a good thing. I leaned forward, ready for the grand finale now.

"Besides," I added smoothly. "Justin will let Atticus sleep in the cabin with us."

Her eyebrow rose. Enough that I could tell the tension had gone out of her face. I grinned my biggest smile.

"Us?" she asked.

"Because Seiko just rented your cabin for the next three days *and* she wanted the dining hall."

"What?"

"She's going to stay at Adventura for a few days in the quiet to get ready for her tour, then bring the band in for two days of rock metal jamming." I leaned back to pretend an electric guitar solo, smug that I hadn't spent a single dollar in advertising but still landed a booking.

"Take that rock music, big kitty," I said as I leaned back.

Stella managed a real smile this time.

I motioned for the waitress to bring the check. "We're going to head to the cell phone store, then head back. I think it's time you had a phone again."

"But—"

"No buts. It won't be that expensive to add to our family plan. Justin's on it too, for what it's worth. Which he thinks gives him the rights to date my sister, but we're still debating that point. Besides, Joshua won't be able to track you through my family, right?"

A look of relief crossed her face when she nodded.

"Thanks, Mark."

I winked at her. "You save me, I save you."

Chapter Seventeen

STELLA

A blue-eyed, brown-haired man with broad shoulders and a quick smile met us when we returned to Adventura. Laugh lines framed his tanned face when he smiled. I felt a little swoony under his masculine mein.

"Justin," he said as he shook my hand with a firm grip. "It's good to meet you."

At his feet sat a muscled black dog with a charming quirk of his ears. He looked like a German Shepherd without the brown coloring. Big dogs had never really been my thing. Grandma preferred the little yappers. But the moment Atticus licked my hand, I adored him. He whined and shifted, as if he wanted to move closer, but didn't budge.

A good sign.

"The gladiator returns," Mark cried as they slammed into a hug. "Took you long enough, brother."

"It's not too hard choosing your sister over your ugly mug."

Mark laughed, hands spread in surrender. "Fair enough." Then he knelt down, giving Atticus a full scrub on either side of his rib cage. Atticus licked his face with what I figured was a happy whine, because Justin laughed.

Already, my nerves felt more settled. Back in the folds of the mountains, away from people, felt much safer. Atticus would not only alert us to the mountain lion, but people, as Mark had pointed out. And the likelihood that Joshua would search here for me was low anyway.

This will work out for the best, I told myself again, desperately searching for Grandma's natural positivity.

My muscles unwound a little bit while Mark and Justin started to talk. I couldn't even lie to myself about it: I felt better *because* I was with Mark. Although I didn't understand exactly how, I knew that he'd notched up in my mind. Gone from client to friend to . . .

Something.

Friends had never made me feel physically safe before. Not like Mark. Nor had they talked me out of my darkest, most frightening moment without a single thought to their own safety or situation.

No, Mark was something else. The question that haunted me was *what.*

Mark and Justin, now lost in conversation about the mountain lion, headed back to the house. I followed not far behind, then slipped a hand into my to-go box, grabbed a slice of leftover bacon, and pulled it out. Atticus trotted faithfully at Justin's side, then suddenly stopped. I grinned as he whirled around and trotted over, then gobbled the bacon up and remained next to me, nose to the white styrofoam.

Before we made it all the way in, I gave him one more slice with a mental note to order some really delicious dog treats the next time we bought groceries.

Strategic alliances at the ready.

* * *

Seiko arrived the next morning.

A long night of restless tossing and turning kept me up until 4:00 a.m., when I finally slipped into a jagged sleep and woke up at 6:00, bleary-eyed and frustrated by dreams of Joshua and orange parkas.

With a growl and pathetic attempt to get into a better head-space, I packed up all my things and moved into Mark's cabin. At his insistence, I had the entire attic at my use. He'd stripped the bed, replaced the sheets, and cleared off a table that I suspected had once held all his unfolded clean clothes. The attic smelled like an alluring mix of aftershave and pine. The perfect scent combination to describe Mark.

It soothed me for a moment, but five more emails from Joshua brought my energy right back down to a witchy level. As usual, I left them unopened in my inbox. I could block them, but for some reason, they made me feel like I had some visibility on him. Like it kept a tab on whatever his brain was doing, even though I didn't look at them.

I assumed Mark planned to sleep on the couch, but I doubted even *he* knew where he'd end up. So I sat at his desk downstairs, paperwork cluttered around me and my laptop, and tried to forget Joshua. To lose myself in saving Adventura and Mark, because I couldn't save myself these days.

Maybe I didn't need to price out every single aspect of Mark's rental plan right this second—down to the cost for cater-ing, including the gas it would take JJ to bring the food that, at some point, he'd agreed to provide—but the numbers soothed me. Digging my fingers back into the calculations, formatting spreadsheets, and mind lanes soothed my agitation.

"Seiko just texted me that she left," Mark said as he stepped out of the bathroom, toweling his wild black hair. "She'll be here in forty-five minutes."

I snuck a quick glance up, then froze. He'd forgotten to put a shirt on after his shower, and the half-naked view from the first moment that I met him lay back before my eyes. Only now I knew Mark better. For some reason, that made his thick, sculpted body even more beautiful.

With a hard swallow, I forced my gaze back to the table.

"Great," I said, and managed to sound just this side of strangled. He riffled through a laundry basket on the couch, grabbed a shirt from it, and pulled it over his head. The ease of it was oddly intimate.

"What are you doing?" he asked.

"Just running the numbers before she gets here. Did we already figure out the cost for housekeeping?"

"No cost." He sauntered past me to the cupboard. "I'll do it."

"Heaven help us all," I muttered.

"I heard that. "

"Cleaning supplies cost money." I chewed on the bottom of my pen. We were talking details now, and Mark tended to tune out when those came up. But I needed them. Details were the only certainty we had.

"Like ten dollars maybe?"

"Depends on how thorough you are," I quipped back. "Water. Laundry. Cleaning supplies. Your time. That sort of thing all has a cost attached to it. If it were me, I'd figure it all the way out but . . ."

"We don't even have the official license yet." He waved a spoon through the air. "I'm not worried about $10 cleaning fees yet. With my other HomeBnB's, don't we just have a general fund to figure this out with?"

A *general fund?* What in the doggone world did that mean?

"You pay a cleaning company," I pointed out to the sound of running water behind me. I didn't dare look at him. My eye roll would be so great it would knock him over.

"Right." The water turned off. "Well, we'll figure that out later. Seiko is a friend that's willing to pay to use our space, that's it. We can still move ahead without that detailed of a cost analysis."

With a sigh, I pressed a hand to my forehead to hide my irritation. He wasn't entirely wrong, but it wasn't being smart either. Mark's ability to pay his bills was narrowing with every day that passed. A mere $50 could make a big difference. The details he hated so much *mattered*.

But how to make him see that?

I shook my head. Time to move onto the next hurdle. "Did she pay you cash or with an app or a check?" I asked.

He frowned. "Hadn't thought of that."

Of *course* he hadn't.

"How long is she staying?" I tried next.

"Three days?"

Why was that a question? My blood felt like it was getting too warm. I forced myself to take a deep breath and calm down. I knew Mark didn't like the details, just as I knew this would be a hard aspect of working with him. Expecting him to change was just wasted effort, but didn't alter the fact that I *wanted* him to pay attention more. To care about the little things more, because he should.

"You're not sure how long she will be here?" I asked.

"Not officially, no. But three days sounds right."

"How much did you tell her it cost per night?"

"I didn't."

My eyes scrunched close. They'd cross permanently with my heightened vexation at this rate. How *had* he survived this long? Suddenly, I was catapulted back to our initial days working together, when I frantically tried to find a different accountant that would be a better fit, but felt so bad for him that I didn't have the heart to pawn him off.

Gritting my teeth, I forced myself to calm again.

"Mark, we need to know how long she plans to stay because we still have to find other people to book it, right?"

"Right."

"So you didn't capture payment yet and we don't know how long she's staying?" I asked, poorly hiding the irritation in my voice. Now I had no way of getting an accurate accounting until Seiko arrived. Seemed pretty unprofessional to say, 'Hi, thanks for coming! Please give us your money for a previous undisclosed amount. Oh, how long will you be here?'

Mark didn't seem to notice. "No payment yet, but I'm not concerned. Seiko will pay."

"And if she doesn't?"

Now he sounded tense. "She will."

"That cannot happen going forward, Mark. We—"

A knock on the door interrupted me, and I glowered at his back as he crossed behind me to answer the door. Seiko's bright voice entered the room before her, and the melodic tint made it abundantly clear she was a musician. Mark wrapped her in a big warm hug with his thick arms and I lost all my patience then. Seiko would think of me as some psycho woman that couldn't stay in a room, but I had to get away.

While Mark greeted her, I ducked out the back door and headed toward the kitchen. One more second in that room with Mark and I would absolutely explode.

Justin stepped out of the kitchen door as I approached, the screen slamming shut behind him. Atticus trotted behind him, tongue lolling. I'd saved a cheese stick in my jacket pocket just for this moment. Atticus, the wise dog that he was, sidled right up next to me. While Justin waved and headed back toward his little cabin back in the trees, I slipped Atty another treat.

"Good boy," I murmured and rubbed him behind the ears. He finished the cheese, then bounded off when Justin whistled.

With a sigh, I stopped, turned, and headed for the lake. I needed to work through this frustration before I saw Mark again. Mark and I had been working together for years now. This sort of annoying back-and-forth wasn't new to either of us. Why

I'd expected him to go through a cost-analysis report with me before he'd even had coffee, I had no idea.

It likely meant something else was bothering me, and if I didn't sort it out, I'd keep being annoyed with Mark and that wasn't fair. Mark was Mark. I accepted that.

Because heaven help us all, we lived together now.

* * *

The lake rippled quietly at my feet as I sat on the edge of the pier and let my toes dangle in the water. The cool water was a soft kiss on the tips of my skin. A bright blue sky unfurled overhead, and the gentle whisper of a breeze wafted by. It smelled like the gentle decay of leaves, and crisp air, and it made me think of pumpkins.

While my toes played with the water, my mind jumped back to the conversation at the restaurant when I'd panicked about my parents. I hadn't been in the car with them when they died. They were on their way home from a weekend together, celebrating their tenth anniversary.

It was the happiest they'd ever been, Grandma had always said.

Then tragedy struck—and wasn't that just like life? You finally find a happy spot, but forget that black ice always lingers beneath happy spots. So the moment you focus too much on feeling good—BAM.

Happy feeling over.

The chill that wrapped around my heart told me *something* lay there. I put a hand on my chest, as if I could warm my heart back up. Unable to bear the lurking question a moment longer, I grabbed my new phone, dialed grandma, and pressed the speaker to my ear. She answered two rings later.

"Hello?"

Her bright voice brought tears to my eyes. "Hey! It's me. Sorry, I had to buy a new phone with a new number."

"You're crying."

I laughed, but it was thick. "I said like fifteen words!"

"And I know you better than anyone on this planet. What's wrong?"

A big, fat tear plopped down my cheek and splashed my jeans. My throat tied together, unable to work for a moment. *So much!* I wanted to say. *Everything has fallen apart. I'm in a world I don't understand anymore and I'm afraid for my life. I think I feel something for a guy that's only supposed to be a friend, but I don't know what that feeling is.*

She waited patiently until I was finally able to croak out, "Did my parents struggle before they died?"

If the question startled her, she gave no sign. "What do you mean?"

"You told me that before they died they were so happy. That it was the best their life together had ever been. I just . . . I was thinking about them today and remembered what you said. I guess I just wanted to know what it meant."

Two empty mom-and-dad-sized holes had always existed in my heart. Over time, they ached less. I didn't think about my parents much, except at the big moments. Getting my period. Prom. High school graduation. College graduation. The moments when I wanted them to be proud of me or comfort me or explain the world to me. While I missed what they would have brought to my life, I didn't actively mourn them anymore. I'd been so young, time had forced me to move on.

But fear lingered within me still.

"Of course they struggled. Your Mom had a hard time getting pregnant before and after having you, so that put a lot of pressure on the marriage. But it seemed like a few months before their death, she had come to terms with it more. Had accepted that they wouldn't have more kids and threw herself into loving you. It was the brightest I'd seen them together."

The momentary storm of tears passed. I wiped them off my cheeks. Grandma had said the same things before years ago, which was probably the last time we'd really spoken about them. But such a truth hadn't affected me the way it did now. Hadn't tied me up in knots.

"Why?" she asked softly.

I blinked, my gaze on the far side of the lake where a thick band of brushes and trees occluded the bank. Gentle ripples moved across the top of the water. My toes had turned cold, so I dragged them out and pulled my knees to my chest, then wrapped my free arm around them.

"I had a moment today."

"A moment?"

Robotically, I relayed what happened with Mark, careful not to tell her where I was. I played Mark off as a friend, but felt as if she could still hear the truth in my words. The slowly dawning realization that I kept mentally pushing aside to deal with later. Repeating what I felt in that storm helped pull the thoughts out of my head so I could make sense of them again.

"I can't help but think I've been living quietly because I'm afraid to be happy." I sighed, my breath heavy. "Like . . . if I allow myself to be happy, I'll die, just like them."

The words sounded ridiculous outside my brain but were terrifying inside it. Grandma didn't laugh, and I didn't pull them back.

Nonsensical or not, they were exactly how I felt.

Happiness meant misery.

"Oh." She breathed the word, as if it were delicate glass. With it came a new tone of understanding. "You are afraid to be happy. You're right. I can see it."

I nodded, then realized that was absurd because she couldn't see it. Tears streamed down my cheeks again and I wiped them free, unable to respond a second time. Across the way, a mournful bird call released from the bushes. The echo of it seemed to ricochet through my chest.

"That makes sense, Stell." Her words were calm, factually stated, but still filled with compassion. "They were happy. You were happy. Then it was all taken away from you and you had to start over. Maybe you associated happiness with loss in your mind because you don't want to go through it a second time."

My nostrils flared as I sucked in another breath, but failed to speak again. Instead, a little sob peeped out of me.

"Is that why you live so softly?" Grandma asked. "You've lived and breathed your job for a while. You stopped talking about your favorite movies. You just seemed to . . . fade into the machinations of your life. Like you hid from something. It's why I've nagged you to get married for so long," she tacked on with a wry laugh. "I've been able to tell that you haven't been happy for a long time, but I couldn't put a finger on why."

Hearing those words from her made me visibly wince. How could something be so obvious to everyone else, but not to me?

"Why didn't you say something?" I cried. "Why didn't you ask?"

"I didn't realize it until this moment, honey. I'm sorry."

"No, it's not your fault. I'm sorry, Grandma. I just . . . I'm sad that I've lived the last four or five years trying to hide from something as silly as happiness. I mean . . ."

I trailed away, unable to articulate just how strange it sounded, even to my own ears. Yet how right I knew it to be.

She fell quiet, and I was glad for a moment to pull my ragged thoughts back together. A headache had started to collect behind my eyes and I felt emotionally wrought after the last two days. Exhausted, but better.

"I'm sad for you too, Stell. But now you know, and that means you can choose something better. Every day is another chance, isn't it? You make it what you want it to be. Dreams don't happen. Dreams are *made*."

The bright words struck a deep chord within. A chord that had been dissonant for years and suddenly came back into harmony when I realized she was right. I had been hiding behind an understandable, but powerful, subterranean fear that I could lose everything all over again. The rocking of my five-year-old world had ripples that still reached me today, as an adult. But they didn't have to frighten me anymore.

Hadn't my worst fears just happened anyway? Hadn't I lost my apartment, my job, my clients, and for the time being, any supposed friends?

And yet here I stood.

Alive.

Alive and *well*. Happiness wasn't out of my reach after a great loss. In fact, I was doing better than I would have ever thought. More joyful than I had been before.

That meant something.

"Thank you," I whispered.

"Anytime, my love," she said. "Are you going to be all right?"

Pounding headache notwithstanding, I felt more unburdened than I had in years. Like the clearing of a storm.

"Better now than ever," I said in a throaty response. Life had taken away so much of what I cared about again but had given me a second chance. A new start. Now, I had the insight I needed to choose to be happy and not be afraid.

After a few more minutes of checking on her, her Bunco club, her stocks, and feeling reassured that nothing out of the usual had come into her world—namely Joshua—I ended the call with a deep-seated relief. My thoughts whirled around each other, but this time in a good way. Cleansing. Removing the debris of the past.

It forced me to stare at the future in a way I normally never thought about. The future would come and I'd be in it. That had always been the extent of my thoughts.

But now I could *make* that future.

I lay back on the pier, my freezing toes back in the water, and I closed my eyes to enjoy the sweet taste of fall sunshine. A languid half-sleep slipped over me until the slow, gentle tread of shoes on the pier interrupted the silence. Then the rustle of fabric and a weight settled next to me.

When I opened my eyes, Mark sat next to me. He leaned back on his hands and stared out at the lake. His profile was silhouetted against a perfect sky.

"I talked to Seiko." He chewed on his bottom lip. "She's fine paying $175 a night, plus $200 for the dining hall for a day. I upped it from $150 because you had wanted to pad the numbers a bit, but I couldn't remember how much. She's going to send it to me on the same app that our HomeBnB people pay, but she said she doesn't need to sign a contract. She's doing this as a friend because she knows it's our first time trying it. She also said she'll let me know if anything is missing or needed so we can do it better next time."

Relief filled me. "Thank you."

"I'm sorry."

He sounded like a little boy, a bit lost. I frowned.

"For?"

"Not being organized. For frustrating you. I could be better at details. It's a habit of mine to pawn them off on other people and not follow up, and the follow-up is my responsibility. So . . . I'm sorry. It can be hard to work with me."

Slowly, I straightened up until our shoulders nearly touched. I pulled my knees back into my chest and mimicked his gaze on the other side of the lake. The gentleness of this moment was at odds with the riotous feelings in my chest now that he sat next to me.

"I was being too sensitive," I said. "I woke up on the wrong side of the bed, and I'm sorry too. I think I need to redefine my expectations or . . . just be more malleable. I get too deep into the details that I become obsessed when sometimes the details don't matter as much as I like to think."

"What can I do to make this easier for you?" he asked. "I'm not afraid of criticism or feedback. I can change things about myself if needed—or I can at least try."

He paused as I thought his question out. The vulnerability I heard masked within it created a little fissure in my heart. Yes, Mark could be hard to work with. Yes, he had so many ideas and things running through his mind like wild squirrels that he missed things, and those missed things were important. But he was willing to take the truth. He would change what was needed in order to make my life easier. He'd even apologized when I was the one that should have done it first.

And I held a deep-rooted loyalty to him I'd never be able to explain.

Perhaps it was my new outlook on life, or maybe just a letting go, but I reached over to put my hand on top of his, then threaded my fingers through his and squeezed.

"Nothing," I whispered. "I don't think you should change anything about yourself, Mark. We'll figure out how to communicate better and this won't be a problem. You save me, I save you."

He sucked in a sharp breath. My stomach curled with heat when he flipped his hand over so our palms touched in an oddly intimate gesture. The feeling of his fingers wrapping around mine sent fire through my arm.

He turned to look at me and frowned. The beat of his heart pulsed through his throat as he gently whispered, "You've been crying."

I nodded.

His gaze narrowed. "Why?"

"Because," I murmured, "I think I'm . . . happy."

He didn't pause to contemplate the absurd dichotomy of my response. Didn't realize how at-odds it sounded, even in my ears. Instead, he put a hand around my neck, pulled me into his space, and pressed his hot lips to mine.

I folded like a house of cards.

His other arm snaked around my waist, softening my collapse against his chest. I twined my arms around his neck, ran my fingers through the soft hairs at the back of his head. When he deepened the kiss, I felt it all the way to the edge of my body like a shot of fire.

Mark yanked me closer until my legs straddled his lap and there was no space between us. Both of his hands found my hair, tugged on it. His arms wound around my waist in a locked embrace that took my breath away. Nothing existed in the gap between us except a fiery passion that I'd never felt.

Not once.

When my breath ran out and reasoning blurred, Mark pulled away. Both of his hands framed my face. His fingertips scrubbed my scalp and his thumb brushed across my cheek. My stomach flipped over and over as I stared into his hazy gaze, thick with passion.

Instead of speaking, he pressed one last, lazy kiss to my lips. Then he wrapped me in his arms, pulled me into him until my face was buried in his neck, and I breathed deeply for what felt like the first time in my life.

MARK

My brain stopped functioning.

When Stella and I finally untangled ourselves from the end of the pier, I felt fuzzy around the edges. She didn't protest when I wrapped her hand in mine and we wordlessly walked away, the quiet lake at our backs. Neither of us spoke—not sure I'd be capable of it—as we stepped back into my cabin and the silence there. She resumed her place at my desk but blinked at her laptop.

I sat on the couch and ran a hand through my hair, ignoring my phone as it rang.

My mind was too busy as it replayed that kiss to hear the obnoxious ringtone. The sparkle of tears that had lingered in her eyes when I first arrived. A mixture of vulnerability and chaos in her gaze. The way she'd slid onto my lap and kissed me back like we were about to die.

Maybe I had.

Because that is how I'd want to go.

The stupid phone rang again, but I ignored it. Lost in thoughts of the hint of spearmint that lived on her breath and what *else* I wanted to do with her now.

"Mark," Stella drawled, drawing me from my thoughts. "Are you going to answer that?"

With a jerk, I pulled myself from my thoughts and scrambled for my phone. Heat rose to my cheeks as she quietly chuckled. An unknown number flashed across the screen, so I rejected it.

There was just one thing I wanted to do.

With a low growl, I tossed the phone on the couch, stalked to the desk, and pulled her back into my arms. Stella melted against my chest like butter, her lips instantly on mine as I yanked her to me. For what felt like an eternity, Stella let me kiss her. Let me realize that what happened out there wasn't a fluke, and it wasn't an imagined hope.

No, the heat between us was real.

Before I let it go too far, I pulled away. Stella blinked as I held her at arm's length, a note of confusion in her expression.

"I want to keep kissing you for the rest of my life," I said before she could misjudge my intent, "but until we save Adventura, that's not feasible. And I think I need to take a moment and make sure you're okay with this."

For half a breath, I feared she'd run away screaming. Realize that she'd made a mistake and now she had to fix it. Instead, a warm smile filled her eyes. Whatever changed in her, I had no idea. But the Stella that walked away from the pier was different than the one that went out there.

"Very okay," she whispered.

Unable to help myself, I smiled. "Me too."

She moved toward me as if to resume our new favorite activity together, but I rallied all my control and held her back. My finger lifted.

"Ah! One more thing."

A silent eyebrow rose.

"What is this to you?" I asked carefully. "I need to know now if you're wanting a friends-with-benefits thing or if this is you wanting . . . more."

The words felt as heavy as my bumper plates. They were awkward in my mouth as if I couldn't force them past my teeth. But the last several months on that stupid dating app had taught me that people brought all *kinds* of ideas to relationships. For all I knew, Stella just wanted to kiss off some steam and resume where we'd been before, as friends.

For my sake, I sincerely hoped not, because I had a dark feeling I was halfway in love with her already.

Stella paused for a moment, and I could almost see her brain moving as she worked out what to say. Enough time to let me doubt what I'd said. *Too fast, idiot,* I told myself. One make-out session didn't a girlfriend make.

But maybe I wanted it to.

Because I was tired of them not sticking. Tired of trying again and again and again to find a spark. Now I had a raging inferno in my hands, and I wouldn't be able to settle for casual. There wasn't enough time in life to make me want that.

The same sort of silence had always come on our phone calls after I pitched her my crazy ideas, the ones she never stood behind. My heart hammered in my chest, but I didn't take the question back. Because we were grown adults and grown adults could figure this out.

"More." She squeaked it out, cleared her throat, then said it again. "More. I want . . . I want more with you, Mark."

"More."

I repeated it almost breathlessly. She smiled and a hand came up to touch the side of my face. This all felt so fast. I woke up this morning worried about staring awkwardly at her while we lived under the same roof because I couldn't keep my eyes off her. Now I had permission to kiss her, to hold her, to . . . *be* with her.

My mind spun.

"Me too," I finally said.

Her smile illuminated her face, brightening her already doe-like eyes, and I lost all my willpower. In one step, I had her crushed against me again, our lips connected, bodies pressed until I didn't know where she started and I ended.

This time, Stella pulled away a few years too soon. Her fingertips played with the hair at the edge of my neck, sending shivers down my back. Then she pressed her forehead to mine, closed her eyes, and drew in a deep breath.

"Thank you," she whispered.

I pressed a kiss to her forehead and pulled her close with a shaky breath. She burrowed into my neck with a little sigh as I tightened my arms around her. As Lizbeth would say, *sweet baby pineapple.*

We were in *big* trouble now.

Chapter Nineteen

STELLA

Mark left twenty minutes later.

The moment the door closed behind him, I let my head drop to the desk with a groan. Silence answered back, and I was grateful for it. The solitude gave me the chance to pull myself back together in the whirlwind that had become my life.

Joshua possibly here, possibly not.

A sort-of argument with Mark.

Dealing with hard truths from the past.

Kissing Mark.

And then again.

And again.

Another groan escaped me. Not that I regretted the kiss—no one could regret a kiss (or all twelve) like *that*—but what it meant. The force I'd put behind it. The abandon with which I'd thrown myself into his arms.

Deciding to let go of false beliefs from my past and be happy was one thing. Jumping into a pool of happy-kissing the next moment was another one entirely.

With that thought bright in my mind, I threw my hair in a high ponytail, changed into a comfortable pair of sweats, an old race t-shirt, and a jacket. I shoved aside the paperwork and my computer. Mark had faith that Seiko would help us iron out this idea, and we waited for official word from Lizbeth on licensing anyway. We needed to find our next booking, but I couldn't do that without him or more information.

So I would trust him.

Work could be stopped to do something else this time, which was, sadly, a difficult concept to wrap my mind around. But I did it anyway.

I needed a run but didn't have the guts to go on my own. My brain still felt like scattered butterflies. I wouldn't be paying attention the way I should in order to be safe from the overly-adventurous mountain lion. No new prints appeared this morning, thankfully, and no protest barking from Atticus in the night.

Instead, I set to work on this cabin. Mark wasn't a slob, but he wasn't tidy either. It needed a little . . . touch. Not too much. Not back to the sterility of my former apartment. But enough that it didn't feel messy. The work gave my mind space to unfold. To wrap around the tingly feeling that Mark's kiss had left behind. The way my lips still burned and the giddy fireworks thrilled in my stomach with each recollection.

I grabbed a laundry basket tucked near the back door, where a stacked washer and dryer stood in the wall. Then I walked around, plucking free his clothes, his socks, his jackets, and shoved them all inside. His random bits of paper went with it, as well as a weight lifting book and an old DVD case that didn't have a DVD in it. Then I shoved it under the desk where he could find it.

Once that was done, I finished with a few other warm touches. A blanket across the back of the couch. Magazines on top of the coffee table. My favorite coffee mug hung next to his over the sink. The sight of the two of them together gave me a moment of wry irony.

"This is going to be great," I whispered, still hearing echoes of grandma's optimism in my ears from our call earlier. "This is going to be great."

It would be.

I felt that.

But I also felt that same twinge of fear—albeit much quieter—that worried it would all go away. The heat of his arms replayed through my head. The bracing smell of pine and man and sweat. My skin prickled with goosebumps when I remembered his eagerness to touch me again, like a drowning man.

Mark, I felt in my core, was the best of men.

Resolve filled me again. Allowing myself to be happy wouldn't be easy, but it could be simple. Joshua still hung over my head. My utter lack of plans and steady accounting work followed next. Setting those aside to let myself be in the moment would take some practice, but at least I'd do it this time. Years lay behind me where I *didn't* let myself be happy. No more of that.

I'd pulled myself from the hamster wheel and now I stood in the vast, big world. The openness could swamp me, but I wouldn't let it.

No, dadgummit. I'd be happy.

With a satisfied nod, I headed up the ladder to unpack a little more, eager to be surrounded by the smell of Mark until he returned home.

* * *

The front door flew open with a *bang* three hours later.

Startled, I jerked up from my spot on the couch to see Mark strolling inside, two brown grocery bags in his arms. He grinned over the top of them when he saw me. The mouth-watering smell of Chinese food floated with him.

"Grabbed us some dinner," he said as he kicked the door closed. Once he set the bags down on the table, he grabbed something out of one and pitched it to me. I caught it and then laughed. A bag of dark chocolates.

"Thank you."

He winked and tossed his keys onto a nail in the wall. A brisk wind had blown in with him, leaving his cheeks reddened at the top. He had a glint in his eye when he headed toward me, then pulled me off the couch and into his arms. Any fears I'd harbored that all those kisses had been a fluke, or he'd want to run away after this and not talk again, dissipated in another warm kiss.

"That," he murmured after he pulled away, a chilly knuckle stroking my cheek, "is worth coming home to."

I grinned, my arms around his waist, still feeling heady.

"I like the sweats look." He peeked around to take in my new attire.

"Yeah?"

"Oh yeah. Very sexy."

"You have strange tastes then," I said with a laugh, but couldn't deny there had been a small part of me that wondered if he'd get weird when I turned casual. I so rarely turned casual these days.

He kissed the tip of my nose and stepped back to peel his coat off. "Any word from Seiko?"

I shook my head. "Peeked out there and looks like she started a fire and the lights are on. Otherwise, she hasn't needed anything."

He pumped a fist, then rummaged through one of the bags. "Bought some groceries but I already put most of them in the kitchen. The coffee, creamer, and other stuff can stay in here. Took a wild shot," he said as he pulled two styrofoam boxes out, "and figured you were a kung pao chicken and lo mein kind of girl."

I grinned. "Well done, sir."

He smiled again in that lopsided way that turned my heart

upside down. "Great. I went with broccoli beef, as one does, and fried rice. And I am willing to share."

While I rummaged through the other bag and put things in the fridge—creamer, small milk, and some pre-peeled hardboiled eggs and cheese packets for his post-workout snacks—he slipped into the bathroom to change. When he emerged in an almost-too-tight t-shirt and gym pants, I felt a flood of heat through my entire body.

We settled into dinner across from each other at the table, where he unabashedly played footsie with me.

"So," I drawled as I speared a piece of chicken. "Seiko seems quiet, and easy, and it's kind of her to help us out but—"

"We need to get our next booking."

He leaned back in his chair, a grain of rice on his lips. I nodded and had a sip of chocolate milk I'd stolen from the fridge.

"Yeah."

His teeth clacked together as he fell into thought, and I let the silence ride. Lizbeth's ghostly involvement in the moving parts of this left me feeling half-blind. What licensure? How long did it take? What were the next steps? He mentioned something about social media, but where? What would she talk about, and in what capacity?

The urge to talk to her followed, but I set that aside. For some reason, I didn't feel great about talking to Lizbeth. Maybe because Mark had once had—probably still did, on some level—strong feelings for her. Or because she held a more firm place in his life than I may ever hold.

I shoved those thoughts aside. They didn't feel great to think about. When I turned my attention to Mark, he'd stared at the ground, still lost in thought.

"Mark?"

He blinked out of it, then shook his head. "Sorry. I have a

few more leads I can follow up on. Some other people that I can talk to that may be interested."

"Are they pity people?"

He snorted. "No, but almost."

That didn't feel great either, but he dove back into his food. Didn't seem to bother him that his plan for keeping Adventura halfway relied on the charity of others, but it wasn't a thought I wanted to voice. The congenial, warm air between us was too nice and I wanted to bask in it a bit more.

"I grabbed a few things for Seiko while I ran to the store," he said. "I'd forgotten shampoo and soap for the bathroom out there. I'll get a firmer date and time for when her band will be here, then we can do the official booking."

"Thanks."

"After we eat, I'll send some texts." He waved his fork around as if to illustrate his point. "We'll find someone."

A hundred more questions rose to the tip of my tongue. *What's your online plan? Is the website live? How long until we can book online?* I quelled them for later. Before I could speak again, he grumbled about spam calls but didn't seem to need a reply. I let him speak through things while I half-listened, my thoughts still churning in the background.

Once our appetites slowed and I folded my container closed to eat the rest tomorrow, he lifted both his eyebrows.

"So," he drawled, "you ready for 007 3.0?"

A rush of butterflies in my stomach took me by surprise. I hadn't watched a movie with touchy Mark yet.

Perhaps this would be my new favorite.

"Yes, I am. Are you?"

He grabbed my wrist and tugged, pulling hard enough to yank me to my feet and back into his arms. Then he easily lifted me off the ground. I squeaked, startled to be airborne, and wrapped my arms around his neck.

"Born ready," he said.

Minutes later, we sat next to each other on the couch, the bag of dark chocolates on his lap, and the next 007 movie flickering across the screen. He had an arm around my shoulder and had tucked me into his side. I leaned against him and enjoyed the way he absently played with a lock of my hair.

Somewhere in this day, I'd settled into something that felt like coming home again. The low, warm glow I hadn't felt in so long I'd almost forgotten that it existed. The one that felt like being happy.

And I couldn't hate Joshua for the gift he'd given me at Adventura.

Chapter Twenty

MARK

"If someone knocks on that door one more time . . ."

The drawled threat no sooner dropped off my lips than another *tap tap tap* came from the front door. Stella had the gall to look amused from where she stretched on the floor, having just returned from a run. With the rock music that had been blaring out of the dining hall for the last four hours, there wouldn't be an animal in sight for days.

An exaggerated sigh escaped me as I shoved myself off the couch and headed for the door, pasting on a wide smile as I pulled it open. Seiko's agent, a middle-aged man with an oily black mustache and smile as flexible as steel, waited on the porch for the 1,764th time.

"Can I help with something?" I asked. If he noticed my gritted teeth, the man gave no sign. I hadn't even bothered to learn his name. Another rendition of the same song we heard an hour ago blasted in the background. I loved it when I first heard it after Seiko and I went on a date four months ago, but now wanted to drive nails into my ears just so I'd never have to hear it again.

"Water bottles." The man pushed his lips up in a strange duck-face imitation. "They're looking for chilled, bottled water."

"There's a tap in the kitchen."

The man's eyebrow rose. "About that—"

"Have a good day."

Stella schooled a chuckle when I slammed the door in his face and groaned when he knocked again.

"Don't get that door," I muttered. "Not one more time."

She held up two hands in silent acknowledgment, then slowly straightened. The last three days of living around each other had been . . . blissful? Was that a word? Sublime? Something that straddled the world of this-is-stuff-of-dreams and I-can't-believe-she's-into-me, whatever that was.

A particularly off-pitch chord reverberated through the air again. I gritted my teeth as Justin slammed the back door shut behind him.

"When," he muttered, "are they leaving?"

Atticus slunk in behind him, heading straight for Stella on the floor. She laughed as he licked her face to death even though he'd just returned from the run with her. The dog couldn't get enough of her.

"Tonight," I said.

"You're sure?"

I wasn't, but I couldn't take away his hope. "I'll make it happen."

He nodded, then sank onto the couch and rubbed his temples. Stella straightened from where she'd been lunging on the floor and winced when another crash of drums rippled through the forest.

"Well," I muttered. "At least mountain lions won't be a problem."

Stella ran a hand along the back of my shoulders as she walked to the ladder. The trail of her fingers against the sensitive part of my neck made me shudder, and it took all my willpower not to spin on my heels and race up that ladder after her. Instead, I contented myself with remembering that we'd watch another 007 movie tonight—our favorite nightly tradition—and then make out afterward.

Amazing how the loneliest time of my life could flip around so quickly.

Once Stella disappeared, I turned my attention to my phone. The driving beat outside didn't help my internal anxiety. None of my contacts had returned my messages. Apparently, no one within my circle of influence, Seiko aside, wanted to rent a crummy cabin on the edge of a summer camp.

Who knew?

My phone buzzed with a text from Lizbeth that set my hair on end.

Lizbeth: Sorry, Mark. I haven't been able to get to the zoning question with the city answered. It's all weird because you're technically between Pineville and Jackson City. I'm not sure which jurisdiction you're under. We need to call but I haven't had the time.

Mark: No worries. I can take care of that.

Lizbeth: Then let me email you some information that you'll need.

Mark: Has the HomeBnB been set up yet?

Lizbeth: No :(We have to resolve this first.

I tilted my head to the side to crack my neck and release some tension. *No* meant that so many things were left undone, and until they were done, nothing could be rented. Lizbeth was helping me because she wanted to help, but unpaid labor was also unreliable, even in a family. Without paying her, I wouldn't ask her to make this a priority over her new marriage.

Still irritated me though.

Mark: Send me everything you have and Stella and I will take it from here. Thanks for all you did, sis.

Lizbeth: Sorry! It's just been so busy.

Mark: It's all good.

The casual *sis* was a mental tactic I employed the moment after I found out JJ had proposed and she accepted. My reasoning at the time had been sound. If I thought of her as a sister, I couldn't crash hard into the deepening attraction that felt like a freight train. It hadn't worked, but I kept at it so long it was second habit now.

Tonight, with the smell of Stella's shampoo in the air, Lizbeth was the last thing on my mind.

A stretch of silence seemed to make the air hum. I looked up, shocked at the strange quiet in the aftermath of hours of rock music. Were they done?

Were they leaving?

Another *tap tap tap* came on the door. This time, it was Seiko. She grinned at me, though she appeared tired. When she spoke, her voice sounded hoarse.

"Hey Mark, thanks again. We're all done here. It'll take a while to get the equipment broken down and moved out, probably just a few hours, but the guys and I have to head out to some other things."

With a quick hug and a wave to the other band members behind her, I shut the door. Justin let out a heavy sigh and rested his head back against the couch. Stella emerged from a steamy shower, her hair wet in sexy strands of blonde and a deeper brown. I blinked.

Stella.

Shower.

Stop.

Before my brain went any further, I shook myself out of it. "They're gone." I averted my gaze from her. "Well, the music is gone. Her crew is still cleaning up."

"Great."

Stella peered out the window as she pulled a comb through her hair. A new problem occurred to me—how did I diplomatically get Justin out of here so I could get my arms around Stella?

A nanosecond before I barked at him to get the hell out, his phone rang with an irritating Dave Matthews cover song, and he grinned. Seconds later, he'd bounded off the couch and said, "Hey Meg" on his way out the back door.

One problem solved.

4,000 to go.

Instead of moving onto the next issue, I drew closer to the siren song reeling me in and stepped behind Stella. She paused as I trapped her wrist, stole her comb, and sank the teeth into her hair. When I pulled it through, the hair gave way like strands of silk.

Stella sighed.

I wanted to trap that sigh on my lips and kiss the rest of it out of her, but settled for the rhythmic whisper of the comb through her wet strands of hair. The motion soothed even me, and not even the HomeBnB zoning question could concern me. Stella watched Seiko's team packing up from the dining hall, winding cords around their arms and hauling amps into the back of a rental van. But I had a feeling her attention wasn't even out of these four walls.

"I just texted Lizbeth."

The words rushed out of me. She didn't respond but made a

little noise in the back of her throat. The expected tightness of her neck had come, however. For some reason, she didn't seem all that comfortable when I spoke about Lizbeth.

Might be the raging crush I had once admitted to that seemed so silly in comparison to Stella.

"I asked her to send me everything she has done for the HomeBnB and to turn the whole thing over to us."

She turned around, strands of hair dropping out of the comb as she spun to face me. Her face had a faint blush from the warm water. Stella hardly ever wore makeup. Tonight, her skin was scrubbed clean, tinted with the faintest scent of apricot. I took a step back before her warmth could draw me right onto those lips and out of my train of thought.

She smirked. She was onto me these days.

"Why?" she asked.

"I think this is something you and I need to control. Lizbeth is busy and it's not fair to ask her to do so much of it without getting paid."

The desire to say *I told you so* seemed to burn right out of her eyes, but I ignored it. She'd mentioned once (or twenty times) over the years we'd worked together that I couldn't run a successful business on free labor from family. I had, at least for a while, but saw her point now.

"Besides." My hands found their way to her arms. I wanted to put my palms on her face and draw her into me but settled for this instead. "You've been asking a lot of questions that only Lizbeth could answer, and I think it may cripple us. So if you're willing, maybe we can work on it together?"

The slow smile that crossed her lips was all the answer I needed. Since she'd said (or smiled) all she needed to say, I finally crushed her against me and got lost in the feel of her mouth on mine. When she pulled away, I tried to follow, but she laughed and put a hand on my chest to stop me.

"First of all," she murmured, eyes bright, "yes, it will be

much easier for us to do it and I'm happy to help. I need to earn that free rent, right?"

"Right," I growled, but she wasn't fooled. Her fingers dropped to the top of my collar, where she played with a little tuft of hair that had appeared there. It sent all my thoughts barreling away from Adventura and right back onto her.

"Secondly, we need to—"

"Get another booking."

She sighed. "Yes."

I groaned and ran a hand through my hair, her spell broken by the stench of reality. When I forced myself to back away from her, she wisely didn't follow. "I know! None of my leads have come back so . . . we're just going to have to see what we can do on social media. Maybe I'll go into town and accidentally run into people."

She snorted and glanced outside. Night threatened on the distant horizon. The sun went below the mountains long before sunset here, which cast Adventura in early shadows, and nights had become chilly. A skiff of snow threatened to fall tonight, which meant I'd need to get more firewood.

"I was hoping the next booking would start tomorrow," she murmured.

The hope on her voice had faded to an almost indiscernible trail and I felt the usual flare of irritation that deadlines gave me. We were something like a week away from needing to make payments. While I had a few aces up the sleeve, they were absolute-disaster-only aces and I had to exhaust every avenue before I even looked that way. All desperate chances aside, we still had a few days to scrounge something up.

"I had some ideas," I said slowly. That sentence wasn't the kind of thing I could just spring on someone, I'd learned, so I monitored her reaction. She lifted her eyebrows in silent question. Uncertain she *really* wanted to hear them, I scoured her expression, but saw no evidence to the contrary.

"You ready?" I drawled.

"Hit me."

"Okay." I leaned back a little. "What about an RV park?"

She blinked, but no scoff came right away so I went with it. "RV Park?"

"In the winter, for a small fee, RV's can park out here. It's surprisingly hard to find good places to park in the wild."

"What about hook-ups?"

I scowled. "We couldn't offer too much. I do have a water hook-up for boondocking. I mean, JJ and I lived out of an RV for almost two years before it fell apart. Maybe we could provide electric, but I'd have to see . . ."

"Literally lived in an RV?"

"Oh yeah." I nodded with a grin. "That was after the bus, so I freaking loved the RV in comparison. Traveled the US, hit every state in a year. We set the RV on fire in a desert in New Mexico and said our farewells once it died. The point is, I think we could carve out some 'private' spaces here."

She tilted her head to the side, eyes narrowed. "You and JJ were really close, weren't you?"

A pang in my chest took me by surprise when I nodded. "Yeah. Brothers. Twins. That whole shared-a-womb-thing. But more than that. We were the Bailey brothers."

She hummed low in her throat, then patted my chest. "I don't hate the RV idea, but what would you even charge?"

"Great! And I don't know. I'll put feelers out. Also, about horses—"

She immediately shook her head. "No horses."

I threw my hands in the air. "Why is everyone so against horses?"

"It's not the animal, it's the man."

Before I could puzzle that one together, she distracted me by touching my bicep and forcing me to look at her. I blinked away the haze that came over my thoughts when I could smell her.

"I trust us to figure it out, Mark."

The easy words, spoken as a no-doubt-intentionally-sexy whisper in my ear while she slipped behind me toward the kitchen, slammed into me with all the force of a sucker punch.

Well . . . that was a first.

Friends, dates, girlfriends, acquaintances—whatever all those other women had been—had never said the T-word before, and definitely not where my business was concerned. Certainly, there had been no *us* in the picture. I had so many loose strings of business in my life at any given time, most of the women I dated didn't even try to catch up. They heard the word *entrepreneur* and dropped interest, or listened politely with a tight smile and glazed eyes that begged to be put out of their misery. When ideas flowed from me, they became anxious, even more bored, or convinced I had ADHD.

Stella's sexy little comment had either helped my confidence, or paralyzed it. At this point, I was just trying to stop my racing mind from reacting to her proximity and get back to the point at hand: saving Adventura.

Blinking, I jerked myself from those thoughts and spun to face her. After the shower, she'd changed into an oversized pair of sweatpants, a pair of fuzzy slippers, and an old shirt. A black jacket covered her arms from the chilly air through the windows. While I'd been lost in thought about my hands on her body again, she'd thrown her hair into a messy barrette that made my stomach do funny things.

The business-professional accountant, Marie, must have been a joke. Stella was all casual ease and smoky glances, like warm honey.

I prowled over to her again with another low growl. She laughed as I buried my face in her neck. Then I stayed there, because it felt entirely too nice to be the one held.

"Say it'll be okay?" I whispered.

She put her arms around me, hands splayed across my back.

"It's going to be fine, Mark. We'll make some dinner and get to work on it first thing tonight, okay? Once we have a plan, we'll get to work finding our second booking. Then we'll curl up, pretend to watch 007, and make out."

My eyelashes brushed her neck when I closed my eyes and let out a long breath.

"I thought you'd never say it."

The sound of her laugh bounced through the cabin as I pulled in another breath, all wound up in her. Apricots. Lavender. Peach. Each scent wound through my mind and settled the fireworks that exploded like warnings. Technically, her cabin lay empty tonight. She could slip back over and sleep on her own again once we cleaned it, but she hadn't mentioned it and I wasn't about to bring it up.

Stella was right. She had to be right. We'd figure something out.

Because if we didn't figure this out, Maverick would give up on it. He was a friend, but not a fool, and no fool held onto a bad investment.

Then I'd lose everything.

* * *

A pair of chattering teeth and a panicked voice woke me out of a dead sleep that night. I bolted up, startled further awake by a wash of bitter cold air.

"M-mark," Stella whispered. "It's s-so c-cold in here."

She crouched next to the couch where'd I'd racked out after our movie. My quilt was wrapped around her shoulders and a pair of thick socks on her feet. Her face was little more than shadows in the deep mountain night, illuminated by the dim light of stray appliances in the kitchen area. I rubbed my palm over my eyes, catching a glimpse of snow flurries just outside my window. The sleeping bag fell away from my chest when I sat up, and I almost swore.

It was freaking *cold*.

"Sorry," I mumbled. "Didn't know it was going to snow."

A pathetic pillow of coals had died down in the hearth, almost as cold as the room. Stella grabbed some firewood and brought it over while I resurrected what I could from the ashes and tossed some dry kindling on top. Within a few minutes, baby flames crackled around a new, dry log. Stella sat with her back to the fire, eyes bleary with sleep. The tip of her nose appeared to be red.

"Sorry to wake you," she murmured.

I scoffed. "Yes, I would have much preferred you freeze to death, Stella Marie. How dare you?"

The firelight caught her eyes in a sudden, startled expression that warmed into a smile. Was it because I said her full name? I'd tried to keep it to just Stella as she requested, but there was something easy about the way *Stella Marie* rolled off my tongue. The goofy grin cut me all the way through the chest as I stared at her, distracted from my intent until a pop startled me back to the moment. With a shake of my head, I turned back to the fire and tossed another log on. Stella shivered next to me while I built it up, huddling close to the warmth.

We sat there in silence, the smell of burnt wood around us, when Atticus's eerie bark cut through the night. Stella sucked in a sharp breath, her eyes darting to the window. I put a hand on her shoulder.

"He's barking toward the lake," I murmured, knowing she'd be worried about it being Joshua. "Not the road. Besides, that's a different bark. That's not a person bark. It's a bit wilder."

When I stood to peer out the window, there was nothing to see but deep shadows and the occasional flash of a snowflake right next to the window. But the resonance of Atticus's warning, like a low reverb, meant he barked away from us.

"Cougar?" she whispered.

I sincerely hoped not.

"Or he just got twitchy," I said to play it off. Of course it was the cat. I strained to hear, wondering if the creepy, undeniable sound of a mountain lion interrupted Atticus's deep staccato barks. Nothing that I could tell for certain, nor likely to hear inside. Stella stood and came to my side, a wary glance outside. I wrapped an arm around her, grateful she hadn't gone to her own cabin.

"It's kind of creepy when you can't see anything outside," she whispered.

I pressed a quick kiss to her forehead and she burrowed closer to me, blanket rustling. "Will Justin be okay?"

"The Gladiator? He's probably the one that'll scare the cat off. It'll take one look at him and scamper."

Atticus had quieted for a moment. I thought about getting on the radio and calling Justin, but didn't want to increase her concern.

"I don't have many winter clothes," she whispered suddenly, and I laughed. She sounded so small and tired while she stared at the falling snow.

"C'mon, Stella Marie. It's time for you to go back to bed."

With a little coaxing, and the fire brightening the room again, she let me guide her to the ladder and nudge her upstairs. The attic felt even colder than the basement. The chimney crept through the attic against the far wall, so it would eventually warm up. But the two windows by my bed kept it chilly on winter nights.

My intention was to tuck her in and give her a lingering kiss to sweeten her dreams—and my own—but when she slipped back under the covers and grabbed the front of my shirt before I could back away, my resolve weakened.

"Stay, please?" she asked quietly. "I don't want anything to happen tonight, I just . . . I'm a little scared."

The plea in her voice shattered me.

"Of course."

Stella scooted closer to the wall while I stretched out next to her and arranged the covers over both of us. She'd already layered the bed with the extra blankets I'd stacked at the end just in case. How long had she been shivering up here, alone? She hesitated on the sheets next to me, stiff like a board.

I broke the hesitation in the air by pulling her close. With a relieved sigh, she molded her body into mine. I curled my arm around her back to close the space between us and ran the tip of my fingers in a circle on her shoulder. She splayed a hand on my chest, her hair spilling across my shoulder. The light scent of apricot still rose from her skin and curled in my nose.

"Thank you," she whispered so softly that I wondered for a moment if I'd just imagined it. She tilted her head, tucked her face into my neck, and her breathing evened out moments later.

For the next hour I stared at the ceiling, paralyzed to the same spot. My heart raced as the thought *I fell in love with Stella Marie* ran through my mind like a busy ticker tape over and over and over again. I didn't try to stop it, because it was true.

And I knew I couldn't tell her.

Not yet.

Because of whatever amazing thing we had going here, I wasn't willing to break with reality. And in reality, women ran away from me all the time.

But not this one.

This one would stay. So I grabbed my phone, logged into my dating app, navigated to my profile, and closed the account with great relish.

Mark Bailey was finally off the market.

And hopefully for good.

Chapter Twenty-One

STELLA

"Marcus Aurelis Bailey!"

The sound of a woman calling up the ladder jerked me out of sleep with a little cry of shock. A warm hand on my arm, followed by a groan, brought me the rest of the way. I blinked, half tangled in dreams with mountain lions and Joshua and Mark before memory served. Mark shuffled next to me, his body radiating heat despite the cool mountain air outside our little cocoon.

Right.

Weird night.

"Go away!" Mark shouted toward the direction of the stairs. He tucked his face back into my neck.

"Mark," I whispered. "Who is that?"

"My annoying-as-crap little sister."

My eyes flew open. "What?" I squeaked quietly. "Megan is here?"

"Apparently."

His hard-as-a-rock body was curled at my back and warmer than a stove. My nose felt nippy with cold, but the rest of me was toasty. An obscure white glow seemed to fill the world outside.

"I haven't even seen my gladiator yet, Mark," Megan called, sounding closer now. "I came to say hi to you first because Justin says you've been whining about how much attention you're not getting."

Panic woke me the rest of the way. I tried to shove him off the bed before Megan came up here and found us like this. What a great introduction that would make. When I yanked the covers over my head, Mark chortled.

"Mark!" I hissed. "She can't find us like this! She'll—"

He laughed then, a deep, rolling timbre that cut all the way to my bones. "Point made," he called to Megan, having mercy on me. "You win two best-sister-ever points. Go see your gladiator and come back. I'll be awake by then."

A long silence passed where I remained frozen, ready to leap out of bed, before Megan grumbled something about getting stuff from her car first and the door shut with a thud behind her. Mark growled, hooked an arm around me, and pulled me back down.

"She'll be a while," he murmured against my neck. "They haven't seen each other in like three days so they're going to pretend as if it's been a year and makeout forever."

My defenses were low this early, and before coffee, so I gave in to the warm lure of his arms and sank back to the covers. He yanked them back over us and snuggled close again. His warm breath caressed my neck in a gesture that felt like an embrace itself. With a sigh, I relished the feeling of his arms around me and heat on a frosty morning. What had I been missing all these years?

This. All of this.

Mark hummed when I absently ran the tips of my fingers across his growing stubble. It prickled gently.

"Did you know she was coming?" I asked.

He shook his head. He still hadn't even opened his eyes. The relaxed contours of his face were more wrinkled in the morning but somehow gentler. Calmer. More at ease and . . . normal.

"Do you think—"

"She'll love you," he immediately said.

"I wasn't worried about that."

"Good." He rolled slightly away to yawn. "Some people are scared of Meg at first, or maybe just the reputation for being a bad-ass that precedes her, but she's really chill. Maybe protective, but chill."

His comfort wasn't working. Until he'd said something, I hadn't felt that nervous about it. But now I wondered if I should. Before I could dive too far into that thought, he kicked the blankets off. Chilly air replaced the lovely warmth we'd been snuggling in and I fought off a scowl. If Mark saw me protesting, he'd probably burrow back in for the next hour, refuse to let me go, and then Megan would *really* have a great first impression of me.

"C'mon," he yawned, a hand held out. "I'll make the coffee. Let's get this over with."

* * *

With that ominous thought, I trailed above Mark down the ladder and into a mostly-warm cabin.

Certainly wasn't as cold as last night, but still chilly. A blanket of fog lay on the world outside. The storm had moved on not long ago, leaving wisps of fog clinging to the canyon walls. Scudding clouds crossed a low gray sky. Wet snow bowed tree branches to the ground.

Not far away, out the window over the sink, I caught a glimpse of a woman in black yoga pants, furry boots, and a head of dark brown hair jump into Justin's waiting arms. He caught her and whirled them both around in a sparkling eddy of falling snow. Atticus bounded happily through the drifts around them, barking.

That adorable reunion calmed the tension that still clung to my ribs with tenacious fingers. Although the mountain lion was the most likely culprit for Atticus's late-night barking session, in my mind I hadn't been able to rule Joshua out entirely.

Mark yawned every thirty seconds as he puttered around, built the fire back up and fired up the coffee machine. I stumbled around coffee cups and pods and tried to pull my thoughts together.

A quick warm shower, a new set of clothes, and pulling my hair out of my face did wonders to restore my brain. When I emerged from the bathroom, Mark had some semblance of humanity restored to his face. He didn't wake up well most days. This sleepy, cozy morning seemed even harder to untangle from, and I wished we *could* have snuggled in bed all morning.

He opened his mouth to say something, but the back door opened. A snowy Atticus bounded by, shaking snow all over the place. Justin followed, his arm wrapped around the girl that must be Megan.

She ripped a white snow hat off her head as she entered, saw me standing in the bathroom doorway, and smiled. Vestiges of Mark lived in her eyes, and JJ in her face shape. She had his sculpted cheekbones, but Mark's spark of vivacity.

"You must be the infamous Stella Marie," she said.

Something cold came into my stomach at that, but I played it off with a smile. "Infamous?" My eyes widened. "That sounds ominous."

She laughed but didn't release Justin. Or, more aptly, he didn't release her. They stood in the hallway together, looking equally as powerful and adorable as I'd expected. If there was any woman that matched Justin's easy confidence, Megan was that woman. I envied her natural presence in a room.

"I'm Megan," she said. "My dad told me how much he likes

you. Mom is dying because she hasn't met you yet. And may I thank you, on behalf of our entire family, for saving Mark from the world's *worst* ideas the past couple of years."

A paper cup sailed out of the kitchen to land right on the back of her head. Megan glared good-naturedly at him, but Mark feigned innocence. Justin pulled her farther into the cabin, and only then did I notice that she carried a couple of sacks.

"Breakfast burritos, brother!" she called and tossed them onto the table. "I bring them as a peace offering."

Mark wilted into a chair and grabbed the closest bag. "All is forgiven!" he declared in a grating operetta. Then he tossed a foil-wrapped something to me. "Stella, these breakfast burritos are the best. You gotta try them."

Any awkwardness that might have come from the fact that I clearly slept in Mark's house with him never arose. Justin, Meg, Mark, and I cluttered around the small table barely big enough for two and fell into an instant discussion about breakfast foods. Megan spent most of her time staring or laughing at Justin. He kept a sturdy arm around the back of her chair and returned the doting attention.

My stomach curled at the breathtaking sight of such . . . abandonment in the face of love and happiness.

Watch out, my brain wanted to scream at them. *What if this all goes away? What if you lose each other?*

But I turned that away and, for the first time since Megan arrived, looked at Mark. He caught my gaze and winked. The rankled, crinkly feeling inside me faded. His hand found my knee and rested there while he leaned back in his chair and said to Justin, "So, Atty had a good time last night."

Megan eyed his arm for a moment but said nothing.

Justin let out a long breath. "I think your kitty came to visit, but I can't be sure. Haven't looked for tracks yet."

"Hear it?"

Justin shook his head. "Nah. I wouldn't let Atty out of the

cabin until I could get a rope on him." He motioned behind the cabin. "He was barking toward the lake. I'll go out soon and see what I can find."

"Probably obscured by now." Mark glanced out the window. Wind blew snow into swirls, but none fell from the low ceiling anymore. Justin shrugged.

"I'll try."

Megan's eyebrows rose as she swallowed a bite of burrito. "Found a new pet, Mark?"

"Well, no one wants me to get horses . . ."

She laughed, then leaned back in her chair and brought her feet onto the seat. Justin ran a hand over the top of her back.

"I ran into a guy named Benjamin when I stopped for coffee at the Frolicking Moose," she said. "They've opened for to-go orders now that remodeling is almost done. It was Maverick's brother."

"Benjamin is working there now?"

"No, just visiting. Ellie was running it. Have you met Benjamin?"

Mark's head tilted. Megan's tone had changed just enough to tell me there was more to what she said, but I couldn't figure out what it might be.

"The MMA fighter?" he asked.

She nodded. "He's here for a few months."

"Why?"

"Hoping to get ready for a fight." Her eyebrows rose. "But he's causing quite a stir in town. A reporter from Jackson City tried to corner him for an interview. Maverick was pretty pissed off when I got there."

Mark's eyes widened. "Seriously?"

She shrugged. "Apparently, Benjamin is very private. He can't find a place to get rid of the press."

For a moment, I couldn't tell whether Mark's sudden fascination had something to do with Benjamin himself or the commotion caused in such a small mountain town. Did Mark follow MMA fights or something?

Mark dug around his pockets—he was still in his sweats—for his phone. Then he held up a finger and disappeared up the ladder. By the time he got to the top, he was already speaking to someone.

"How are things?" Justin asked me, and I was grateful he picked up the conversation next. "Any new bookings?"

"Not yet. We set up a plan last night. I received everything from Lizbeth and was able to get my head around what needs to be done. It took a while, but I feel like I have a grip on it now."

"Another spreadsheet?" he asked with a grin.

I laughed. "Yes. Several. It felt wonderful."

"You sound like Lizbeth," Justin said, and I felt a lightning bolt all the way to my heart. The sudden realization that I could just be a shadow of the woman Mark really wanted hit me right then. Could Mark have attached on to me because I reminded him of Lizbeth? From what little I'd seen from her emails and the company, she was organized, on top of things, and not afraid to be a bit bossy.

Familiar, indeed.

Megan glanced at me with a sly smile, saving me from a sudden, breathless spiral. "You must be a saint, Stella, to stay here with Mark."

There was a teasing note in her tone, but it set my teeth on edge all the same. The urge to rise to his defense overcame me in a flash.

"Not at all," I replied quietly. "Mark is . . ."

Only a moment of hesitation lay in my broken response, but in it, I comprehended that I had a choice. Throw myself into a clear path with him, or hold back. Despite Megan's obvious love for her brother, I couldn't help but wonder if it was comments like *you must be a saint to stay with Mark* that had Mark bracing himself whenever he felt like he was too much. Whenever he wanted to be himself but wasn't *quite* sure what the response would be.

I tilted my chin up.

"Mark is amazing and I'm incredibly grateful that he's putting up with me."

An inscrutable expression crossed her face. In the space of a few seconds, she rotated through several emotions. Surprise. Annoyance. Then a sort of clarity. Justin cleared his throat and squeezed her shoulder. She blinked, pulled out of it, and opened her mouth to say something, but Mark thudding down the ladder stopped her.

"Sorry!" he cried, snatching his coat off a peg on the wall. He stepped into boots and didn't bother lacing them, but did stop to press a hasty kiss to my cheek before he grabbed his car keys and yanked the door open. "I'll be back in three hours!"

The slamming door escorted him out.

All of us stared at each other, stunned in the wake of his quick disappearance. Seconds later, the Zombie Mobile roared to life.

Megan leaned forward. "You're right, Stella," she said. "He is amazing. Thank you for reminding me."

"I—"

She held up a hand to stop me. "You did the right thing. Sometimes I need to be put in my place."

Chastising his sister. What a great first impression. Despite my concern, I could tell I'd earned Megan's respect. And maybe that wasn't an easy thing to earn.

"He's crazy about you, you know," she said. "I can tell. I haven't seen Mark like this . . . ever."

"Like what?" I asked, my voice raspy.

"Like himself," Justin said with a laugh.

"Normally when Mark has a date or a girlfriend, he's different. Subdued. Quiet, even. And yes, such a thing *is* possible." She frowned. "Just . . . different. This idiot is the same idiot that

I grew up with, and that is very telling. I mean he just up and left in the middle of breakfast without explanation and no one here batted an eye."

Justin laughed again. "Definitely being himself."

My heart registered an emotion deeper than I'd ever expected to feel. It thudded around my chest for a while, like it wasn't sure where to go. I didn't know what to do with it, so I just let it flail for a few minutes until I could wrangle it back under wraps.

"Thanks." I swallowed and managed a wry smile. "I think."

Megan studied me without reservation. "Just don't break his heart? He's had it broken so many times. He's . . . the divorce wasn't easy, and although he'll lie to me until the day he dies, I can see his face when Lizbeth is around."

My eyes widened.

Megan smiled. "Yeah, I know how he feels about Lizbeth. Mark thinks he's so suave and mysterious, but the man wears his heart on his face."

"Does JJ know?" I asked.

Both of them shook their heads simultaneously and my lips twitched with a smile. Had they already reached that point in their relationship where they thought the same thing? Was that a phase?

"Doubtful," Megan murmured, "although JJ does know Mark better than anyone else on this planet, so maybe."

She looked to Justin with a questioning expression and he just shook his head and said, "Nah. JJ doesn't see it."

"If he does," Megan continued with a shrug, "it certainly hasn't concerned him at all. Mark takes on a lot. He's always been the glue between us siblings and it's weighed on him. Even though he wouldn't admit it. Just like JJ leaving has been hard."

"I won't break his heart," I whispered.

And the promise rang all the way into the deepest caverns of my heart because it had the same echoes of trust that Mark had in himself. Maybe he really was rubbing off on me in great ways.

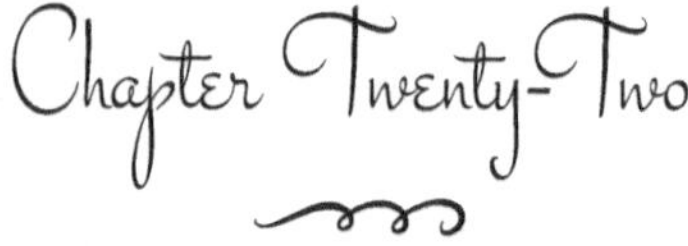

Chapter Twenty-Two

MARK

Leaves scattered past my feet as I crossed the parking lot of the Frolicking Moose and stepped inside. To the right, four women crowded around the back of a car. Three of them were bent to their phones, the fourth had her eyes darting at the coffee shop ahead of me, then back. Despite the chill, their short skirts fluttered in the wind.

I grinned.

This was better than I expected.

When I stepped inside, Ellie's light eyes peered at me from behind the counter, where she stood at the drive-thru window. Normally, she had a wild look in her eyes. She was a true child of the outdoors. I'd been hiking with her, and she'd always been a beast. There was a drive of competitiveness I admired about her, but something dim lived in her expression now. No doubt that had everything to do with Devin Blaine's unexpected departure.

"What're you doing here?" she asked, then passed a drink to someone outside. Ellie had always been tough and hard to impress, but now that Devin had ditched, she appeared to have moved to permanently pissed off.

"Hey, Ellie."

She stared at me. I stepped up to the counter, which was a mixture of old and new. Some of the wooden beams that the construction company had pulled down from overhead were repurposed into new cabinetry to keep a mountain-like feel. Lizbeth had created half a dozen Pinnable boards that she talked about constantly while the Frolicking Moose went into full reconstruction in the spring and early summer. Instead of an old fishing stop pretending to be a coffee shop, the new Frolicking Moose had been reborn as mountain funky—a perfect blend of new and old.

That was Bethany—constantly turning things around and making them better. Maverick included.

"Mav is here, right?" I asked.

She nodded. "Upstairs."

"Thanks."

"Did you see the creep in the car?" she asked, tilting her head to the right with a scowl.

"Yeah, on my way in."

"What's he want?" Her gaze darted to the clock above the front entrance. "I've tracked him there for twenty-three minutes. If he's there for seven more, I'm confronting him."

Trust Ellie to know every single person that surrounded her and for what amount of time.

"He's not here to cause trouble for *you*," I said. "I recognize him."

Her lips rounded into an O when understanding dawned. The guy was a reporter at the Jackson City Gazette. He'd done a piece on Adventura after it opened up.

"You doing good?" I asked. "I miss having you at Adventura with your sister."

Ellie's lips thinned. There were all kinds of unspoken sentences there. *With Devin,* I could have added, but didn't. *Miss seeing you joke around with him. Miss the way he always made you laugh so much.*

"Great," she muttered, then softened. "And thanks. I'll head out your way soon."

"Hey, I'm sorry about Devin."

If her jaw tightened any further, her teeth would snap. She shot me the coldest of glares, but I ignored it. Ellie was just like my dad, all bluster.

"Did you want something to drink?" she asked frostily. I headed for the hallway and called over my shoulder as I slipped to the back.

"Not today, thanks!"

The short hallway led to a pair of winding spiral stairs that the fire hadn't touched. From the loft came the low murmur of male voices. While I climbed, I forced my heart to slow and my mind to calm. If I wanted to take this opportunity, I had to be *very* careful, and very casual. I grabbed the newspaper that I'd balled up in my back pocket as I took the last few stairs.

When I reached the top, an open door into a brand new loft greeted me. Two brothers, equal in height, stood with their backs to me. Maverick, the one with the half-metal leg, stood on the right side of the room and studied paint cans with a tilted head. Benjamin, his younger brother, held a roller in his hands. Ben was tighter and more bound, like a fighter. His hair was cropped close to his face these days, but I'd seen it in between fights, when it was occasionally longer.

"Mav, you suck at colors," Benjamin said. "What is fuschia anyway?"

"Shut up."

The walls were half painted with primer already when I knocked on the door frame. "Interrupting anything?" I asked.

Mav glanced back and grinned. "Hey! Wondered where you've been." Benjamin looked back when Mav smacked him in the arm. "Ben, this is Mark. He's the one that owns that summer camp I was telling you about."

Ben nodded with a jerk of his head. "Good to meet you." I returned it. Then I gestured to the loft and whistled low.

"Looking good, Mav."

What had been a tiny attic room that Bethany and Lizbeth barely managed to live in had grown with the coffee shop. They'd renovated the Frolicking Moose to the side, adding a larger dining area as well as a back room for client meetings, parties, or book clubs. The attic followed suit, large enough they could rent it one day. Once Ellie moved out, I had no doubt they would.

"Thanks." Mav set a hand on his waist. "Feels glacially slow getting it all finalized, but we'll get there. The plumbing up here has given us some issues, but I think I've gotten it all worked out now."

"Now that you've got competent help, you mean." I gestured to Ben with a tilt of my head. Ben snorted.

"How are things?" Mav asked. I didn't miss the undercurrent in his voice, but I did ignore it. Instead, I tossed the newspaper on the wooden floor and it hit with a satisfying slap.

"Just came to see if you needed some help."

Benjamin shifted back a step and glanced at the newspaper, then me. No doubt he'd already seen the front page article of the county newspaper, but I did love an unforgettable entrance to make my point. Benjamin regarded the image of his face on the front cover, then looked at me in silent question.

"There are four women in the parking lot, by the way." I gestured with my thumb. "They're pretending to be looking for a place to eat but I think they're waiting for you to come out. If you look closer to the hair salon, I recognize a reporter from Jackson City waiting in his car."

Benjamin swore under his breath, shot Maverick a sharp glare, and turned back to the roller brush sticky with primer. Maverick sighed.

"I failed you, brother." Maverick clapped Ben on the shoulder. "To be fair, you're the jackass that had to get famous. I really thought you'd be left alone here."

Maverick confirmed my suspicions. Benjamin, three months away from his next fight, needed a place to train and prep. He needed a camp away from the distractions of life because he had sponsors to satisfy. No doubt he'd run to Pineville to hide away, but it wasn't working out so great.

"Maybe you *can* be left alone," I drawled.

Maverick tensed slightly, no doubt anticipating my coming pitch. Like recognized like. While Maverick was years ahead of me in the business build-up, maintenance, and follow-through, I recognized myself in him all the same. In a near-perfect impression of his brother, Maverick half turned to me with a silent question on his face.

"You have a fight coming up," I said to Benjamin. "But there's no place to really train here and there's certainly no privacy. Not with the space you need, anyway, because this fight is the career maker. You're either on top, or you're down, and your focus has to be absolute."

"Tell it to me already," Benjamin said, but he'd turned my way and crossed his arms across his chest. Like a freaking cobra, those arms. Perhaps my idea would be beneficial for everyone right now. Stella included.

"Adventura is out of the way, has space for you to train and fight that's winter proofed, and cabins for you to live in if you don't want to make the drive. The wifi is better than in town and there's no through road. I own, with my investor," I quickly added when Maverick cleared his throat, "all the land around it except for what backs up to National Forest. No one comes out there."

"You want me to move my entire camp out here to train before the fight?"

My heart hammered like a wild thing now because I at least had the instinct to know that this could close one of the biggest deals of my life. Not just in sheer timing—because it could save everything—but in reputation. Having Benjamin in my world would be no bad thing.

Above all, one more male on my property left Stella that much safer.

"No," I countered. "*You* want to. But it's not going that well, is it?"

Benjamin hesitated, and in those three seconds, I saw everything I needed to know before he closed back down. Something wasn't right in his world. His sponsors should be paying for this, but they must not be. Or maybe something personal had come up and he was ducking the limelight.

Why else would he be here of all places?

"There's space for mats, a separate gym, a kitchen that could feed as many as you need," I continued because I sensed the opportunity to press it. "And so many mountains to climb. We live at 8,000 feet elevation, so there's a definite lack of oxygen. You can have an entire cabin for just your team, if you want. There is plenty of space at Adventura."

Benjamin's head tilted back slightly.

"What's in it for you?"

Time to be brutally honest, because if I wasn't, Maverick would be later. "Mortgage payments," I said easily. "Summer camps are terrible investments in the winter."

A hint of amusement flickered through his eyes. "The media are a problem these days," he said slowly. "So why should I trust you?"

"Because Maverick trusts me."

Benjamin glanced to Maverick, who immediately nodded. The lack of reticence in his response gave me intense relief. For several long moments, no one said a word. I waited and willed myself to hold still for the first freaking time in my life.

Benjamin's sharp gaze had narrowed. "What kind of equipment can you support?"

"All of it. I have a cement-floored dining hall bigger than the closest gym in Jackson City and already have all my own weight stuff in a large shed that I use. You could bring whatever you want. Or whoever you want," I added.

"How long is it available?"

"Long enough to get you to your fight and then some."

"Can you guarantee privacy?"

Could I? I wasn't sure what *guarantee* meant in his world. People could still find Adventura if they learned where he was. But there was only one road in and out and we could gate it if we had to.

"Yes."

Another interminable silence reigned until he loosed his arms and said, "I'll come to look at it this weekend. Saturday at noon."

With a confident smile, I held out my hand, thankful it stayed steady when Ben clasped it. "See you then," I said. "Maverick can give you my number. I'll text you directions."

"No need. I'll find it."

Maverick sent me a knowing smirk as he, too, shook my hand. Then his expression dropped.

"Meant to tell you that some guy swung by today."

"Oh?"

"Yeah. He was asking about you. We were the only ones here when he stopped by. Didn't tell him anything but thought you'd want to know."

Something cold settled in my stomach. Stella had given me descriptions of Joshua before, but not enough that I'd ever recognize him if I saw him. He sounded perfectly normal enough.

"Tell me about him," I said.

"Baseball hat. Normal height." He tilted his head back and forth, as if uncertain. "5'9" I'd bet. Blonde hair. Hazel eyes. Not overly muscular or impressive. Seemed nice, but asked enough questions that it turned my radar on. Questions about where you lived. If you took tenants in your camp. How often you came to town, that kind of thing."

"Ask about a woman named Stella or Marie?"

"No. Just you."

Could be anyone, technically, but I had a crawling suspicion it wasn't an accident. As irrational as Stella said she felt, something told me that this situation wasn't as innocent as she wished it were.

Benjamin had clued in now, listening to Mav with an eyebrow raised. "The guy that came earlier?" Ben asked him.

Mav nodded.

"Got a problem you need some help with, Mark?" Ben asked with a low drawl. There was a wicked glint in his eye that told me he *wanted* a fight. I knew the feeling.

"Not yet," I murmured. "But maybe soon enough."

Ben eyed me. "You could take that guy."

"It's not Mark that needs to worry," Mav murmured. "It's his lady. Lizbeth mentioned her to me last night."

The words *his lady* ran through my mind like a reverberating echo, and I let them roll. Yeah, Benjamin needed to know she was mine. Because she was. Benjamin made a disgusted sound in his throat.

"Take that guy out hard, Bailey."

My knuckles cracked when I squeezed my fist too hard. "It's going to be my pleasure once we can find him."

While Benjamin turned back to the wall that still needed primer, Mav caught my attention again. "Not sure if it was anything," he said, but I could tell something with it didn't sit right for him. "Just thought I'd let you know."

"Thanks, brother."

When I turned to go with one final head jerk, Mav stopped me.

"You got this handled?" he asked. He meant Adventura. He

meant the mortgage. He meant everything that was, most definitely, *not* handled and would be due someday soon. I couldn't remember when.

"You know it!" I called over my shoulder with my usual, laissez-faire verve. He must have bought it because neither of them said a word as I descended the stairs, my thoughts a storm.

* * *

The Zombie Mobile creaked and groaned as I lumbered out of Pineville and into the canyon. Most likely, I imagined the feeling of being watched but felt even greater concern and sympathy for Stella now. Was this unsettled feeling what she'd been living in for weeks now?

Bastard.

With JJ and Megan at the camp with Stella, I took a detour off the highway and onto a familiar dirt road. By the time I made it back to Dad's property, the sun was overhead and my stomach grumbling. Dad would probably have tuna, egg salad, and old bread. His weird favorites, for some reason. When I skidded to a stop, a figure in a broad hat slowly looked up from where it sat near the creek. I chuckled.

The old man had fallen asleep fishing.

When the truck door slammed, Dad straightened up and waved a lazy hand. His fishing line had gotten tangled up down the stream in some brambles, but he hadn't noticed yet. Instead, he rubbed a hand over his face and readjusted his hat.

"Good nap?" I clapped him on the shoulder. He grumbled something at me while I grabbed an extra chair propped against the house and brought it over. By then, he'd started to tug on his line again.

"Great nap." He yawned. "You should try it sometime."

I snorted.

"You never did nap," he muttered bitterly. "Stopped that business when you were 18-months old, you monster."

That did sound like me. While I settled into the chair, Dad eyed me from the corner of his eye, then glanced back at the truck.

"You alone?"

"Stella's with Megan and JJ."

He grunted. With the lure returned, he reached for new bait. Unlikely he'd get anything now, but Dad would be aware of that. He always had to have something to do with his hands when we spoke. Getting fish wasn't the point of fishing.

"You liked Stell?" I asked.

Dad cast, chewed on his bottom lip, and nodded.

"How?" I asked. "You saw her for all of ten seconds and spoke three words to her if that."

"You've talked about your accountant before. When you texted me and said she was going to stay with you for a bit, and then I saw her," he shrugged, "simple arithmetic."

"So why did you like her?"

"She's got an honest face." He shot me a perturbed look. "And she might be the only person on this planet you've ever listened to when it came to all your businesses."

"She's brutal that way."

He laughed. "Besides," he drawled, "she's the only one that didn't seem afraid of me."

"You have a good eye for people."

He shrugged.

Ah, Dad. Silent, steady observer. JJ was too much like him by half. While relieved to have his approval, I couldn't act surprised. Dad was an open book when you really knew him, and he was that way on purpose.

I fidgeted in the chair for a moment, trying to figure out how to voice my next topic. Conversations with Dad were a lot like speed dating. Bullet points. Get to the purpose. Say the important stuff. Move on. Mom was more like a long, country drive. She'd extrapolate all over the place, wander into side roads, get lost in a topic, and be happy every second. Meanwhile, Dad couldn't fathom keeping up with it.

No wonder that marriage crashed and burned.

"Say it," Dad barked.

"What?" I asked.

"You're fidgeting. That always means you're not sure what to say."

I sighed, still grateful for his observation. "Stella's in trouble. Ugly trouble, and I need some advice."

He motioned for me to continue with a wave of his hand, then had a sip out of what looked like coffee. Then I told him everything I'd learned about her and Joshua from the moment she arrived. What the feds said—and didn't say—when she first reported it. Her fear of being paranoid and irrational. Right down to Mav's report today.

Dad's frown grew with each passing minute.

"Stella . . . she keeps saying her life isn't a movie," I said with a shake of my head. "That this can't be real. Some kind of denial, probably."

"Shock," he countered. "She's in shock."

"That too. But now *I'm* starting to wonder if this is more real than I'd thought, and I'd already thought it was pretty real. If that guy asking about me was Joshua, it probably means he's here and he's up to no good. I don't like that. Not at all."

Dad's lips thinned and eyebrows thickened, a sure sign he was thinking. I let the silence go, appreciating the quiet tinkle of the creek that calmed me. Repeating the story only made me more agitated. I leaned my forearms onto my knees.

"Feds aren't going to help because it's not really their jurisdiction," Dad finally said. "Until he actually makes a move, a threat, or harasses, there's nothing *anyone* can do."

"So I'm supposed to let that happen? Hell, no."

"No," Dad drawled, "didn't say that. I'll let the guys at the station know, tell them to keep an eye out. Get me a photo of him and we'll send it their way."

While that made me feel better, it wasn't enough. What if Joshua made a move? He only needed access to Stella once to do irreversible damage, and that wasn't acceptable to me. There were, of course, no guarantees here. But I wanted one. In all my life, I'd never wanted a guarantee more.

"Restraining order?" I asked.

He shrugged. "She doesn't live here."

"She does. She lives with me. Adventura is her home now."

Dad quirked an eyebrow. I met his stare and all the thousands of words behind it that he didn't say. Thankfully, he kept that locked away.

"Has she changed her drivers license?"

"No."

"Does she have proof of residency? Something official sent to her there through the mail?"

My hope started to feel small.

"No."

"That would be a first step. Even if she does do the restraining order, she'd have to do a temporary one for two weeks, then go before a judge. Do you want her to have to explain this to a judge if Joshua hasn't actually made a move against her? It'll be a disaster. The system is not ideal, but it's how it works."

On instinct, I fought back a curse in front of my father.

"So what do I do?" I asked.

"You get me the picture and description and any other information you have so I can pass it along. Then you watch, be careful, and wait. Let Atticus stay with her as often as you can. Don't leave her alone. That kind of thing."

"I don't like that."

Dad chuckled humorlessly. "That doesn't matter one bit, boy."

I already knew that.

I just hated it.

With a sigh, I ran a hand over my face. "Thanks, Dad. I appreciate your help. I'll get you all that stuff."

He nodded, running his tongue over his teeth. He tugged on the line as he slowly reeled it in, but I could tell his thoughts were far from Adventura.

"You still have the Sig Sauer?" he asked.

The handgun he'd taught me how to use when I was a teenager was safely locked at home. Normally, I only carried it while hiking or out on the trails in case the kitties or bears became a problem. Maybe I'd have it with me a little bit more, just in case. But even that wasn't comfort enough.

"Always," I said.

He grunted but didn't need to say more.

"Let me know," he said. "I'm always happy to come fishing there if you need me around for a few days."

His gaze met mine, and the steel-hardened sheriff in the depths of his eyes gave me great comfort. If nothing else, Stella and I weren't alone. My entire family would have our backs if we needed it.

"Thanks, Dad."

"Always, son. Always."

* * *

Light from Justin's cabin, tucked back in the trees and just within shouting distance, caused a faint glow out of the forest when I finally returned back to Adventura.

The sun was still an hour or more away from setting, but the sharp mountains cast early darkness here. The faint sound of Megan laughing trailed out from the kitchen, and I wondered where Stella would be. I'd texted Justin a few hours ago, and he'd confirmed they'd be there all night, so I'd run to a few more places. Hotels, for one. Did a little sleuthing on my own. Of course, I didn't know what I was looking for, so it had all been pointless.

Not even that much work could stop a knot of dread from forming in my chest. But it wasn't entirely about Joshua. The closer I got to my cabin, the more dread I felt about seeing Stella again.

In hindsight, it was wrong to leave that morning the moment I had an idea. I didn't think my pitch to Benjamin through until two minutes before I walked in the Frolicking Moose. My instincts tended to take over and they normally served me well, but those instincts really sucked in the romance department.

Too late, I realized there were a dozen ways I could have been a less-sucky boyfriend today. Abandoning Stella with my sister and her boyfriend so Stella would have the honor of being a third wheel was the worst.

The literal worst.

In fact, I hadn't even texted or explained myself. I could only expect a half-raged-filled woman and all the glares that came with such a situation. Inwardly, I groaned. How did I always botch this up?

This exact scenario had eventually broken all other women in the past.

With a sharp intake of breath, I forced myself to have a bit more courage. Whether she'd be pissed or not, putting it off longer would only make it worse.

My concern came to a fast halt when I stepped back into the house, eager to clap my eyes on her regardless. She stood with her back to me, wearing a pair of yoga pants with lacy flowers, an over-sized white t-shirt, and her hair in a messy bun at the top of her head. Her zip-up hoodie was old, but well-loved, and pushed up past her elbows. A cold draft of air ushered me inside. She whirled around, a scrub brush in her hand and a coffee mug in the other, then broke into a wide smile.

"You're back."

No chastisement. No flood of questions. No annoyed dart of her eyes. Stella just smiled at me.

"Hi." I shut the door and swallowed. "Everything good?"

She nodded, then motioned to the coffee table with a nod. "Great. Just taking a quick break before we get back to it. Megan and Justin are getting some snacks."

A plethora of candy wrappers, pop cans, drinks, and other various food gems littered my coffee table, along with several decks of cards. Ah, the Bailey family tournament. Megan had already baptized Stella into the family, and stupid me missed it because of my lack of curbing ideas.

"Thought I'd clean these before they stained." She held up the coffee mug. "Your sister is hysterical, by the way. And I'm in love with the two of them. If they were famous, there'd be hashtags about them, you know? They're both so . . . "

"Arrogant?"

"Amazing."

I shook my head, unable to believe this. The last thing I wanted to talk about was my sister and her boyfriend. "You're not angry with me?" I asked.

"Angry?"

I cleared my throat and gestured to the door. "I've been gone for so long and—"

"Oh! Yeah. Can't wait to hear it. You must have had an awesome idea."

She waited, clearly eager, as if she wanted me to say it right now. My mind took a few moments to reorient to this alien situation. Slowly, the tension bled out of my shoulders. *Can't wait?* I wanted to repeat in utter disbelief. *You . . .*

Instead of speaking, my brain took over again. In two quick

strides, I'd crossed the space between us. The next thing I knew, her body was pressed against mine, her face was in my palms, and her lips locked with mine. She tilted back over the sink from the force of my descent, but I gathered her up in my arms and pulled her back into me. There wasn't a breath that could have fit between us. Not space. Not air.

Nothing.

What must have been an eternity later, she pulled away with a little gasp.

"Wow."

She blinked. The scrub brush and coffee mug were still in her hands. They'd sloshed the back of my shirt. Water ran halfway down my back, but I didn't care. I captured her for one last, long, lingering kiss and forced myself to step back. To pull myself back together, I turned away and ran a hand through my hair.

Her rumpled grin deepened.

"Wow," I repeated quietly. Inside me, the knot that had choked my stomach slowly fell apart.

While she chuckled quietly to herself, I ripped the wet shirt off, balled it up, and threw it in the washer. She could laugh about this, but I couldn't. No, Stella had rocked me. Sucker-punch to the kidney so strong it rattled my metaphorical teeth. Oh, yeah. She had to be independent, beautiful, *and* accepting.

The nerve.

She also had to be stalked by a total creeper that I'd rip apart at the first opportunity.

"If you're looking to gain a bit of control over that fiery passion I love so much," she said wryly, "I hardly think you taking off your shirt is going to help."

I'd stopped to stare at her. Even with half the cabin between us now, I still felt like I didn't have enough space to stop me from taking this too far.

Unbidden, Joshua's latest appearance sprang back to my

mind. My nostrils flared as I noted her fuzzy boots that hid stockinged feet, then marveled at the absurd normalcy of every second that had just passed. Of course, it felt *so right* that she stood here, looking adorably rumpled and bright. Her expression faltered for a second.

"Mark? You okay?"

I grabbed another shirt, yanked it on, and returned to her side. This time, I leaned both my hands on the table and gripped the sides so I wouldn't be tempted to touch her again. I hadn't planned on telling her about Joshua. She didn't need to be more stressed out, but now that she stood before me, I knew she could take it. She'd want to know.

I'd want to know.

Sober now, she dropped the mug and brush back into the sink, but she didn't move closer. Instead, she swallowed.

"Joshua?" she asked.

I met her gaze. "He's in town, I think."

To her credit, she only paled. There was no gasp of shock or cry of terror. Something like resignation followed.

"Why do you think that?"

With calm precision, I told her everything that had happened and everything that my Dad had said. By the time I finished, she'd lowered into one of the chairs and stared at the top of the table. For a long pause after I fell silent, she simply blinked.

"You'll sleep in this cabin with me," I said as I paced. "There's no going back out to that other one. And I swear I can follow boundaries, I swear I won't make out with you every single minute even though I want to do that much and more. But I want to be close. I'm sure Justin will agree, but we'll have Atticus in here with us. Atty will love it," I added quietly.

An-almost twitch of her lips rose and disappeared.

"We'll make sure that either Justin or I are with you all the time. That'll give this time to blow over. As soon as the feds finish their investigation, Joshua will be a goner and you can get back to normal life with me."

Unable to bear her silence, I sat across from her. Her hands were in her lap or I would have grabbed one. Instead, several burdened moments passed before she shook herself from her thoughts and met my questioning gaze.

"It doesn't seem fair to ask all this of you," she said quietly, but before I could interrupt she continued. "But I'm going to ask all this of you."

She reached out with a hand and I grabbed it.

"Because you're the only person I feel safe with. So thank you. Thank you for . . . caring."

A burden of worry instantly lifted off of me. She wouldn't fight me on this. Tucked in the back of my mind was the terror that she'd leave to keep me safe, but she meant what she said.

I opened a hand. She put hers in it, then I yanked her off the chair and onto my lap. She straddled me, her fingers toying with the soft hairs along my neck. Then she pressed her forehead to mine and closed her eyes.

"I'm a little scared," she whispered quietly.

"I know." I pressed a kiss to her forehead and ran a thumb over her cheekbone. "But I'll keep you safe. We'll get through this together, one day at a time. Okay?"

"I know," she murmured. "I trust us to save each other."

With that, she kissed me again, and the world as I once knew it collapsed around me like a dying star. All that lay before me now, Adventura or not, was Stella Marie. The forest could burn down, the mountain lion could come, or a blizzard of epic proportions could wipe us out for all that I cared.

Stella was all that mattered.

Chapter Twenty-Three

STELLA

The next morning, a tangle of sunlight woke me.

I blinked awake, my eyelids heavy from the late night and an unholy amount of sugar. Megan had brought a few pseudo-healthy-but-delicious treats that she'd nabbed from JJ and Lizbeth after visiting them on her way here. But after Mark returned home, sources of candy I didn't know existed appeared out of nowhere.

Apparently, the Bailey card game was a local legend. Thankfully, I hadn't been half bad at it. When my finesse with numbers was paired with Mark's natural speed, we made a natural team. In many ways, I was quietly realizing.

A twitch of movement near my neck made me smile and brought me all the way out of my sleepy stupor.

Mark lay on his back, eyes closed with sooty, black eyelashes thick against his cheek. His hair was mussed and his shirt halfway up his torso, but he looked little-boy adorable. At some point in the night he'd come up, but I couldn't remember when. I'd felt his heat curl up at my back and I'd fallen back to sleep an instant later.

With no ideas or words streaming from his mouth, I stared

at him, grateful for a chance to study him. A recollection of what he said about Joshua came with it. To my surprise, the choking fear didn't follow. There was uncertainty, of course, but with Mark at my side and the light of day surrounding me, it didn't feel so bleak.

Besides, I wasn't alone and I wasn't paranoid. Joshua was a real threat, and I could embrace that now that Mark had the same heightened sense of uncertainty and wariness. He'd never once thought I made this all up, but now I could see he felt it too. He understood just how out of normal depths this entire situation had become. That validation felt like a gift.

"You," he mumbled, his voice a deep burr, "are so creepy."

Grinning I set my chin on my folded hands. "Why?" I asked. "Because I'm staring at you while you sleep?"

He stirred but still didn't open his eyes.

"Yes."

"It's the only time you're not talking."

He cracked a grin and my heart melted a little more. Moving fast, he wrapped his arms around me, flipped me on my back, and trapped me beneath him. His beard tickled my neck as he nuzzled into me. The weight of his body and the warmth of his skin was the only reassurance I needed that I was in safe hands.

"I have to get out of this bed," he growled, "before I kiss you while I have morning breath. But just know that I want to."

With a long kiss to my cheek, and the burn of his lingering breath on my neck, he disappeared off the bed. I laughed outright when he landed on the floor in an ungracious *thunk* and a string of muttered curses followed.

"Mountain man indeed," I murmured, then doubled over laughing again when he flipped me the bird.

* * *

Half an hour later, Mark placed a hand on the small of my back and spun me around. We'd just finished a quick breakfast with Megan and Justin, who left to change, when Mark pulled me back into his arms. I went willingly, wishing we could stay all day like that.

"Yes?" I drawled.

He grinned. "I have an idea."

"It's clear by that gleam in your eyes, yes."

"Then I won't disappoint you. There's a snow storm coming up this weekend. It's supposed to drop a foot here in the mountains. Which means it'll probably drop a crud more. They're anticipating ice on the roads because it's supposed to be warm the days before the storm. Rain + freezing temps = ice. So the highway may be closed for a bit. I want to get supplies."

"Okay," I drawled.

He tightened his hold on my waist. The edges of his eyes crinkled a little, as if with concern. "Come with me into town. We'll get you out before we hunker in for a while."

"But . . ."

"I know. Joshua was likely in Pineville yesterday, but we're going to Jackson City. And if that creeper is watching us, so what? What will he figure out that he probably hasn't already? That you're with me? That I'll beat the hell out of him if he even looks at you?"

His arms clenched, so I put a hand on his right bicep. He relaxed and looked adorably sheepish. The color had heightened on his cheeks.

"Sorry," he mumbled like a guilty child. His gaze dropped. "I just . . . I don't think you should have to hole up here, afraid for your life, when I'm with you. You know I'll keep you safe."

The idea of Mark against Joshua was an interesting one. Joshua wasn't a wimp, by any stretch of the imagination, but he did lack Mark's brawn. More than that, Mark had a force of willpower the size of a bull and the passion to drive someone all the way to the end of their life. His ability to protect me from Joshua wasn't in question.

The wisdom of venturing into the world to taunt Joshua, however, was. Even if Mark could beat Joshua, did I want to take that chance?

Not at all.

"My dad was right," he continued, as if he could see the war in my gaze. "Joshua hasn't made a move yet that we can act on and he may not. So why put you through more trauma and hiding? Besides, I'll be with you the whole time. Justin and Atticus will stay here while we're gone."

The situation with Joshua didn't seem as terrifying in the light of day as it always did at night, nor when Mark wasn't with me. But it seemed . . . reckless to go out into public notwithstanding.

However, the lure of civilization did call. Visiting with Meg and Justin had been restorative, but it would be nice to see people again. Even if I didn't talk with those people, there was a sort of community power that came from being around others. The noise, energy, and action. I craved just a bit more normal chaos for a while.

Megan was planning on just one more night here anyway before she went to stay with her Mom for a night. Mark and I would have plenty of time to figure out a way to save Adventura. And possibly kiss way too much.

Which idea I liked *very* much.

"Okay."

He'd opened his mouth to say something else, but snapped it closed. Startled, he blinked several times. I smiled.

"I'll go," I said. "I'm not super comfortable with it, but I also think that you're right. Joshua probably wants to have some power over me. To make me feel afraid. To . . . live small. If you will be there with me, I'll go. And thankfully, because as much as

I love your house, these walls do kind of get small. Plus, I'm having a big craving for Mexican food."

Mark grinned, gave me a quick kiss, and then another, and finally took three steps back with a charming little wink.

"Then let's go! We have delicious burritos and toilet paper to buy."

* * *

While Mark made obnoxious motorcycle noises and steered a cart around a grocery store in Jackson City, I picked a card for grandma's upcoming birthday and made a mental tally of what we had left to buy. Not to mention the fact that Mark had exactly zero dollars in his accounts.

I knew because I checked them daily.

The $500 that I'd originally given him lay in my pocket, and I silently tried to conspire a way to get him away from the checkout line so I could pay. We still had no second booking—not to mention the massive incoming storm that would surely detour tourists—to fall back on.

"Chocolate or caramel?" I asked.

He scoffed. "Always caramel."

"Fine. Try this one on for size: Cheery Bees cereal or the generic equivalent?"

"Generic." He tossed a small carton of OJ into the basket. "Always generic. C'mon, Stell. You're my accountant. Aren't you the one holding me to a budget?"

I laughed, eager to find more fodder for questions. Grocery shopping with Mark had been enlightening, to say the least.

"Sparkling water or plain?" I asked next.

"Chocolate milk."

"Not an option!"

"Always an option," he whispered dramatically. For every piece of junk food he put in the cart, I managed to squeeze in something with healthy value. The nasty sugar wafers, however, he just wouldn't part with no matter what I promised to give him instead, which was saying something.

His phone rang. The word *Mom* flashed across the screen with the call. My gut clenched from the unexpected surprise. Sara, his mother, had been a frequent topic of conversation between Megan and Mark the past evening. She was mentioned here and there, mostly with warmth, but sometimes the normal annoyance that comes with children and siblings. Mark was, clearly, close to her on several levels. The idea of meeting her caused me nerves, right up there with *losing my job* and *former boss unleashed.*

Meeting the Mom was a big deal. In an involved family like Mark's, it was probably even bigger.

"Ma!" he called. "Where are you? We're in aisle twelve already."

I tilted my head to the side. What did he just say?

Mark shoved the cart to the side of the aisle, then turned around, the phone still pressed to his ear, and waved an arm. A woman at the other end lifted her hand. He grinned and hung up, shoving the phone into his pocket.

"You told your Mom we were at the grocery store?" I whispered.

"Oh yeah," he said, as if this was totally normal. "She lives and works up here. She meets me at my errands all the time."

"Seriously?"

He shrugged. "Why not? Then we get to see each other."

Seconds later, a woman uncannily like Megan collided with him. He wrapped her in a big bear hug that would have made me jealous had it been for anyone else. She had dark hair in a short ponytail, and, from what I could see, kind eyes. When she pulled away, those eyes danced with amusement.

"You must be Stella," she said with a broad grin. "The girl that has made my son so happy."

Heat flared to my cheeks as she yanked me into a hug. Doggone it, but that sounded both hilarious and ominous at the same time. Mark rolled his eyes and mouthed, "Sorry. So dramatic."

As if he had *so* much room to talk.

But, to my astonishment, he didn't try to soften or take back what his mother had said. Then again, Mark wasn't the kind of guy to get embarrassed.

Sara pulled away and held me at arm's length. A maternal warmth emanated from her, and for just a moment, I wanted to curl up in her arms and ask her to play with my hair. She squeezed my arms, unapologetically excited to see me, and said, "Megan called me last night and gushed over you. Megan doesn't gush, so take it as the highest compliment. It's been a while since there's been any report of a woman in Mark's life to stay. I had to come over to meet you."

Like it wasn't a big deal that his family had been speaking about me, and in such warm terms. That his mom had stopped by the bread aisle, for heaven's sake, just to meet me in a quick whirlwind.

No wonder Mark had such power. When he had people like this surrounding him all the time, why wouldn't he be a force in the world?

As unconventional as it felt, standing next to the whole grain oats and wheat bran, I couldn't help but love Sara. She held onto me with one hand on my arm while she grilled Mark in the way that only a mother could. He accepted the torture of a caring mother the way any male adult would—with so much eye-rolling I thought he'd lose his irises in the back of his head.

But once she finished and embraced him again, he held her tight. Asked her about her latest date. Her newest haircut. Her raise. For a few minutes, they chatted back and forth while people whizzed past as if no one else were there. All the while, Sara didn't let go of my arm.

Within minutes, we laughed like old friends.

And then she was gone as quickly as she came, with warm hugs and cheek kisses for both of us. In her absence, I felt like I'd just endured a glitter whirlwind and all the sparkle had left again.

"She is . . ."

"Extra, right?" he drawled. "She's *so* extra."

"Amazing."

He winked. "I know. She's pretty great. You know what else is great? French toast, baby. Grab me some grains."

He balked as I grabbed a whole grain variation, then tossed his cheap white bread back on the shelf, but eventually acquiesced because I shoved the cart forward and ran my hand along his arm just to distract him. The trick worked. He shivered, completely distracted from food.

We pressed on, my heart on fire for so many reasons I didn't try to understand.

People cluttered the aisles, and the eggs and milk were almost gone by the time we arrived at the dairy section. While I still felt paranoia about who could be watching me, the confidence in Mark's tone rang out earlier.

I'll be with you the whole time.

And what if Joshua did come? What would it mean? Well, so many things. With so many people bustling around, the warm weather outside belying the incoming storm, and the feeling of Mark's hand on my back, it just didn't seem that scary. Somehow, I was able to let go of thoughts of Joshua. To smile at strangers. Although I scanned every face I could find, the same crippling fear didn't accompany it.

Once Mark steered us toward the front of the store and slid into a spot at the checkout, I made a few more silent plans to get rid of that junk food. A thirteen-year-old wouldn't even buy that much.

No wonder he worked out so religiously.

"Oh, toilet paper." I snapped my fingers, able to execute the act just as I'd planned. "We almost forgot that."

He held up a finger and turned to leave, then stopped and shot me a questioning glance. I smiled and nodded toward the back of the store, letting him know I'd be fine. He disappeared just as the cashier grabbed the first item I'd stacked on the belt, if a guy with shoulders like that *could* disappear.

Once he was out of sight, I turned to the cashier, a middle-aged woman with a quiet smile and fluffy hair. Then I passed her two one hundred dollar bills.

"Can you accept this now so that he doesn't try to pay?"

She lifted her eyebrows, then winked. "Of course."

"Thanks." I grinned. Winning felt good. The energy of the store felt good. Then I proceeded to cull at least half of the junk food he'd piled on and asked her to reshelve it. She laughed and tucked all the sugary boxes onto another counter. While she prattled on about a story with her neighbor and a particular brand of window cleaner that we were buying, I glanced around.

Even though I felt silly for doing it, I couldn't help myself. The busyness of the store made it impossible to track people around me, but seeing faces helped. Maybe at least gave a false sense of—

A quick move jolted my gaze back to where I'd just looked, near the back door. My heart leaped in my throat when, for a second, I could have sworn I saw Joshua in an orange parka. His neatly arrayed hair. Strong but lean shoulders. The perpetual smirk of one side of his lips. But the sense faded away.

Paranoia, again.

I turned half my mind back to the conversation with the cashier and tried to smile at the right time, but couldn't help the jarring feeling left behind in my body. Like someone had kicked me and I couldn't quite get my breath back. Maybe this hadn't been such a great idea. Maybe the close, ragged edges of the mountain felt safer. Maybe—

My breath whooshed out of me, as if literally kicked, when I looked back up and right into Joshua's eyes.

He stood on the other side of the store, near the exit, in an orange parka and a pair of jeans. He stared right at me without a waver in his expression or . . . much expression at all at first. Seeing him wouldn't have been so frightening if he didn't look so utterly . . .

Nothing.

Then his gaze hardened. His lips pressed together. My heart slammed against my ribs for several seconds before I could recover my wits. The woman continued to prattle while she typed in the code for bananas, and the world moved on, but my gaze didn't falter from Joshua's. Not for a second.

Suddenly, all the memories rushed back.

The awkward silences at work after he'd said something inappropriate. The way he'd watch me walk to my car. The feel of his eyes on me in a meeting. Emails upon emails upon emails. The hidden pictures of his current wife.

All the pressure of his intensity felt like a heavyweight on my shoulders.

Now, he stared back at me with rage, frustration, resentment, and the bitter dregs of something gone very, very sour.

At that moment, I knew I'd made a mistake.

I'd vastly underestimated his sense of entitlement and the way he showed up in the world. His desire to not only scratch back at anyone that harmed him, like a festering cat, but to destroy. I'd assumed that Mark's larger-than-life personality and foolish sense of confidence made him safe from someone like Joshua. Joshua who lived far more quietly, but not less dangerously.

Most of all, I'd underestimated everything that Joshua had

to lose. Had the company let him go? Did his wife find out and divorce him?

Or was his sense of being in love with me delusional enough to push him to this point?

It all came back to me at that moment, when the fury of a thousand suns seemed to channel from his gaze into mine. We'd always played a game. Cat-and-mouse. From the first day, I rejected his advance to this very moment.

And I'd just been ignoring it.

Joshua wasn't here because he was an angry, thwarted lover. No, Joshua was here because he was *livid*, probably on the verge of being destitute, and desperate. I was the one that got away.

When no one had ever got away.

My throat ached as I stared at him, hardly daring to breathe until a light touch on my arm pulled me from the trance. I blinked, looked at the cashier who must have asked me a question several times because she stared at me like I'd lost my mind, and realized that several people stared at me that way.

"You okay?" she asked

Her voice swam through several layers of thought before I managed to nod. "Sorry," I mumbled. "Yes."

"It's $205, dear. You got any more?"

Numbly, I passed over another $100 bill. My gaze darted back to the exit, but as expected, Joshua had left. No amount of searching helped, because he was gone. He'd made his point. He'd delivered his jab. He'd effectively cut off any hope and exhilaration and normalcy I'd started to feel again with Mark.

Just then, Mark nudged his way back through the line and at my side, a container of toilet paper in hand. The cashier dutifully rang it up and passed me my change. I barely registered Mark's annoyed exclamation once he'd realized I had paid. Then, like it happened years later, I felt his touch on my elbow.

"Stella?"

Concern colored his tone.

"Outside," I rasped.

Even I wasn't sure whether I was telling him I'd explain myself outside, or whether I wanted him to know that there was something outside. To his credit, Mark simply glanced around, got the change, thanked them for their help, put an arm around me, grabbed the cart, and led me away. I stiffened as we passed through the doors where Joshua had stood, but he wasn't there.

Just as he wasn't in the parking lot.

Or near the car.

Or anywhere.

But now I could feel him. The power of that ugly gaze. The wrath behind the fire. The utter desperation of a man that may have nothing left to live for *but* to win. No, Joshua was coming.

And there was no way to stop him.

Chapter Twenty-Four

MARK

By the time we made it back to the car, Stella trembled.

I slung the grocery bags in the seat, shoved the cart with a bunch of others, and climbed inside. Her fingers shook against mine when I grabbed her hand and steered us away from the parking lot. What I wanted to do was pin her against the truck, wrap her in my arms, and help her speak. But I had little doubt as to what happened, and if Joshua was even *maybe* near, she'd want out of here.

So I settled for holding her hand as we disappeared down the canyon, toward Adventura. A warm fall sun beat down, as if scoffing at the idea of snow that was supposed to descend.

By the time we returned, her uneasy breathing had calmed. She tracked every car that passed us, but especially the ones that followed behind. No one seemed to tail us through the canyon, and just to be sure I pulled off once or twice. No one followed and she didn't ask what I was doing.

Silently, we unloaded the groceries into the kitchen fridge, then the creamer and snacks at the cabin. Not for the first time, I thought about the almost-desperate need to remodel the cabin.

It was all just a distraction, though, from what really simmered beneath the surface.

Joshua. Joshua. Joshua.

Finally, Stella paused, her hand halfway to the table, when she realized there was nothing more to put away. Then she turned to face me and her eyes were drawn. The rage I battled ebbed slightly in the face of her fear.

"Stell?"

Without a word, she stepped into me and buried her face in my chest. Relieved, I wrapped my arms around her and waited. Minutes passed while she breathed into my shirt. It wasn't until I felt something damp that I realized she was crying. To comfort myself, I ran my fingers through her hair.

"I saw him," she whispered.

"I figured."

While she explained what had happened, goosebumps formed on her skin. I kept her anchored against me as I listened, but my mind spun with ideas in the background. Could I call the owner of the store to look at the security tapes? Call Dad, for sure. Confront this guy myself? Go to all the hotels in Jackson City and see who is booked there? No, that would never work. Hadn't in Pineville, anyway. Plus, there were too many places a guy like him could disappear here. For all I knew, he'd pitched a tent in the forest.

I didn't realize how far into my thoughts I'd spiraled until a little sniffle drew me out. Sheepishly, I realized Stella had pulled away and been staring at me. Her fingertips touched my face.

"Where are you?"

"In my head, beating the sh—"

"Mark, it's—"

I pushed her hand away. "I'm sorry, Stella. I'm not mad at you. It's . . . him. I need to call my dad." I shoved a hand through my hair and began to pace. "He can let his buddies in Jackson City know that Joshua is confirmed here. He's already passed on the pictures and information we sent earlier this morning, so he can send them to Jackson city."

"But Joshua still didn't do anything *wrong*."

"He looked at you."

She laughed, but it was forced. "Yes, he looked at me. How dare he? He walked into a grocery store and he looked at me."

"With the intent to frighten you! It's a threat, Stell."

Her hand grabbed mine, stopping me. My whole body had become tense, and under her touch, I only calmed slightly.

"I need to lift," I muttered. "And throw something very heavy many, many times."

A half-smile found her. She nodded.

"You should."

"Or we could go on a run together."

She nodded. "We could."

Her calm softened me. Why was I the one freaking out? She should be able to do that. I should be the calm, steady one in the face of danger. But isn't that how we saved each other all the time?

"I'm sorry." I closed my eyes and pressed our foreheads together. The steady warmth of her breath on my cheek reassured me. "I'm sorry."

"Don't be."

When she curled into me, I pulled her close. We stood there for several moments before she tilted her head back to look at me. I tucked a piece of hair behind her ear.

"I have to confess something," she whispered.

"What?"

"I paid the Adventura bills."

I frowned. "The mortgage is an automatic withdrawal."

"Right, but you needed more, so I mailed in the credit card payment and the rest of the mortgage. Justin took it into town with him the other day."

Several questions bubbled to the surface all at once, but

before I could ask any of them, she said, "I paid the credit card a little bit early, and did the minimum balance with a little bit extra."

"But—"

She pressed the tips of her fingers to my mouth. "I did it a few days ago and didn't want you to know. I know you never check and would be upset so I didn't want to tell you until it was already done."

If I hadn't been so heated already, maybe I wouldn't have felt the bubbling frustration under my skin. The humiliation. The annoyance. The—

"You save me," she whispered, "I save you."

All the tension died down. A rare tear seemed to have formed in her eyes and they sparkled there now.

"We save each other," I finally whispered.

She smiled, and it was mixed with relief. I pinned her to the wall and kissed her breathless. Stella had bought us—literally— another four weeks to figure something out. With any luck, I wouldn't need four weeks, but the fact that she wanted to save me as much as I wanted to save her rang something deep in my chest.

For the next day or two, we could enjoy the sunshine together before the storm. I wouldn't let her out of my sight. Joshua would leave us alone, and we'd be happy here in the fall mountains, when life was still vibrant before it faded into cold and quiet. Benjamin could come check the place out, she'd realize we had saved Adventura with his willingness to set up a training camp here, and we'd celebrate with another 007 movie.

Somehow, I had to believe that everything would be okay.

Chapter Twenty-Five

STELLA

While Mark and Benjamin stood in the dining hall the next day, arms waving as they mapped out something with *mats* and *bumper plates*, Atticus and I slipped away from the kitchen.

Benjamin had arrived alone in a black SUV with shiny rims and thumping bass. Despite arms like mountains and an intense expression, he had a warm smile. Mark had an interesting way of playing off of other people's energy in different situations. Instead of his usual vivacious self, he'd been more subdued and even-keeled with Benjamin as they spoke. With the muscles I could see moving beneath Benjamin's jacket, I had no doubt he'd destroy whatever opponent waited for him in three months.

The fresh fall air had turned chilly and gray, with a loamy blanket of clouds racing from the far horizon, when I headed toward the woodpile. Pre-emptive snowflakes fluttered down in anticipation of the big storm that was supposed to start soon. A warm lunch sat in my stomach, and my phone lay heavy in my pocket. My mind skipped around a few movies I wanted to snuggle up and watch, but there were chores first, and I sort of loved that.

Atticus lolled around on the ground while I restocked the cabin, swept up the dried pieces of bark scattered around the hearth, and puttered around Adventura. I stayed within earshot of Mark while I cleaned out the cabin where Megan had stayed. Mark looked back for me often, but kept the rest of his focus on Benjamin.

Once all the main chores had been settled, books updated, and dinner set in a crockpot in the kitchen, I grabbed a coat, my phone, and headed for the lake. Atticus trotted happily next to me, content to stay at my side while Justin ran Megan to her Mom's house in Jackson City.

After this, I'd never live without a dog.

Or Mark, if I could help it.

Mark caught my eye as I hit the footpath. I showed him my phone, pointed to the lake, mouthed *grandma* before he looked for Atticus, and gave a quick nod. With a storm like this, we may need to hole up for days. I'd rather enjoy the open space before the snow collected *too* heavily.

Minutes later, I sat at the edge of the pier, legs crossed, and stared at a grumpy sky. An unusual *thud, thud, thud* rocked beneath me. When I peered through the slats and into the water, I could just make out an old canoe stuck under the pier.

Mark really needed to audit his equipment better.

I made a mental note to ask him about it later, then dialed grandma, eager to hear her voice. She was like hot chocolate on a cold day. Atticus foraged through the trees at the edge of the lake, looked up every now and then, then turned back to his nose work. Seconds later, the ringing stopped.

"Stella Marie?"

I grinned. "Hey, grandma. Happy birthday!"

"Well, it's about time you called. And let's not talk about birthdays." Her voice dropped. "It's rather gauche."

A laugh bubbled out of me. "I'm sorry, it definitely has been too long since I called. But yes, we're going to talk about your birthday. Your life should be celebrated, especially when you're in your 80's!"

"You could call me every day, Stella Marie, and it wouldn't be enough. Not until I can hug you again. My birthday is fine. My stocks are up. Ranger brought me a new pen. The staff sang to me at breakfast, and rumors of an ice cream cake are circulating around those of us that aren't diabetic. Enough about birthdays. How are you? Tell me everything."

Her creaky voice soothed the rattled soul inside me. She always underplayed her birthday, then overplayed mine. It was our favorite game.

"The mountain getaway continues to be wonderful," I said, "and it's so lovely up here. I wish you could see it. I'll snap some pictures. There's a storm blowing in and it's just starting to snow."

"Sounds magical. Is it that boyfriend of yours?"

Shock rendered me momentarily surprised. Had I mentioned Mark to her? Yes, but not with that word.

"Boyfriend?" I asked.

"The one that brought me the flowers a while ago. Oh, what's his name?" She tutted under her breath while my heart turned to ice. "Something with a J. He called to tell me happy birthday this morning. Wasn't that kind of him? Joe, was it?"

"Flowers?" I repeated needlessly.

"Jonathon?" she mused. "No, that's not quite it . . ."

"Joshua?"

"That's the one! Nice guy. Bit . . . unusual though. He said you met at work. Why haven't you mentioned him? Seemed pretty odd that he was all the way down in Florida, but I do appreciate the thought."

My spine straightened with a snap. Joshua had visited my grandma. When? How? What . . . The questions filled my mind like a snowglobe. I had to force them to settle by taking a deep breath.

Was he trying to frighten me? Threaten me? What was his game? Why fly all the way to Florida from Cincinnati to talk to my grandma?

Unless *that* was how he found me.

My latest number with Mark hadn't received any calls or texts from Joshua or an unknown number, but that didn't mean he didn't have it. Could he track just a phone number? Locate me that way? Probably somehow . . .

"Grandma, Joshua is . . . he's not my boyfriend. He's . . . a delusional man that I used to work with."

"What?"

The confusion in her voice cut at me. This is exactly what I wanted to spare her from. Following me was one thing, but my grandma? I licked my lips and fought for control.

"What did he say to you while he was there?" I asked instead.

Flustered now, she fumbled around. "Oh, we talked about you and your job and how much you love numbers and how you were taking a little sabbatical to be in the mountains for a bit. He helped me program your new number into my phone."

My eyes closed. The sneaky, nasty devil. He must have been there days ago, got my number, and somehow tracked me here. He clearly had access to my clients' information. Had he known I was at Mark's? Made a wild guess, then confirmed it?

"I see," I murmured.

"Stella Marie, is something wrong? Is he not your boyfriend?"

"No, grandma. Joshua is a sick man that's following me. I left my job to get away from him, in fact. It's why I'm in the mountains."

"Oh, dear." Horror filled her tone. "And he was here. I talked about you. Was that wrong? I didn't know, I—"

"Grandma, you did nothing wrong."

"Are you safe, Stella Marie? Have you called the cops or—"

"Yes. Very safe. Mark, my real boyfriend, is here with me all the time. Where I am is safe and you don't have to worry about that. Has Joshua called or come back since his first visit?"

Dismissing the fact that I easily called Mark my boyfriend—and felt about ten years old for it—was easy. Mark was a natural part of my life now. Horrifying circumstances aside, I couldn't wait for him to meet grandma.

"No. I'm sorry I forgot to mention it to you," Grandma said. "He came a week or so ago. Maybe more? It just . . . it slipped my mind. You know how things are slippery these days and—"

"You did great," I said firmly. "Thank you for telling me now."

"I'm worried about you, my girl."

"No need!" I forced a bright tone. "I'm quite happy and safe, grandma. But thank you. How is the Bunco club?"

We moved onto safer topics while Atticus roamed the reeds along the lake edge at my back, caught a scent, and nosed his way into the trees. Grandma didn't recover her usual vivacity. I could feel the burden in her responses.

Silently, I cursed Joshua over and over again in my head. How dare he?

How *dare* he?

For the first time, I wanted to get my hands on his neck and have my own revenge. He'd intentionally frightened me both at work and here. He'd *stalked* me. Made my work life miserable, my home life frightening, and tried to get me to commit fraud. Now he wanted to clutch at whatever happiness I'd created without him.

My fingers were tight on the phone. My heart raced in my chest. We spoke for longer than usual as I tried to change topics and get the relief back in grandma's voice. By the end of our conversation, she sounded more reassured, but wary.

"You're really okay?" she asked.

"Really okay," I murmured. Heat warmed my cheeks. "I love

Mark, grandma. Really love him, like Mom and Dad loved each other."

The truth thickened my throat, but not with fear this time. Mark had brought life back to my world. Light. Intensity. He splashed a palette of colors into a gray storybook. This was real life.

This was love.

The sound of a little yelp from Atticus drew me back to the present. I glanced behind me to see a quiet, tree-lined bank but nothing more. He often nosed himself into a bone he couldn't reach or something sharp.

"Well, I better get going," I said as I tried to find Atty's dark coat amongst the shadows of the trees. The sound of Mark talking to Benjamin in the distance gave me a modicum of comfort, even though the quiet had become *oddly* quiet. Still, I couldn't wait for the day when all of this wasn't necessary. When I could just live and breathe and run without fear.

"Okay, Stella Marie." Grandma sighed. "Well, send me a picture of this hunky Mark, please? And I'll let you know if I hear anything else from this Jonathon character."

"Yes, of course."

"Love you."

"Love you too, grandma."

Once the call ended, I pushed the phone back into my pocket. The cold seemed to drive into my bones as snow thickened in the air, falling in fat flakes that obscured the other side of the lake. A warm fire would feel most welcome right now. I couldn't wait to get back inside.

But first, I had to find Atticus again.

"She was a lovely woman, you know," drawled a quiet voice just behind me.

My spine froze into icicles as I slowly spun around. Joshua stood a few feet away, hands in his pockets. A little wind stirred the golden hair on top of his head.

The past few weeks hadn't been kind to him. Stress had ravaged his face into gaunt lines and sallow skin. With no news from the company and no friends I could really poach updates from, I had no visibility into what had happened to him. Did the CEO find out about the federal investigation and fire him?

Had Joshua realized what I'd done and run away before things got ugly?

His brow furrowed into the same dark intensity that captured my attention at the grocery store. For some undeniable reason, I had the feeling that he expected me to pay for his sins, and I couldn't fathom why.

"You've been a most inconvenient woman for some time now," he murmured. "I think it's time to stop playing chase."

Too startled to respond, I could only stare as he closed the distance between us with a single step. He leaned forward, eyes alight with something sinister when he whispered. "So good to see you again, my love."

Just as I gathered a scream, he grabbed my throat and shoved me down. My legs gave way under his bent knees as he pushed me into the lake. Cold water washed over my skin and through my hair. My chest bucked. My scalp prickled with the pain of such cold water sloshing all the way over my head. The freezing lake encompassed me with a belly-jerking shock.

I surfaced with a desperate gasp.

Then all went black.

MARK

A tingle had started in my neck.

While I toured Benjamin around the rental cabin, we discussed his use of it as an office to watch videos of his opponent. There were other cabins littered throughout the area that could easily house him, but they'd need repair. The cobwebs didn't seem to bother him on first inspection, even though we'd get rid of those easily. Still, it highlighted the fact that we had improvements to do.

These were details I should have paid attention to before I toured him around.

My mind silently tallied the costs of updating the place. Justin would do the work in exchange for free rent, and the honor of dating my sister, but the supplies would cost. I shoved that aside. Investments, all of this. I'd figure it out if Benjamin did a down payment.

Snow collected rapidly in the air now when we started back to the kitchen, like sheets of fake snow in a globe. My breath frosted in front of me, collecting on a cloud before I walked through it. With a little shiver, I thought of snuggling Stella in front of the fire tonight. Suddenly, cold winter nights sounded like a dream.

"It has potential," Benjamin said as he twisted around to look at the main camp area. "But I'm not really looking for a Rocky thing, you know? The benefits of altitude could be gained in Pineville just as easily, and without the drive or isolation."

"The isolation is a problem?" I asked.

He frowned. "Only for one reason," he muttered, but it didn't seem to be aimed at me, so I let it slide.

Something stopped me on the stoop of the kitchen. Mountain air was almost always calm during a snowstorm, but this felt markedly different. Deep in my gut, an unsettled feeling shook me up. I stopped to listen.

Benjamin paused behind me, one eyebrow cocked.

"You hear anything?" I asked.

He shook his head, hands stuffed into the front pockets of his jeans, but I felt his attention rise. No Atticus snuffling around. No sounds near the lake where Stella had gone. Trees obscured my view of the water, but I should be able to hear something. Besides, it was cold and getting colder. She wouldn't stay at the lake long.

"Just a sec," I murmured, and took off toward the lake at a jog.

"Need any help?" he called.

"Stay there for just a second."

The empty pier came into view less than a minute later and my stomach twisted with it. "Atticus? Stell?"

A quiet, wintry world replied. The lake was a clouded sheet of glass that reflected the low, tumultuous ceiling overhead. Snow collected in a ring at the edge of the lake. No tracks returned down the path to indicate she'd gone back to the cabin.

Something wasn't right.

"Hey, Ben!" I called.

"Yeah?"

"Check for Stella at the cabin?"

"Sure."

While he took off, I stepped over to the bank. The rapidly gathering snow revealed two slight indentations of shoes, definitely too large to be Stella's, but with no clear destination. They stood there, facing the lake. Amidst them were several dog prints, tracks that meandered back and forth. Some slightly smudged, muddy dog paw prints decorated the planks on the pier, as if Atticus had been dorking around as usual. He certainly hadn't been barking at all.

I straightened.

"Atticus?"

A growl, then a bark, came from the ring of forest around the edge of the lake. With a muttered curse, I slipped into the trees, calling his name. Less than a minute later, I found him tied to a tree. He stumbled over a rope, his bark plaintive. The snow around him had been trampled in a circle. On the ground was a massive bone, like a cow joint. He alternately sniffed at it and tried to chew on the rope. A foul smell came from the greasy bone as I approached. Poison?

Whatever it was, Atticus didn't seem to have tried it.

"Bastard," I hissed and kicked the bone out of Atticus's reach. We'd have to come get it later and destroy it, just in case.

If there had been any doubt whether Joshua had shown up, it was just erased. He'd probably lured Atticus with poisoned food and tied him up with the hopes he'd take it. Atticus whined as I untied him from the tree, but kept him on the rope. He wasn't trained for search-and-rescue, and would probably just mar any footprints I could track. Still, he had his uses. Together, we headed back to the bank.

By then, Benjamin jogged up. He shook his head.

"Not there."

I yanked my phone out of my pocket and dialed Justin as I crouched next to Atticus. The strange smell emanating from the bone wasn't on Atticus's breath. He appeared normal as he pushed against me with a low whine.

Justin answered with a quick, "Hey Mark."

"Joshua's here, and he's got Stell. I think he tried to poison Atticus, but I don't think Atticus took it. Get my dad and whatever officers you can and get up here now."

"Where's Stella?"

My voice sounded grim when I muttered, "I don't know." My gaze darted to Ben. "We're going to go find her now."

Benjamin immediately nodded.

"On our way," Justin said.

Justin hung up and I straightened. Something didn't look right here. It wasn't until a splash of out-of-place color caught my eye that I realized it.

"Son of a—"

Benjamin pointed across the lake, his eyes landing on the exact same thing as mine. "That canoe supposed to be there?"

"Definitely not," I muttered. "You going to help me take this bastard down?"

Benjamin spread his arms. "Say when."

Benjamin, Atticus, and I jogged along the perimeter of the lake. Snow fell in sheets now, occluding the view of the other side. Skirting some marshy areas, an arena where we did campfires in the summer, and thick bracken along the banks slowed us down. By the time I reached the canoe, at least twenty minutes had passed. Sweat ran down my back, staving off the cold.

The haunting silence of the mountains taunted me.

You're too late.

Joshua maybe had a twenty-minute head start at most.

Benjamin and I could easily close that gap. He'd kept up with me so far. MMA fighter or not, living up here conditioned me far better for speed than he would be right now, but at least he wasn't a liability.

Carefully, I worked my way to the canoe through the reeds. Benjamin followed, not surprisingly agile amongst the slippery snow and bracken. The snow fell fast enough that any tracks were faint, but it was clear that two people had clambered out of the canoe. What appeared to be water droplets dotted some parts of the snow. Was Stella *wet*? Surely Joshua wouldn't be stupid enough to get in the lake.

Or would he?

No, that didn't make sense, but my dread tripled anyway.

"What's up?" Ben asked, puffing.

"I think he pushed her in the lake," I murmured.

"What?"

I pointed to the water droplets. "This is water. See how the snow is gone? The holes in the snow, but not by the lake edge? Doesn't make sense. The paddle is in the canoe, so it's not splashing."

"But why?"

"Silence her, probably. You didn't hear anything, did you?"

"Nope."

"He got her out right under my nose somehow. She'd be too shocked from the cold to scream if he pushed her in, and it could happen quietly."

Benjamin's expression darkened. If Joshua was dragging her into the forest after a plunge in the lake, she'd drop temperature fast. But if they moved quick enough to get away, it would hold off anything but mild hypothermia. Still, Stella wouldn't be comfortable. If she stayed out in this all night or they stopped too long?

This would get ugly.

I cleared those thoughts, blood soaring past my ears as I

strained to hear any sort of struggle. Atticus waited with an impatient whine. I kept him on the rope at my side so he'd stay quiet and ready for when I needed him.

"C'mon," I murmured quietly to Benjamin. "I see where their tracks are going."

With Stella's life on the line, my thoughts slowed into an oddly even pace. Steady instead of wild. I thought clearly because at least Joshua had given me the advantage of home turf.

While I followed what I could see of a trail into the woods, my thoughts ran to the forest behind the lake. Eventually, if Joshua cut to the northwest sharply enough, they'd run into the main road within a mile. But there was thick forest to work through, and gullies that wouldn't be easy in this snow. Visibility was obscured already, and if Stella was cold, she'd stumble. They wouldn't move as quickly as we could.

The likeliest scenario was that Joshua would get lost and they'd stumble around the woods until they both froze to death in the middle of the night. Unless he knew enough to head straight west or north. They'd eventually encounter the road or the river and the highway.

The urge to call out to Stella, let her know we were coming, came every five seconds. Instead, I kept quiet, prowling along their primitive trail. Enough snow had collected that they left clear tracks. Stella was still struggling.

"Struggle on, girl," I murmured as we dove deeper into the forest.

Chapter Twenty-Seven

STELLA

My teeth chattered so hard against my gag I thought they would crack. There wasn't a lot I knew about hypothermia, but at least I knew *that* was a good sign. Despite being so cold I thought my bones would break in two, my mind was clear.

Joshua's grip on my upper arm was so tight it ached. The bandana he'd tied around my mouth was soaked now. The driving snow froze parts of it, so when my teeth crashed into it, it cracked with ice. My head throbbed. He'd walloped me across the face and stunned me into silence while he'd hauled me onto the pier, then into that wretched canoe beneath the dock. Should have sunk it while I sat there, talking to Grandma.

Had he just been lying in wait for the perfect opportunity to appear? Or was it sheer luck that that canoe was there? There was no way to tell.

Now, prickling pins moved all the way through my body. The wet water had already dried my hair into heavy chunks that were painful against my scalp. They felt like medusa snakes, crunchy and cold. Joshua dragged me behind him, my hands tied in front of me. My fingers were exposed to the air. I could only feel their painful edges now.

Maybe thirty minutes had passed since he hauled me out of the water, tied me into silence, and shoved me into that hidden canoe. Wisely, he'd already locked my hands before I got in the boat, so attempting to tip us over would have been my death. But that didn't mean I went quietly, attempting to leave as obvious a trail as possible as we flailed around the forest.

I had to believe that Mark would eventually see that out-of-place canoe. Still, it didn't stop the questions that streamed through my mind.

Where was Atticus? What would happen next? Why didn't Joshua say a word? Was it part of his disappearing act to be totally quiet? If Mark was on our trail, then the less noise, the better.

Joshua hadn't said a word after he'd pushed me into the lake, and that seemed far more ominous. I'd expected a maniacal prattle. Him to say his plans and reveal everything he'd felt so far, the way it happened in all my favorite movies. But this was cold-blooded reality, and reality was unnervingly silent.

He paused, not for the first time, to gain some bearings. For as thorough as he'd been with snatching me, he seemed uncertain. He consulted no map or GPS. While I knew very little of the terrain here, likely not much more than him, even I felt totally lost. Eventually, if we kept moving north, we'd hit the river that the highway followed. That's all I knew. The forest could be disorienting on a clear, warm day. With so much snow and quiet, we might as well have been in a different world. Still, I thought I knew the vague direction of Adventura, and that was behind us.

If I could *just* get this shivering under control and his attention to lapse, I could try to break free. But it was far more likely I'd freeze first.

"J-j-josh," I struggled to say around the gag. "I'm f-f-freezing."

He grunted. Likely the only thing that would save me was to keep moving. My feet were totally numb except for a painful crash through my hips whenever I took a hasty step behind him. Perhaps the movement would be enough to stall the inevitable hypothermia. I'd only been submerged for a few seconds. Surely, it would take hours for a real effect to happen if we kept walking.

That would at least buy time for Mark to find me, assuming we stumbled around the forest that long. Joshua must have a car hidden somewhere. A plan. *Something.*

Without a word, Joshua angled us toward a dense canopy of trees on a ridge with rockfall. Navigating those rocks wouldn't be easy with this wet, dense snow. With my hands tied, I'd probably fall and bash my face.

Not that I'd be able to feel it.

With relentless determination, I pushed off the abject fear that lived like a wild thing in my stomach. No, this wouldn't be the end of Stella Marie. Grandma would *not* bury her last loved one. Mark would *not* save Adventura without me. This is what we did. We saved each other.

Mark would save me.

With that burning hope inside my almost-frozen body, I followed behind Joshua as we stumbled toward a towering outcropping of rocks. Before we made it halfway up the rock field, an unearthly scream broke the silence. My blood, already cold, turned to slush.

Joshua stopped. "What," he muttered, "was that?"

"M-m-mountain lion," I tried to say, but it was garbled through the gag. The eerie sound came again, this time directly ahead of us. It seemed to widen and echo across the air with painful wails. The grating noise made the hair on the back of my neck stand up. A movement drew my gaze up, and my heart crashed into my stomach.

On a ledge of the rocks above us appeared a long, lithe

animal. A sinewy tail became a large, catlike body that stood on a tree branch and peered straight at us. The upper lip twitched as the mountain lion sniffed our direction.

Fear pooled in my trembling stomach. Of all things I'd expected, this was not it. Not that ridiculous mountain lion. The insanity was almost too much to bear.

New questions and fears ran through my mind at top speed. Was I supposed to look bigger or smaller? Bigger, I thought. But how? The cat slipped to the edge of the branch and onto nearby rocks without taking its eyes off of us.

Joshua stumbled back a step.

"It's massive," he whispered.

Massive didn't do the beast any credit. While I didn't know much about mountain lions, this one appeared so thick I had little doubt it was mature. It licked its lips. Corded muscles moved on its front shoulders as it prowled down the rocks and toward us. The snow continued to fall between us. Was this the creature that had been prowling around Adventura?

Undoubtedly.

Not for the first time, I both wished for Atticus and feared for him also. How thorough had Joshua been in his attempt to steal me? Had he killed Atticus? The thought brought hot tears to my eyes. I didn't dare ask as I blinked them back. Hope was too precious to destroy.

Part of me wanted to throw myself closer to the cat—surely Joshua would leave me behind then—because I wasn't sure which was the greater danger anymore. I could bumble my way back to the lake on our trail and hope to get there with my frozen limbs.

But would the mountain lion let me go?

Also doubtful.

Joshua stumbled back another step when the mountain lion stepped onto a lower rock, whiskers twitching. Joshua grabbed onto the back of my coat, keeping me in front of him as we backed away. A rock slid out from beneath him and we both almost went down, but I righted us at the last minute.

"Easy there, lion," Joshua crooned while the cat growled. For every step back we took, the mountain lion took another one forward. Snow fell on top of my already frozen head as we skimmed through trees. A new sort of numbness moved through me.

This is good, I thought, foraging through my brain for any positivity that would keep my dimming hope alive. The mountain lion had certainly slowed us down. If we could hold still, Mark would find us all the sooner.

Although he may not have realized yet that I was gone. Without movement, the cold would set in with surprising force. In which case, there were three things trying to kill me tonight.

My whole body shook in another round of shivering as Joshua crouched down and picked up a fallen branch. The mountain lion stalked toward us, body low to the ground, paws deliberate with every step. It let out a low growl that turned into another scream.

Joshua waved the branch so wildly it almost crashed into my head.

"Get back!" he screamed. "Back!"

For just a moment, he'd let go of me. I took a step to the side but fell to my knees as the cat advanced with a hiss, its back curled. The unnerving, grating sound echoed through the forest. Joshua grabbed the branch with both hands.

"Get back!"

Yes, I thought as I tried to stand without the use of my arms. *Sing, kitty. Sing. Bring Mark to you.*

Joshua jerked me to my feet when I tried to stumble away again. "Don't do anything stupid!" he snarled.

The mountain lion shrieked and ran at us with an arched

back and puffy tail. I suppressed a scream and fell on my butt. Joshua skirted ahead of me to jab the branch at the mountain lion.

I reached up and ripped the gag off.

"MARK!"

Joshua jerked back to me and barked, "Shut up!" but the cat lunged closer. Forced to whirl back around, he swung the branch at the mountain lion with another cry. I shoved back my feet with all my awkward power and stumbled in the slippery snow.

"HELP! I'm over here!"

Joshua feinted after me, but the cat advanced on him. Joshua stopped with a livid growl, eyes on fire with frustration.

My voice cracked as I shoved through snowy trees, screaming Mark's name. Snow and ice landed on my neck with a painful sting as I barreled through the snow, tied arms held up to protect my face.

Joshua's indecipherable bellow rippled through the trees next. "Stella!"

The tips of my fingers had turned blue as I tried to wrench my hands free from the hastily tied rope and run at the same time. Buying my only chance, I tried to head back the way we'd come. My thoughts were too scattered and narrow to think of a path, I just went.

The distant sound of a bark came next. I stopped, my breath arrested with hope. "Atticus!" I screamed. "ATTICUS!"

The feeling of something hard slamming into me from behind followed. My cheek scraped snow seconds later and a warm gush of blood fell from my nose. Joshua grunted from where he lay on top of me.

"Don't. Move," he wrenched out.

The scream of the mountain lion still issued behind us, more startling and raw with every second that passed. Joshua stood back up, a foot pressed into my back that kept my breath from returning full force. I tasted metal in my mouth.

Darkness swam before my eyes.

Chapter Twenty-Eight

MARK

The sound of Stella's scream made my already heaving heart flop around in my chest.

"MARK!"

I skidded to a stop on the icy grass. Their trail had been clear, but they'd still had some advance on us. Even though daylight still remained, the world had grown dim and the snow fast. Now, she'd sounded close, but not close enough. Driven by pure instinct, I hauled down a rough ridge in her direction. Ben's heavy breathing followed not far behind me.

Without stopping to check on him, I pressed harder. Atticus bounded easily next to me when she screamed his name. I reached down, yanking the rope off his neck.

"Get her, boy."

Atticus bounded away, barreling through the trail. My chest burned and my legs throbbed, my ankles sore from sliding on the slick grass and ice. But I didn't really feel it, driven to desperation by the shrill scream. I prayed Atticus followed the sound of her cries.

What felt like an eternity later, a bark sounded not far ahead. I glanced up to see a low rolling hill just as Atticus disappeared over the ridge. Stinging snow slammed in my face like tiny little icicles as I gained the ridge, silently grateful for all those trail runs JJ and Megan dragged me on.

When I crested the top, I skidded to a stop. A snarling Atticus stood not far from Stella and Joshua at the bottom of the hill, near a rocky hillside that led to an outcropping of tall, oddly-shaped rocks. Joshua had one foot planted on Stella while she tried to crawl away.

Meanwhile, a mountain lion crouched in some nearby bushes, ears planted back.

Of course.

Atticus barked and pranced in weird circles, not far from the feline, but out of range of an immediate paw-swipe or lunge. His barks rang through the quiet night, punctuated only by hisses from the mountain lion.

I immediately stepped back behind a tree, and motioned for Ben to do the same as he closed the distance between us. Joshua hadn't seen us yet. My attention turned back to Stella. She lay on the ground with a pool of blood staining her face in the snow, but presumably alive.

And fighting.

She struggled now, but seemed to be out of breath. Rage bubbled back up under my skin. He'd clearly hit her with blood like that spouting all over the place.

"Atta girl," I muttered.

Benjamin came up next to me, shoulders heaving. "Is that a damn mountain lion?" he whispered incredulously.

"It is."

His gaze darted between Atticus, the mountain lion, and me, then he shook his head in disbelief. "This place is friggin' nuts," he muttered.

"We need to surprise Joshua," I whispered. "And we have to move fast. With Atty distracting the cat, Joshua's going to expect us, and he's going to move with her fast. You go around the back.

Drop back into that gully." I pointed to the bottom of the hill he'd just climbed, then pointed west. "Loop around and come up behind. I'll stall him where they are right now."

Ben nodded. "Got it."

With one last glance at the mountain lion, Benjamin skittered back down the hill, into a draw, and moved his way around the flank of the hill.

"Enjoy," I muttered.

With Atticus prancing and snarling, the mountain lion retreated slightly, belly to the ground as it hissed with its ears back. Stella tried to push off the ground. Her hair had clearly frozen into chunks. So she *had* been in the lake. The thought made my stomach seize.

Thankfully, Benjamin moved faster than I'd expected. A flash of movement caught my attention out of the corner of my eye, far enough behind them that Joshua hadn't seen it yet.

I advanced.

"Stella!"

Her gasp rippled through the forest in a silent moment between canine and cat. Joshua, who had been warily watching Atticus and the mountain lion, leaped to action now. He grabbed the back of Stella's neck and yanked her against his chest. She moved with a cry of pain and my entire body twitched. I clenched my fists and forced myself to calm. My moment with this loser would be glorious.

The gleaming hilt of a knife appeared at her neck. Stella cried out, her chin already bathed in blood. Her entire body trembled. A gag hung around her neck, frozen and inert.

Oh, yeah. This bastard was going down.

"Get back!" Joshua screamed.

Both of my hands lifted in the air, but I took a shaky step forward, as if a rock had given way. There were thirty feet between us. I could cross that in less than ten seconds. He'd need less than half of that to slit her throat. The math wasn't reassuring.

"Joshua, let's talk," I called.

"Don't say my name and don't act like this is going to end well for anyone if you so much as step in her direction," he snarled. "If my guess is right, we're fifty yards from the road. So you are going to stay right there while I drag her away from here. Then we are going to get into my car and we're going to leave. Do you understand?"

My arms lowered.

"I have a better idea."

Stella's lips had turned dusky. They trembled so much I didn't think she'd be able to talk, even if she wanted to. Still, her eyes were clear. Afraid, but lucid. A good sign.

Joshua laughed. "This isn't a negotiation."

"You leave Stella and I leave you. It's a get-out-of-jail-free card, Joshua, and I think you should take it."

"She is the prize!"

"I think freedom is a better prize," I shouted over a burst of icy wind, "don't you? The moment you hit that highway, there are going to be deputies checking every single car that passes. We've already put the plan into motion. If you leave with her, you don't have a chance. If you're clearly alone in your car? Well, that's a much easier escape plan, isn't it? Because I'm willing to bet that you know there's no other road out of my canyon."

His nostrils flared. It was a lie, of course. To my knowledge, there was no roadblock planned, although that was a great idea that had come too late. But that didn't matter. Because now he was cold, stuck, and outnumbered. Desperation made for a terrible negotiation.

Vaguely, I attempted to track where the mountain lion had gone, but assumed it wasn't far. Atticus prowled around still, hackles raised. Hopefully, the cat hadn't moved its attention to Benjamin.

"You think I'm going to believe that?" Joshua asked with a wild half-laugh. "Even if it's true, who said I was taking the highway? Maybe I have a camp here."

"Then you might have a purring visitor in the night. Mountain kitties love to stalk their prey, you know, and now it has your scent."

His nose twitched. Without taking my gaze off of him, I attempted to watch for Benjamin. Didn't matter that I lied about the mountain lion either, although it could be true. Uncertainty would follow Joshua, and that bought me time.

"Listen, Joshua, I get it. You want Stella, but this isn't the way to do it. She's going to die if you leave her out here. If you do have a camp, you'll need a fire in this weather, right? Everything is soaking wet so that will be almost impossible. Not to mention the fire will draw the police. The deputies will have dogs out looking for you that can track you. If you don't take my offer now, this plan is doomed."

Stella's nostrils flared. She winced as Joshua shifted, wild eyes darting to where the mountain lion had been crouching under the bush. Atticus prowled around, hackles up, alternately sniffing at bushes and then barking.

"No." Joshua said it firmly. "This is not how it happens. I take Stella. You deal with the mountain lion. That's how this ends."

"That's up to you." I half shrugged. "But the longer you wait, the less chance you have of getting out of here alive, whether it's from freezing to death or that cat or the police already on their way. Joshua, give her to me and get out."

My heart thundered when movement closed in behind them. I guessed that Benjamin would be twenty yards away and hopefully silent, but he wouldn't know about the knife. Joshua hadn't given any indication that he heard something.

I straightened, then acted like I stumbled. The dirt and snow at my feet gave way, sliding me farther down the hill, but closer to them. Stella let out a muffled cry. Joshua jerked up, the knife pressed firmly against her neck again. She grabbed his arm, clawing at it, but he only tightened his hold.

"You have one knife, Joshua," I shouted furiously, "and if you plan to cut her throat, you better move fast, because I will be on you in less than five seconds. There will not be time for you to survive what I have planned for you."

Joshua snorted, but another flicker of doubt had registered in his gaze as he studied me. That moment of hesitation brought the knife away from her throat just slightly. My heart nearly stopped when Stella's gaze caught mine.

Then she dropped.

Chapter Twenty-Nine

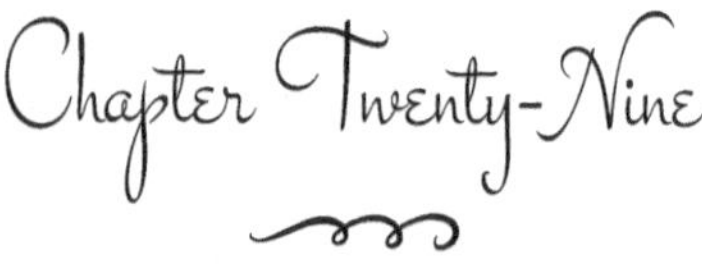

STELLA

Mark looked like a livid vision through the gently rotating snow.

Flakes fell so thick and gauzy I almost couldn't see him. But he stood there, an avenging god, carefully controlled rage in his eyes. He didn't even have a coat, just one of those zippered hoodies, over his shoulders that seemed miles wide compared to Joshua. Joshua's gaze darted between him and Atticus, who hadn't taken his attention from the mountain lion that appeared to retreat.

Who do you fear the most? I wanted to whisper to Joshua. *Because both will tear you apart if you let them.*

In the face of the knife that pricked at my neck, all thoughts of the cold had fled. The blood from my nose had nearly frozen to my face and crackled on the edges now.

All my focus rested on that knife. The pulse of my heart as it beat against the blade. My careful steady breaths. Every now and then, the cat would let out another low warning growl, and Atticus would bark all over again.

So the question remained: What would kill me first?

When Mark stumbled and shouted, Joshua's entire body

tightened. As if he'd finally measured himself against Mark and realized how lacking he was. The blade moved away from my throat the tiniest amount in that moment of hesitation. Through the pounding in my head and the waves of tremors that slipped through me, I understood it would be my only chance. Not on any planet could Mark get from there to me in enough time to save my life, and he knew it.

I knew it.

Now I wouldn't let Joshua have the satisfaction. It was time for *my* revenge.

With a grunt, I shoved Joshua's arm away from my throat and dropped to the ground. My sudden, unexpected weight shifted Joshua's balance, and he stumbled forward. The knife slipped, grazed my throat as I fell, then disappeared in the snow at our feet.

A second later, the sound of a *thud* connected on top of me, and Joshua's weight was gone.

Another body had come from somewhere, tackling Joshua to the ground in a flurry of snow and rolling bodies. Benjamin popped out of the haze of white, his legs wrapped around Joshua's waist and his arm across his throat. Joshua thrashed uselessly in the snow.

With a cry, I tried to scramble back to my feet, but stumbled on the rocks. Another pair of arms caught me. Mark appeared, his warm hands on my face.

"Stell. I've got you."

My knees toppled, but he caught me.

"Mark! I . . ."

"I'm here."

"He . . . I thought . . . a-a-and—"

Mark hauled me back to my feet, then grabbed the zipper of my coat. "Take this off, Stell. We'll discuss all of it when we get back home. For now, you've gotta warm up."

My hands trembled as I attempted to wrench the half-frozen coat off. He yanked it free, tossed it to the ground, and reached for my soaking wet shirt. When he ripped it off over my head, I let out a cry. Snow fell on my shoulders and soaking bra. Cold rushed over me all over again.

"W-w-what are you doing?"

"It'll take us at least thirty minutes to work our way back through the trees, maybe twenty by the road," he said, ripping his own jacket off. "You can't be wearing those clothes that whole time. You have to start warming up sooner, at least at your core."

Bare arms slipped out of his jacket. He only wore a short-sleeved shirt beneath his winter jacket, which he jerked around me, then zipped up while I pushed my arms through the sleeves. They were warm from his heat, thick with his reassuring scent.

"Wh-what about you?"

"I'm fine." He scoffed. "Hot as an oven."

Joshua's muffled shouts had faded. His eyelids slowly lowered until his body went limp. Just before he passed out, Benjamin released him, then held out a hand to Mark.

"Atty's rope?"

Mark tossed a rope his way. With surprisingly deft movements, Benjamin shoved a half-delirious Joshua onto his stomach, then tied Joshua's hands together. Still sluggish from almost passing out, Joshua didn't even protest. Just made weird, half-mewling sounds.

Mark put an arm around my shoulders and pulled me close, but turned to Benjamin. "You got him?"

"Hell yeah."

"It'll be faster on the road. Follow my tracks back and I'll send someone to pick you up. Sound good?"

Benjamin nodded, then sent a hard *smack* against Joshua's head. "Go. Get her taken care of. Joshua and I have some chatting to do about how we treat women around here."

"The cat is retreating, I think."

"I'll feed Joshua to him if I have to. We'll be fine."

"Atty, stay. Follow me, Stell," Mark commanded quietly. "We'll be back home in no time."

MARK

"I-I can r-run."

Stella stuttered the syllables as soon as we spilled out of the forest and onto the road. Two sets of tire tracks broke through the snow on the road, which gave me discernible relief. Justin had already made it back, and likely my dad with him. They must have been hauling through the canyon to get here so quickly.

"Are you sure?" I asked.

She nodded as her body wracked with another shiver. The blood on her face made her cold face paler than usual, and her hair had frozen in weird clumps along her head. Fatigue showed in all her movements.

I hesitated, then nodded. If she could do it, the sooner, the better.

"Let me know if it hurts too much? I'll happily carry you on my back, but this would be faster. Warmer for you, too."

I kept a hand on her back as she slowly shuffled forward with a grimace, then waved it off when I asked. We moved in a slow walk/jog, but it was faster than I'd expected. About fifteen minutes later, twirling red and blue lights greeted us as we stumbled back to Adventura. Two bodies moved near the front door, and a third lingered in the cop car.

"Justin!" I called. "Dad!"

Seconds later, Justin jogged across the parking lot, Dad striding out with his long steps right behind him. Justin slowed in front of us, eyeing my bare arms and her frozen clumps of hair with incredulous eyes.

Dad was only a few steps away. "What happened?" he asked.

"Benjamin is back on the road." I jerked my head back. "He has Joshua tied up. I told him I'd send you. Atticus is with him if the mountain lion hasn't gotten them."

"Mountain lion?" Justin cried.

"It's a long story."

Justin reached a hand out to Stella's shoulder, concern in his gaze. "Are you all right, Stell?"

She nodded, but it wasn't immediately clear from her violent shivering.

"What happened?" Dad asked again.

"I'll explain it all later. Dad, can you get Ben and Joshua? I don't want anything to happen to Ben or Atticus."

He already fished for his keys in his pocket. "I'm on it. A few more deputies are on their way, just like you asked, but the canyon is ugly. Might take a bit to get them here through the snow. Get her inside. I'll take care of this out here."

Stella followed as I led her through the parking lot, Justin on her other side. Heat blasted us in the face when we shoved into the house. Justin shut the door behind us.

"Meg!" he called.

She appeared from the side room. One look at Stella and concern lit up her eyes. Only a moment passed before she'd taken the situation in and stepped forward.

"Hey Stell."

"I'll get the shower going," Justin said.

"I'll help her get in," Megan said, then reached for her.

"Geez, girl. You're a literal bloody popsicle. C'mon. I happen to be a professional at this. This might really suck at first, by the way. Rewarming hurts, but the fact that you're shivering and talking is an excellent sign. I hope the other guy looks worse."

Within seconds, Stella was whisked away from me and into Megan's comforting, quiet prattle. It smoothed over the strange edges of this situation and made it not so frightening to release her. The door to the bathroom firmly shut. Justin reappeared, his expression still shocked as he stared at me.

"You all right?" he asked.

My hands shook when I collapsed into a chair, put my head in my hands, and said nothing. He put a hand on my shoulder and squeezed.

"Whatever happened out there, she's okay now. You did it, Mark."

For lack of any better response, I just nodded. The whole scene replayed itself in my mind with the feeling of seeing it from a different point of view. The knife at her throat. The rage in Joshua's voice. The fear in her eyes. For several minutes, I spiraled there until Justin clapped me on the shoulder.

"Get up," he said firmly. "Get upstairs, get a change of warm clothes. I'll get some coffee going and the fire built up. Do whatever you have to do to pull it together, all right? You can crash later, but not now."

His commanding tone shook me from the stupor. I ran a hand through my hair. The frozen strands had thawed, and it felt wet between my fingers. He was right. Stella needed me now.

"Yeah, thanks."

Justin extended a hand, which I took, then yanked me off the couch. He met my gaze. "You did it, Mark. You saved her."

Relief flooded me.

"We saved each other," I said quietly.

Justin grinned. "It's how the real ones work." He sobered. "Get changed so you can warm up, then get back down here for coffee, all right? It sucks after all you've gone through too, but you need to get yourself together for Stella. She looks like she just about died three times over, she'll need you. You'll have time with her once we can get this sorted out. It's going to be okay now, Mark. You'll both be okay."

Chapter Thirty-One

STELLA

Hours later, the final deputy nodded to Mark's dad.

"Thanks, Jim, always good to see you. Let's make it under better circumstances in the future, all right?"

With a laugh, Jim shut the door on him.

Atticus sat on the couch not far away, belly full of warmed canned chicken and rice. A special meal for the hero dog. A quick call to the vet had cleared Atty of immediate poisoning issues, but just to be sure, he had an appointment the next day. Justin kept a firm eye on his every move.

From the moment I stepped out of the bathroom, my hair blown dry at Megan's insistence, the house had been filled with Mark's family or deputies. Benjamin stayed long enough to give his version of the story, then left with a promise to be in touch soon.

"You're a wild man," he'd said to Mark as he left. "A manimal. Can't wait to set up here."

Now, Megan and Justin spoke quietly across the room where they snuggled near the ladder, his arms around her. The warm scent of cream of chicken soup filled the air. Crusty bread bowls littered the small table, some half-filled, thanks to the dinner JJ and Lizbeth had brought with them. Sara, Mark's mother, had puttered around the house cleaning everything while hovering over me with a loving, protective touch. Now, the three of them were in the kitchen, conspiring over a sugary dessert to keep the mood elevated before they dispersed.

Meanwhile, Mark had remained near me like a shadow while Jim orchestrated the entire crime scene investigation, retirement notwithstanding. Jim's explanations and suppositions thumped dully around my head, and I considered for the tenth time that all of this wasn't real.

Megan's help in a warm shower had been absolutely necessary and had sped the painful rewarming process up. But I still sat by the fire now, wrapped in a pair of yoga pants under my sweats, three pairs of Mark's warmest wool socks, and several layers of long-sleeved shirts. My shivering had stopped, but my nose still ached. Bruising had already started along the bottom of both eyes, making me look like a pale raccoon.

At some point during one discussion with a police officer, Mark had dropped one of his other zippered sweatshirts around my shoulders. His smell had anchored me, brought me out of the weird disbelief that punctuated every second, and I felt instantly warmer.

Despite the heat, any touch of cold air from the storm outside came with another round of shivers. Not all of them were from the cold.

Joshua had been loaded into the first cop car that had arrived and eventually taken away. Several people had spoken with me, and I'd answered all their questions while slowly sipping whatever warm drink Justin shoved at me next. The coffee restored my mental abilities with surprising speed. The general busyness in the cabin whisked away thoughts of Joshua. Of mountain lions. Of freezing in the depths of the forest.

Mark and I still hadn't spoken outside our desperate conversation on the road. There hadn't been a chance for me to say all the things that I wanted to say.

Jim stood with his hand on the doorknob now and faced me. I stood at the fire, a mug of tea in my hands. What looked like a glower was, I imagined, deep concern. That Mark's father would give me that look sent a warm bolt through me.

"You'll be okay, Stella Marie," he said quietly. "You're one tough cookie."

I managed a small smile. "Thanks for everything, Jim."

He winked. "My pleasure. I've missed this. The good stuff always happens after you retire," he finished in a mumble, then turned to his son. "Call."

"I will." Mark embraced him with a manly back slap. "Thanks, Dad."

Megan shuffled forward and grabbed her coat off a hook. Snow fell even harder now, accumulating on the porch in piles already inches deep. "We'll walk you out, Dad." She turned to Mark. "Then we'll go hang out in the kitchen and help with dessert for a bit. Give you some time. I'll usher Mom home after that, okay? She won't dote all night long."

He nodded. "Thanks, Meg."

Megan gave him a quick hug, Justin smacked him on the shoulder, and they both shuffled out. Mark quietly closed the door behind them. Then he sighed, leaned his head on it for a moment, and let out a long breath. The silence rang through the cabin, at odds with the bustling environment that had moved around for the last several hours. I opened my mouth but closed it again when he straightened and swung around to face me.

Fatigue lined his features. A thousand other things, too. Concern. Fear. Worry. After we'd returned, he'd changed into a pair of workout pants and a long-sleeved shirt that pulled tight across the shoulders. He'd watched me carefully, and stayed close. Like me, he'd seemed to carefully avoid any direct interaction, as if that would force us to acknowledge and face exactly what happened.

"Stell," he whispered huskily as he closed the space between us. With a trapped sob, I let him capture me in his arms and crush me against him. My legs wound around his waist as I tried to claw him closer. A little cry peeped out of me as he tightened his hold.

"I thought I'd lost you," he whispered.

"Me too."

For so many heartbeats I lost track, I kept my arms around him, my body pressed to his. He stood there, holding me in front of the fire, until I pulled back, framed his face in my hands, and whispered, "You saved me."

"No, Stella Marie. You've saved me."

Tears filled my eyes when I pressed a slow kiss to his lips. My fingers found their way to his hair again. His hand slid up my back as I tilted my head to deepen the kiss. He growled, whirled us around, and dropped us both to the couch. His warmth enveloped me from head to toe as he kissed me breathless, pulling a blanket over us as I stretched along with him.

I pulled away to catch my breath.

"Thank you, Mark."

"I love you." He pushed a strand of hair out of my face. "I love you more than anything I've ever known."

Tears filled my eyes again. "I love you too."

He broke slightly beneath me at the words, then swallowed hard. "Can I stay with you tonight? I just . . . I want you near. Forever, Stella. This is it for me. There is nothing but us now."

"Me too," I whispered, then burrowed into his neck and closed my eyes. He tucked me into his side and played with my hair. I tried to memorize the feel of him. The smell of him. The absolute comfort of his heartbeat slamming in my ear.

Because he saved me, and I saved him.

And always would.

Epilogue

"I don't think I've ever been this nervous before."

Mark stared at the building set beneath a bright blue sky. Sunlight pushed through the rental car windows with a curl of warmth that chased away the lingering spring storm we'd left behind in the mountains.

"Not ever?" I asked.

He shook his head. "Nope."

I reached over, grabbed his hand, and pulled his chin until he faced me. Then I smiled. "Grandma is going to love you, Mark. Don't stress about it."

He slammed a quick kiss into my lips, then disappeared. He was already out the door and stretching from the hour-long drive as I chuckled, climbed out, and shoved the keys into my back pocket. Green shrubs, trees, and the quiet shuffle of movement filled the air as I beeped the lock, then reached out for Mark. His hand slid effortlessly into mine, without a second thought, and I tugged him toward the main door.

"She's a pretty easy audience."

"Well, she did give Joshua your number."

I shot him a look of warning—he better *not* bring that up—

and he winked. Joshua wallowed in prison on several local and federal charges. He'd be locked up for a good, long while. Just the way he deserved.

"I'm excited to see her," I said with a delicious little shiver. He squeezed my fingers.

"Me too, Stella Marie. Me too."

He pulled the door open and put a hand on the small of my back as I slipped by, the hot Floridian air ushering us inside. Two steps into the main waiting area, and I came to a quick stop with a gasp.

A banner of balloons and an assortment of people in wheelchairs, walkers, or loafers, waited only a few feet away. Grandma sat in the midst of them, her pillow of gray hair and bright smile like a beacon.

"Welcome!" came several stuttered shouts, and Grandma smacked an old man with a baseball cap that said RANGER across the top.

"Bad timing!" she squawked. "We're supposed to say it together!"

Another poorly timed effort followed, and I giggled into my hands. Seeing Grandma, and her entire Bunco club, sent a frisson of electricity all the way through me. Mark's family had been so warm and accepting. Now, mine could be as well.

She stood up, arms bent and hands on her hips.

"Well?"

With a laugh, I stepped forward and embraced her. She held me tight, her soft skin and the quiet tremble in her voice just like home.

"I'm always glad to hug you," she said in a teary voice. "But that's not what I meant."

Startled, I pulled away. "What do you mean?"

"Well?" She motioned behind me. "What are you going to say?"

I glanced back, then gasped. Mark knelt on one knee a few

steps away. Something glittered in between his thumb and pointer finger. Shock rippled through me as I slowly turned. He smiled, and all nerves, all fear, were gone. Nothing but certainty filled him now.

"Stella Marie," he murmured. "Will you officially be mine?"

With trembling hands, I reached for him. He stood and trapped my hand. Cool metal slid onto my left ring finger. An ostentatious diamond sparkled there, set with smaller ones in a white-gold setting.

"Mark, I . . ."

Unable to finish the thought, I just gaped at him. He leaned forward to whisper, "At this point, it's a good idea to say yes or no."

Laughing, I grabbed his face.

"Yes, Mark. Forever."

He was smiling when our lips touched, and another ragged, unsynchronized, but heartfelt cry filled the air from the Bunco club. I wrapped my arms around Mark's neck with tears in my eyes and held him close.

Grandma called out, "That hunk is my grandson-in-law!"

A deep chuckle reverberated through his chest as he held me close. I'd found my home forever. Now I knew, without a doubt, that I'd never have to run away again.

The moment I walked into the MMA Center, I knew exactly what would happen: snap judgments, a flare of annoyance, and maybe even concern. But I walked in anyway, because desperate times call for desperate measures.

This fat lip wasn't going away fast enough.

On purpose, I stepped inside at 8:50 pm, ten minutes away from closing, so I didn't get roped into a conversation I didn't want. My old black backpack was slung halfway across my back and my maniacal brown curls tamed into something of a ponytail.

There weren't many people left here, which wasn't surprising. The MMA Center was a place for athletes across the country to train in mixed-martial arts, not an every day gym. But Benjamin Mercedy, the owner and founder, had been forced to pack it with weight machines and treadmills and ellipticals for the average mortal to use in order to pay the rent. The giant mats taking up most of the room, however, belied the casual jogger's attitude.

This was a serious place.

A girl across the room spritzed down gym equipment with a

bright spray, then wiped it with a white cloth. A heavy-set guy huffed away on a treadmill below a TV with the news streaming across it, ticker-tape style.

My gaze honed in on the girl. Medium height, just like me. Strong, but unassuming. She was way more wiry than me. I had thighs thick enough to be proud of, as Mama said, but I sensed an understanding soul in her. She'd get me. No judgment from a fellow woman. I turned toward her, but stopped when a deep, rolling voice to my left asked, "Can I help you?"

The hairs on the back of my neck stood up when I paused midstep. Fantastic. Just who I didn't want to encounter. Benjamin Mercedy himself. I responded without looking over. Maybe I could make it in and out of here without him seeing my swollen face.

"I just had a question about classes." I adjusted my backpack strap. "And what you offered."

"We have a full schedule on the website."

"I saw it."

Silence answered. I closed my eyes and sucked in a slow breath. Obviously, this was awkward. He had to see this. I couldn't talk to the mats on the other side of the room without looking like a total weirdo. Finally, I turned to face him.

As expected, Benjamin stood behind a counter, both of his hands on the desk. He peered at me through golden eyes framed with thick eyelashes enough to flutter away. Longer brown hair normally grew in waves around his face, but tonight he'd pulled the top half of it back. The rest wasn't long enough. His arms coiled in muscles all the way up his neck. They'd probably ripple down his back, too.

His adam's apple bobbed as our eyes collided. I stared right at him to avoid looking at the rest of him and I forced my voice to remain normal. "I . . . I just wanted to see if you offered self defense classes."

His gaze immediately dropped to the fat red line down the

middle of my lip. Maybe I could have passed it off as dry skin or some weird condition, except for the swollen state of the lip beneath it.

Two days later, it still stung.

When his eyebrows came together slightly, I realized I'd lost the game. I dropped all sense of pretense and leaned on the counter in an intentional mimicry of his posture.

"Look," I leaned waved a hand around my face. "I know what this probably looks like, particularly considering my need for a self-defense class. But I'm not an abused woman in a relationship with a crappy boyfriend. That's not what this is. That's not my jam."

A flicker of amusement traveled through those honey-gold eyes before he nodded.

"No, we don't offer self defense classes right now. We tried, but no one came."

"Well that's stupid," I muttered.

He lifted an eyebrow.

My tense body felt like I was preparing to meet a blow to the stomach. That wasn't the case this time. I was just preparing myself for his inevitable judgment. The quiet talk about what my resources were and how I deserved better. Um, no. Not again, please. I'd already been through this with my boss.

This wasn't that.

Except . . . it wasn't far off from that, either. I was potentially one more bad situation away from being a statistic, which was why I just needed someone to get me the basics.

"Do you need some help with whoever did this?" he asked, nodding toward my fat lip.

There was an underlying promise of vengeance in his words that sent a little chill through me. This guy didn't even know me, and I'd very intentionally not allowed myself to know him for the last eight weeks.

What could *he* possibly want retribution for?

"Nope," I replied cheerily. "Tip top over here." I leaned forward again, affecting a casual air. "Can you tell me if you have any plans for opening a self-defense class in the next week or two?"

His gaze narrowed. "What do you need?"

The blood of my enemies, I wanted to say. *What do you think I need if I'm asking for a self-defense class?*

I quelled the burst of inner sarcasm. My bad mood had nothing to do with Benjamin Mercedy. Actually, scratch that. It did. The quiet power in the way he held himself, his muscular frame, and the unassuming way he lived his life was all way too attractive for me to deal with in a constructive way.

Instead of answering right away, I chewed on my bottom lip and looked back to the equipment sprinkled through the gym. My gaze lingered on the lifting equipment, treadmills, and a few other things against the far wall, near the mirrors.

Actually, his question had been a fair one. There were different types of self defense. What *did* I need? Confidence. I needed confidence. Power. Quick reflexes. I needed to be a fighter, and all of that sometime before 3:00 pm tomorrow.

"Safety," popped out instead.

He lifted an eyebrow.

"Wait, stop. I take that back." I waved my hands in the air, thoroughly annoyed now. The smell of marinara and chicken carbonara wafted through the air as I tried to take that back. "Ignore my dramatics. I'm in a safe . . . well, mostly safe . . . situation. I just need to be able to defend myself against a surprise attacker for a few more weeks." My voice elevated a pitch too high. "Not a big deal!"

He stayed cool when he asked, "The one that hit you already?"

"Yes, if you must know," I ground out, then pointed to him. "And he is *not* my boyfriend or my fiancee or my husband so don't even go there. I'm not a victim. He's not . . . an attacker either. It was all an accident. I think," I tacked on, then regretted it when his lips tightened.

Except I *was* sort of a victim in the way that any woman would be against a much larger man she couldn't exactly escape.

The details were murky.

Benjamin frowned. "Look, our roster is full. There's literally no mat time available to host a self defense class."

A curse word slipped out under my breath, but before I could back away, he held up a hand.

"But maybe you and I could figure something out."

"What does *figure something out* mean?"

He tilted his head to the side. "I'll teach you a few things. Self defense isn't that hard to get started with. We'd need an hour, tops, to cover the basics."

"Really?"

He nodded. Despite having a larger-than-life presence with his body, he had a calm way about him. Coming in here had been one of the hardest things I'd ever done, and some days, that was saying something.

"Why?" I asked.

He shrugged. "Let's just say I'm a sucker for a damsel-in-distress."

Three seconds passed while I comprehended that comment. Then my blood boiled. For three more seconds, I saw the world in shades of red. Is this how Talmage felt? Is this why I had a big fat lip? Some genetic predisposition to instant rage when helpful people were just trying to help? Maybe I had too much pride.

Without realizing it, I had taken a step back sometime between the word *distress* and my indrawn breath of rage.

His eyes widened.

"Then find someone else to rescue," I snapped. "This damsel can save herself . . . with a few well-placed self-defense lessons from someone that isn't you," I added for good measure. "I have some pride, no matter what you've judged of me."

I spun and shoved out the front door.

Cool spring air washed down my face as I headed for the mountain bike I'd parked close to the back, out of sight. My bike had been stolen before, and thankfully recovered, but I couldn't afford another fall back. It was my only transportation.

My cheeks had exploded with heat in the ten seconds it took to tell him off. Humiliation had a way of coloring me bright crimson, and I hated it. Damsel-in-distress? *Seriously*? I wanted to throw his own arrogance back at him. I wasn't sitting at home, waiting for the next fist *and* prince charming, thank you very much.

Geez.

Fuming, I jerked the backpack on the rest of the way, grabbed the bike handles, and had one leg almost over the bike when a hand grabbed my ankle.

On reflex, I kicked back with a grunt. Whoever had my leg shuffled at the shifting weight, but didn't budge. They released me. I whirled around to find Benjamin there. My helmet swung from my hand as I wheeled it toward him, but he dodged the flying foam missile like a featherlight ninja, then took a step back and held up two hands.

"Sorry," he quickly said, "I shouldn't have touched you."

Chest heaving, blood thumping, I let my hand rest at my side. The helmet hit my thigh uselessly. Embarrassed at my over-reaction—but seriously, he grabbed my *ankle*?—I took a deep breath.

"What?" I snapped again. "You made your position very clear."

"I want to help."

In the dimming spring light, his face was bathed in shadows. A glimmer of something showed in his eyes anyway, and he tucked two hands into his front pockets. He normally stood with his arms at his side, like a god come to life. His face was usually analytical and serious.

Now it was . . . concerned.

Fantastic. I engendered pity in the man I'd secretly tried to ignore for months now. And maybe—just maybe—that had been a bit of an overreaction. Mama always said that defensiveness meant there was truth in what the other person said.

So . . . there was that.

"I'm sorry," he said. "That came out arrogant and not entirely true. I don't see you as a damsel-in-distress or whatever. I just . . . I want to help you better your situation however I can. I want you to be safe."

My racing heart calmed. I studied him for another short eternity. "I overreacted," I said. "I'm sorry too."

He lifted his eyebrows. Was it surprise or a follow up question? Going with the latter, I stumbled over my own thoughts. Did I want to trust him? Yes. Could I?

Yes.

At least I could sense *that* much beneath the layers of vulnerable bravado and muscle that I sensed held something of a charming man. He was coiled quiet. Deadly precision. Probably moved faster than I could think.

Not probably, he definitely could.

I'd seen the videos of his last fight where he'd destroyed his opponent in a crushing career-builder, then retired and left the MMA world in a sense of reeling shock. No explanation, just walked away and disappeared into a quiet bubble.

There was nothing *normal* about Mercedy, but something told me that everything in him wanted to be.

"I just need someone to teach me the basics in case I need them." I ran a hand through my hair, which had fallen from the loose ponytail and gone full-curl-powered-frizzy at some point after leaving the restaurant. "Like poking eyes or groin kicks or something. I'm pretty open in the afternoon. I work from six to three at the diner Monday through Thursday and to closing on Saturday."

His gaze followed my gesture to The Diner across the way. For several moments, a machine seemed to move behind his eyes.

"Come at 9:00 tomorrrow," he finally said, "just after we close. I'll teach you what you need to know. But it's not going to stop someone that's determined to hurt you. If—"

"You'd do that?"

"Yes."

I rolled my eyes. "Because you want to be the hero?"

"No," he said softly. "Because I want you to be."

My natural snarky response froze in my throat, and all I could do was nod. Geez, what was I doing? Giving Mercedy—it was easier to picture him as a non-god if I called him by his last name—attitude. Not only that, but I'd be alone with him.

For an *hour*.

"Okay, I'll take that." I nodded, hair waving around my face, and held up a finger. "Can I pay you?"

"I don't need the money."

"Great! Then I'll bring food," I said quickly. "Dinner is on me. And it won't be from the restaurant. I'll make it."

A hint of amusement appeared like a crack in his veneer. "It doesn't matter where it's from. And you don't have to bring me food."

I tilted my head back and forth. "Well, I really shouldn't steal food from the place I work, you know? And yes, I do need to give something back. I demand it. Is this a deal?"

Feeling a sense of euphoria for the first time in weeks, I stuck my hand out. It had been too long since I had a real win. Only a few seconds before our hands came together did I comprehend that I'd be touching him.

Him.

Mercedy.

Whom I quietly stalked from behind the diner windows and tried to ignore all at the same time.

When he gripped my hand in his, tiny little fireworks

erupted under the skin of my palm and electrified the rest of my body. I hated that physical response. The pooling collection of heat in my belly that just seeing him caused.

He gave me a short nod, and I couldn't help but wonder if he ever smiled.

"Deal," he said.

"Thank you. I appreciate it. Oh! Do you have any allergies?"

"Nah." He took a step back, our hands falling apart. "I eat just about anything."

Like a madwoman, I wanted to rush forward and snatch his hand back. To cradle his in mine. To imagine what that thrumming touch would feel like on my shoulders. My neck. My cheek. Instead, I let my arm drop back to my side.

"Thanks, Mercedy."

His head tilted back in amusement, as if he didn't know what to make of me. He certainly wouldn't be the first. I climbed on top of my bike, one leg bent as I put a foot on the pedal.

"What's your name?" he asked.

"Serafina. You can call me Sera."

I shoved off, my bike tires humming on the pavement as I pedaled away.

* * *

Go to katiecrossromance.com or any online retailer to grab your copy of Fighter.

I hope you love Benjamin and Serafina.

—Katie

About the Author

Katie Cross is ALL ABOUT writing epic love stories and wild places. Creating new books is her jam.

When she's not hiking or chasing her two littles through the Montana mountains, you can find her curled up reading a book or arguing with her husband over the best kind of sushi.

Visit her at www.katiecrossbooks.com for free short stories, extra savings on all her books (and some you can't buy on the retailers), and so much more.

www.ingramcontent.com/pod-product-compliance
Lightning Source LLC
Chambersburg PA
CBHW061545210726
48287CB00006B/2079